MANY AND MANY A YEAR AGO

SELÇUK ALTUN

MANY AND MANY A YEAR AGO

Translated from Turkish by
Clifford and Selhan Endres

TELEGRAM

ISBN: 978-1-84659-067-2

First published in Turkish as *Senelerce Senelerce Evveldi*
by Sel Yayıncılık, Istanbul, Turkey

This English edition published by Telegram, 2009

A full CIP record for this book is available from the British Library.
A full CIP record for this book is available from the Library of Congress.

Printed in the UK by CPI Mackays, Chatham, ME5 8TD

TELEGRAM
26 Westbourne Grove, London W2 5RH
2398 Doswell Avenue, Saint Paul, Minnesota, 55108
Tabet Building, Mneimneh Street, Hamra, Beirut
www.telegrambooks.com

What is to come will not cause us to mourn for what is gone, says my inner voice. Should I trust it? Does eluding death mean losing the will to live? Is it a reward or punishment? My inner voice warned me once too about my passion for music. It was when I was five and lost in a solo on that unearthly flute, the *ney*. Turning to my aunt, I said, "It's Allah Baba talking, isn't it?"

I

Our neighborhood clung fiercely to the slope of Z. Cemetery. Maybe that's how we managed to dodge the city's wrathful whimsies. Out of respect for the cemetery's silhouette the crooked and careless but god-fearing buildings stood a mere three stories high. In return Z.'s resident winds refrained from harassing the L. neighborhood. Our bazaar consisted of little shops lining two sides of the sorry street, which was prone to flooding. The residents sighed for the lack of a bank or a bar whenever they saw one in one of those cowboy movies. The pharmacist considered himself the street's VIP, priding himself on living in a shanty house in neighboring Ç. As he faded away in the evenings on his motorbike, the factory workers spilled out of the coffeehouses to be replaced by the night shift of gravediggers. In that labyrinth of streets I knew so well I scarcely remember the echo of laughter. It was as if despair were a local disease. I even dreaded the gaze of the babies who crawled around outside their houses, and wondered whether a dream of being rescued from this pit could persist.

While the luckless L. was squeezed from on high by that high-society cemetery, a garbage dump nibbled away at it from below. It was on muddy Selvili Street, running between Z. and the main street, that I squandered my childhood. At the head of the street, on the top floor of Zevk Apartments, lived Aunt Ikbal, a retired matron, and her husband, Celal. She was the neighborhood's needle-jabber, my father's sweet-and-sour older sister, while her husband was its leader elect.

We lived on the middle floor of this woeful building. My aunt had been the go-between for my father, whom she called Humpty Hasan Ali, and my mother. When I heard that I'd come to earth in dire straits during the fifth year of their marriage, I thought it only right to apologize.

"If it hadn't been for me," my aunt liked to say, "your name would have been Saint Yashar, my dear Kemal."

My earliest childhood memory is of watching my father marching on the spot in front of the mirror while he shaved, while at the same time mimicking the sound of every instrument he could muster. At first I was embarrassed by his diva performances, but soon I'd memorized the essence of every instrument, from tuba to trumpet. He would break into a high-pitched whine as he washed his face and with that the show would come to an end. I'd walk away glowing with the satisfaction of having watched a clown and a magician at work. Before I was born, my father had played the tuba as a sergeant-major in the local Air Force band. He retired when he became paralyzed in his right arm. I could hardly believe the respect that people paid him as we walked through the bazaar, almost as if he were an imam. Despite the fact that he was a tall fellow, they never tagged him with the usual nicknames. I was disconcerted, in fact, at how well he wore the mantle of Assistant Cemetery Director of Z.

My mother was a fragile woman due to her orphanage upbringing. It infuriated me when people referred to her as "Servet the exotic beauty." Before her marriage she'd interned as a nurse at the hospital where my aunt worked. It was only after two miscarriages that she managed to deliver, and because of her poor health she had to quit her job. I was at first annoyed by the way she continued to defer to my aunt as if she were still the boss. When she'd finished her housework she'd sit in front of the TV and, if there was nothing on worth watching, start knitting. She seldom interfered in my affairs, yet observed my aunt's and father's excessive fondness for me with some anxiety. The warmth of her distant smile was always enough for me.

The middle floor, with its boring curtain-washing rituals, was ours. The other two floors belonged to my aunt, who constantly looked for opportunities to say, "We had to work three jobs and were indebted to the mafia just to have a roof over our heads." In my childhood nightmares the building grew angry with me before collapsing, leaving us homeless in the middle of winter. My retired uncle's office was in an alcove on the ground floor; every so often its door would open softly and benevolently. To the left of that, where the curtains remained resolutely shut, was the cubicle where my aunt administered injections and meted out pills to the neighbors. She ceremoniously handed over half of what she earned to my father to be put towards my education fund. This transaction, performed always in my presence, embarrassed me to the point where sometimes I had to fight off imaginary cramps. My aunt's son had died in childbirth, and she had disowned her daughter Iclal for marrying an Alevi classmate while a student at the College of Education, so I grew up as a nephew who meant more to her than a son.

My grandfather, who died thanks to the lack of a doctor in a village close to Mount Ararat, was apparently an enlightened teacher. My aunt mourned her father for days, then was shaken from her grief by my father bursting into prayer at the cemetery one day when his arm miraculously healed. With his arm whole, his work tempo became frightening. He gave flute and mandolin lessons to the untalented children of neighborhoods that took two bus transfers to reach, besides offering gilt-work courses to the rich women of Moda on the other side of the Bosphorus. On Saturdays I would go with him and attend English classes in the building where he taught. As far as my father was concerned, even waiting tables was too good for somebody who didn't have elementary English. I understood very well the importance of education to my surviving L., and therefore willingly accepted his fanatic supervision. I was subjected to culture-overload, assignment-checking and oral examinations. I did crossword puzzles, watched documentaries, and read the magazines my teachers recommended. In second grade I memorized the capital cities of innumerable countries—no matter if I confused the Swedes with the Swiss. By third grade I knew the Taklamakan Desert as well as the Bursa Plain; by fourth grade I could discern the Arabic and Persian words that so bedeviled Turkish.

On being told my marks, Aunt Ikbal would remark, "Blue-eyed like your mother, tall like your father, but smart like your aunt, my Kemal."

My father bought my underwear and administered my baths until I finished primary school. When the time came for the soapy torture of my hair and head, he would whisper, "Close your eyes and imagine you're a pilot flying a fighter jet at twice the speed of sound." For him there was no calling more noble than that of the military, no rank higher than a pilot's. I'd keep my eyes carefully shut and visualize myself in one of those shark-like vehicles until the command came to open them again. He combed my hair with a comb dipped in lemon juice to make it shine. Each time it raked through my hair I felt the pressure of a new expectation: my son will become a fighter pilot; my smart Kemal will become an officer; Kemal Kuray, by the grace of God, will rise to the rank of general …

*

Isn't it wonderfully ironic for a sign to proclaim that cemetery administration is the job of the Ministry of Health? My father shared his office, which was next to the ground-floor entrance of that soulless building, with two assistants. I never tired of sitting there watching people pass by. Most of the women workers covered their heads. Their shapeless garments and sullen faces were inseparable from the funereal setting. The men's constant quarreling irritated me, but if I had a good reason not to go back home I could visit the gravediggers' shed and drink tea. By and by I got used to the graves all lined up in orderly rows. Respectful of my marble environment, I wandered among them as if they were an exhibition of sculptures.

The most colorful children of the neighborhood were the wildest ones. I was forbidden to go near them. And they never came near me, out of fear of my aunt. The most exciting activity of the group I finally managed to socialize with was playing five-a-side football for a Coke. One day, when they assigned me to the lowly position of goalie, I stormed off the field and, saying a *Bismillah* under my breath, that prayer to mark an auspicious beginning, I slipped into the cemetery through the back gate. I stopped to catch my breath at the top, feeling as satisfactorily thrilled as the older boys did when they were admitted to the amusement park. For a talented kid who talked to himself in the mirror and built cowboy towns out of old house slippers, inventing solitary games in a cemetery was easy.

There I arranged quests to find, first, the most majestic cypress, then the most grandiose charitable monument, and finally, growing really excited, the most elegant tombstone and epitaph. Eliminating the losers one by one, I picked those that registered the longest and the shortest lives and bore the prettiest and the funniest names. I disliked graves that marked the birth date by the lunar calendar and the death date by the solar calendar more than those that flaunted unrhymed and unintelligible verse. I worried that—God forbid!—an infidel might see those dates and laugh at the idea of 650-year-old people. I can't remember now why I abandoned my project to write to the children of famous businessmen and artists on the matter of their fathers' untended graves.

A marble block as white as a sugar cube attracted my attention one day. At the top left corner of a slab resembling a thin pillow was written, simply, "ASLI." A tender but irresistible force seemed to embrace me, and I shivered. My head ached in a pleasant way. I felt tired. With a murmured *Bismillah* I sat down at the foot of Aslı's grave. As I did, the *ezan* rose up from the city's 3,000 mosques. I bowed my head until it was finished. When I plucked up the courage to face those four letters again my heart beat faster and I glowed inwardly. The size of the grave told me that it belonged to someone my own age. I stood up with the satisfaction of having found my first sweetheart.

I knew that Aslı would enter my dreams that night in

her long snow-white gown. I didn't mind the halo of light obscuring her face like a veil. It would be enough for her to say, "Wait patiently for me, Kemal." When I awoke in the morning to the *ezan*, an angel named Aslı had come into my life and I vowed to remain forever faithful to her, my sweetheart, the Aslı of my soul. We popular boys of the fourth grade were all in love with our teacher, Miss Nimet. I broke the happy news to them that I was now removed from the competition. I didn't mind that they doubted the existence of their future sister-in-law Aslı, whom they would never be able to see in any case.

My hero was the Pied Piper. If I happened to hear the sound of a flute or a zither I would freeze as if bewitched. For some time I believed that if I observed the sky carefully I would actually see the notes fly by. So as not to waste the slightest fragment of music, I would close my eyes and put all the cells of my body on high alert. Baritones, sopranos, the peddlers' cries, the *ezan*, the twittering of birds, the droning of bees, all moved me, even the rhythmical braying of donkeys. My childhood dream was to own a real transistor radio, but alas I had only toys and my imagination. If my father, who was also my homework inspector, ever let me touch his clunky radio, he would observe that "the best music is what a person himself composes." And "no music is more profound than the sky-shattering roar of a plane flying at 15,000 feet at twice the speed of sound." I found this nonsense poetic for quite a time.

I liked the fat boy named Nafiz who sat next to me

in English lessons. During the breaks he would copy my homework, contributing his own mistakes, in return for which he let me listen to his radio on headphones. When we graduated from primary school he wangled an apprenticeship for me at his uncle's music store. My father was okay with me working as long as he could confiscate half my salary. I woke up happy on those calm summer mornings and ran to the bus stop at the edge of Z.

Cisum Music specialized in classical and world music and had six sleepwalkers for employees. My job was to stand in for whoever was taking his annual vacation. In almost no time I became the mascot of the store. That first season I did everything except wait on customers. I recorded the immortal music of many world-famous musicians, starting with Elvis Presley. Aret, our classical-music man who sported an artificial arm, used to laugh at how I pronounced Engelbert Humperdinck. The real prize of my job, however, was to spend time with the cassette player, which we were forbidden to turn off during business hours. Aret was the first to notice my passion for music. He would say, if Tchaikovsky or Wagner was playing, "Don't turn up your nose, kid. Unless you *get* these guys, you'll never be an authentic music lover."

It upset me when the boss found fault with everyone's work. "Even the composers on the album covers frown when he shows up," said Aret. Summoned to the boss's office one day, I was afraid I'd be fired before I could even ask him what the word "authentic" meant. But I wasn't fired. What's more, I got my July salary five days early, and he gave me the good news that I was welcome to work at Cisum the following summer and even during school breaks.

"Kemal, my young friend," he said, "if you want to earn a few tips in dollars and hear a bit of music played now and then, why don't you drop by my pal Hayri Abi's place this evening?"

It was rumored that our building had been inherited by my boss's elderly Greek wife. I'd been to the second floor many times because we used it as a storeroom. The third floor had a door with a plaque on it in French that nobody could decode; nor did they know why the door was always locked. Whenever various coquettish girls fluttered their way up to "my pal Hayri Abi" on the fourth floor, our boss would veer off up after them. I could never understand why a chorus of giggles then filled the shop.

After sorting out the pop CDs that were squeezed in with the Mozarts, I confronted the heavy door of the Ispilandit Apartments and managed, on my second attempt, to push it half open. Immediately a wave of melancholy music pulled at me like a magnet. Magical violins seemed to be dueling with one other, producing a melody that cascaded down the stairs like a waterfall. I could feel it ease the musty smell catching at my throat. This was how, with my hand moving dubiously toward the doorbell, I met the meaning of my life—baroque music—moments before meeting the hero of my youth, Hayri Abi.

In the five seconds it took him to turn down the volume and unlock the steel door, I had an inkling of the unusual messenger work I was about to be assigned. The imperious long-haired creature that appeared before me was in his thirties. I thought I'd seen his type in the cowboy movies. The only clothing he had on was a pair of red and blue shorts. He brought me apricot juice and I felt that he appreciateed the way I looked around the room in amazement. Even in the movies I'd never seen a room like this, with its gray walls and red floor. I would have been impressed by the stereo, which looked like the skyscrapers you see in cartoons, if it hadn't been for the black guitar on the glass table. When I caught my first glimpse of that noble instrument I realized that what I *really* wanted was to be a musician. But while I could always save up to buy a radio, to buy a guitar I would need a really solid reason.

He had me sit on the bamboo divan. I was to call him "Abi"—"older brother"—and think of him as such. He dropped a tape of Chris Rea in the cassette player. I didn't like it a lot when Hayri Abi began whispering to me about my responsibilities because it sounded like he was giving me orders. But when he called me "Kemo" on my way out, I felt as honored as a bodyguard who has just been given his code name.

I started carrying bags whose contents I knew nothing about to the well-to-do districts of the city every other day, sometimes twice a day. I received a "Bravo" and $5 from Hayri Abi when I brought back the sealed envelopes handed to me by those tense young folk who seemed to relax a bit on seeing me. I memorized the addresses on the lists he gave me and then tore them up. I didn't take the usual taxis. I paid no heed to Aret when he said, "That pimp is making you deliver sex videos." Hayri Abi laughed and said, "It's just because Aret can't jerk off. Eros took revenge on him by tearing off his right arm." When he wasn't yelling into the phone in various languages, I would wait impatiently for him to ask, "How about a little concert, Kemo?" The way he played left-handed guitar was amazing, but his repertoire never changed. "I'm going to sing for you the best ten love songs in the world," he would say. Then he'd close his eyes while he played—"Over the Rainbow", "Moon River", "Autumn Leaves"… I often thought of asking Aslı why love songs were all so sad, but I always forgot, maybe because L. was there like a bogeyman to greet me every evening after work.

To keep my father from taking half my earnings, I didn't tell him about my second job. My tips accumulated at Hayri Abi's until they grew into a fund sufficient enough to buy a good radio.

The summer I qualified as a seventh-grader I went back to work at Cisum. Everything was as I had left it. By the next month I had a little three-band radio with headphones. I had never known a happier moment in my life. I decided not to hide the radio from my father. He was as pleased to hear my lie about how I'd bought it secondhand from the neighborhood grocer's delivery boy as the father of a son who's scored his first goal in a football match. At night I used to pray to Aslı not to be upset with me, before falling asleep listening to familiar tunes on unfamiliar stations.

That summer I developed the ability to solve the tabloid crossword puzzles in half an hour and gravitated toward classical jazz. When Hayri Abi proclaimed, "You've got gourmet musical taste," it was the most meaningful "Bravo" of the first fourteen of my twenty-eight years. "Music is to feel, not to understand," he'd say. "The structures of genuine music conceal within themselves poetry, narratives, and images that can't be put down on paper." Perhaps these weren't his own words, I'm not sure.

Even if they wouldn't let me deal with customers, I still wanted to go back to Cisum the summer after I graduated from secondary school, because Hayri Abi had told me that he was going to "orientate me" in classical music. Maybe what added to my excitement was this exotic-sounding word "orientate." On those nights when we watched videos of symphonies conducted by famous maestros, my father assumed I was working overtime. I closed my eyes as those surly men in penguin suits let the oboe or viola perform solo. Maybe my images failed to reach the heights of dream, but in my foggy way I was inventing plots like those of *The Thousand and One Nights*. Opening my eyes again, I would feel calmer, but those ruthless conductors who could hush twenty wind instruments or start thirty violins whining with a single gesture still frightened me.

Then I'd head home on city buses filled with workers returning from the night shift. I wondered whether to reflect on the fact that those poor souls would die without ever hearing the name Vivaldi was just something to bolster my ego. I was never satisfied with the Bach overtures I tried to whistle on the walk home from the bus stop. It came as no surprise that, while I was lost in my fantasies of directing the Berlin Philharmonic or the Boston Symphony Orchestra, Aslı abandoned me.

Hayri Abi had gradually grown more nervous. Though I wasn't making deliveries anymore, he still gave me $5 tips, which I was slightly reluctant to accept. At the beginning of August Aunt Ikbal sent me to England to attend a three-week language course. When Hayri Abi heard that I was going to Bournemouth he said, "That's like going to Siirt instead of Istanbul to learn Turkish." If the school administrators hadn't taken us to London on our first weekend I would never have realized that I was abroad. I complained to my father that the plane home hadn't produced any "authentic" music, but he just replied, "Beautiful melodies can only be felt by airplane pilots and Rumi's grandchildren."

I went directly to Cisum to distribute ballpoint pens with "London" and "Bournemouth" printed on them. Then I planned to see Hayri Abi and give him the CD of Vladimir Horowitz's latest concert. The shop was silent. Aret, who was talking on the phone, lifted his artificial arm and beckoned me over. He wore an irritatingly cynical expression on his face as he dug out of his drawer the third page of a yellowing newspaper and showed it to me. "Gang Selling Drugs to Youth Nabbed," said the headline. When I saw this, and the name Hayri Tamer just below, it was as if the notes of

"Sleeping Beauty" had turned into arrows to pierce my brain one by one. I was afraid to close my eyes for fear I wouldn't be able to open them again. I ran out of the shop because I didn't want them to see me burst into tears. I remember walking without stopping until I reached home. That night in my dreams I saw myself conducting, with great difficulty, the Bavarian Radio Symphony Orchestra in "Swan Lake." I suspected Aslı was laughing and crying at the same time.

I didn't have the heart to give up the radio that I'd acquired with my tips from Hayri Abi, so I sentenced myself not to listen to music for a month. My relations with certain people in the neighborhood seemed about to cool off. I knew they were irritated by my trip to England. If they happened to hear that I'd started listening to classical music too, I might have been in for the "gay treatment." So as not to be excommunicated I decided to be one of them until school started up again.

I'd forgotten that I'd sat the entrance exam to H. High School on the Asian side of the city, a state-run boarding school, but in early September the news came that I'd won a scholarship. Even my mother rejoiced. The first time I walked into the building I thought it was like a jail, then a dead whale.

"Starting high school is the second step to manhood," my father declared (the first being circumcision).

I shared my dormitory room with forty boys who came from districts of the city that I'd never heard of, as well as from neighboring towns. The first night, as though it would identify the traitors amongst us, we all asked each other what our fathers did. When my turn came, even *I* could barely hear myself whisper that he was a municipal bureaucrat. I was studious and disciplined and could never get along with the country yokels who thought that being in a boarding school was synonymous with being on holiday. On a scale from "Gnat" to "Bastard," the nickname they chose for me—"Çakır," "Blue" (because of the color of my eyes, I suppose)—didn't bother me. My mature attitude in comparison to my classmates' was put down to my military ancestry by my weary and ignorant-of-Mozart teachers.

I began preparing for university entrance exams in tenth grade. In order to get an Air Force Academy interview one had to come within the top ten percent of the million or so who took the exam. This I was reminded of repeatedly on weekends when I was home. I was pleased with how my ambition soared whenever my classmates, who were looking for the easiest possible schools, made fun of my hard work. Elgar's concertos offered me moral support as I struggled with science. With the exam looming, my father, who had managed to procure a list of questions asked by interviewers over the past five years, warned me continually to keep my eyes healthy. He had heard, I don't know where, that they were the most important item on the health checklist. "Work hard but don't let anything happen to your eyes!" he'd say.

As it happened, I was in the upper two percent and sailed through the physical and psychological exams without a hitch. When the interview results came in I was duly accepted by the Air Force Academy as their second-best candidate.

I thought it was a joke, at first, when they told me I'd be sharing a room with four other guys. My roommates were from the countryside, sons of government officials. You couldn't say that we had much in common other than having had English prep classes. I didn't really expect them to defer to me as their leader simply because I was the tallest, or came from Istanbul, but I enjoyed their panic when they discovered my passion for classical music. Weekends when I came home my father would finger the white braid on my jacket respectfully, and before I changed clothes we would stroll through the market together. It was embarrassing watching him walk two steps ahead of me, nose in the air, hands behind his back thumbing his prayer beads. But I couldn't help smiling at the disheveled greetings accorded us by the shopkeepers who thought that not jumping to their feet would be disrespectful to the Armed Forces.

The military-school way of life soon became mine. Like the works of Bach, the system was shored up by mathematical principles. I soon learnt that the friend of a person with goals was "discipline." Only six of the 250 students were girls, and those of us who didn't fall in love with Gülay were considered perverts. I flirted for a while with Asu, a second-year student at the nearby sports academy. She was surprised when I broke up with her for saying "Yo dude" all the time. After a while civilian life began to look strange to me. The *lumpen* who obeyed traffic laws whenever it suited them and had no idea how to navigate shopping malls infuriated me—especially those whose boom-boxes constantly blared. My belief was that by choosing to be an officer and taking refuge in classical music, I had rescued myself from the city's chaos and superficiality.

I graduated from the Air Force Academy third in my class, with the rank of lieutenant. Although civilians asked us all the same question—"With so much flying, aren't you afraid of dying?"—only half of the graduating class actually qualified as pilots. My loyalty to the most magnificent mode of transport ever invented by man—the airplane—began on my first day of training. At my first Air Force base—my overture, so to speak—I discovered that seductive symphony which is improvised by the sounds of airplanes taking off and landing. Planes are like purebred race horses when they're above the clouds, powerful and skittish. The excitement that stirred me when I accepted my diploma from the President's hand was nothing compared to what I felt on being authorized to "take solo command of the cockpit."

At 12,000 feet I felt I'd been spirited away from the world's filth and had reached the outskirts of divine tranquility. There I touched eternity. There I could embrace the most meaningful of all music—absolute silence. I was pleased at how my flying skills improved with each flight training. My body would tremble with pleasure whenever I got the order to fly. When I was on the ground I envied those who were in the air. Yes, flying was a test for the body and a ritual for the soul.

At twenty-five I was assigned to the strategic base B. I was the first of my cohort to be awarded the fiercest warplane the sky has yet known, the F-16. I was the youngest member of the team representing our country in the NATO Inter-Army Air Show. When our team was declared champion, and Kemal Kuray number one in the individual category, I felt for the rest of the team, all of whom held higher rank. At twenty-eight I aced the exam for staff officer. Soon I accepted it as normal when people around me singled me out as the future commander of the Air Force. At this time my father, and especially my aunt, wanted to marry me off. But I wiggled out of that by using my officer's training as an excuse. I was happy during that period of my life, perhaps because women weren't a part of it. I'd forgotten to fall in love ever since I hurt the feelings of a ghost.

Now I was counting down the hours that remained for me in the Academy. On a summer morning with 1,551 hours to go, I drew the assignment to head to K. on a reconnaissance flight. North of Sivrihisar I was surprised to see the engine failure light come on. (I believed in my heart that F-16s were *immortal*.) The gauges showed that the engine was losing heat. I tried twice to restart it. Nothing happened. I began to lose altitude and notified the closest base of my coordinates. Three thousand feet from the ground I noted that the area was at least uninhabited. I was forced to abandon my plane in my parachute. In ninety seconds I would have the devastating experience of watching my noble F-16 crash to the ground and explode. I began to weep. I knew that even though I had survived I would always feel the pain of letting a heroic friend, given to me to safeguard, slip from my grasp. A mountain wind caught my parachute and my sweat dried. I could have aimed for the sharp gray rocks below, but I didn't have it in me to challenge nature. "Dear God," I begged, "please let me be a martyr next to the corpse of my plane." I closed my eyes and while I prepared to watch twenty-eight years of my life unravel before me, I must have hit something jutting upward and lost consciousness.

*

I was flown to the nearest hospital by helicopter. After a considerable struggle I opened my eyes; my head hurt and I felt a strange lightness in the lower part of my body. I felt such emptiness that I couldn't answer the doctors' questions. I didn't hear them say how many ribs I'd broken. As they prepared to operate on my right ankle, I remembered how my father had always told me to put my right shoe on first while pronouncing the name of God. I chuckled nervously, but it still hurt.

I was under the care of two dutiful psychiatrists. They thought I was suffering from "post-traumatic stress" but I knew that it was more than that, that I was severely depressed. Despite the handfuls of pills I couldn't forget that moment my plane exploded, and since I couldn't come up with a good reason for its failing, I eased my soul by pleading guilty. It was difficult to keep from snapping at the psychiatrist, who was my superior in rank, so I focused on the spots floating around the ceiling instead, whistling Mendelssohn like a prayer. The first two nights my nightmares jolted me awake, and when I discovered that I couldn't get out of bed I burst into tears.

My family's visits added to the strain. Maybe what I saw in my mother's eyes was the compassion of parents who get over the fear of losing their children. My father and my aunt, on the other hand, were anxious and irritated. Like investors whose efforts have come to nothing, they could no longer swagger around L. as relatives of the future Commander. When my uncle began sermonizing, I had to tell them that my whole body was in pain and would they please leave and stay away until I called them back.

Forty-eight hours later the colonel leading the Accident Investigation Team stopped in with his lieutenant. Despite the sensitive way in which they questioned me I could barely refrain from crying. What finally ended my nightmares was the report they filed concluding that the crash hadn't been caused by pilot error. But my lack of interest in the outside world continued. I was susceptible to sudden headaches, and my right hand had developed a tremor.

They said I would walk again in six weeks, and I did. My appetite returned and I started reading the newspapers. A week later the hospital chief paid me a visit. His tone was carefully optimistic as he told me that my recovery was underway and that my place at the Air Force Academy was being held for me. Flawlessly modulating the tone and dosage of command and advice, he informed me how helpful a period of desk work would be in regaining my concentration. I was sure they wouldn't even let me get close to a helicopter if I failed to resolve my psychological problems.

It was a good two months after the crash before they assigned me to a temporary job at Air Force headquarters. I went to Ankara full of misgivings, responsible for coordinating a top secret translation project on which ten hand-picked university graduates were working while performing their military service. The job had to be finished by the time their term of duty was up three months later. Though they'd all come from good universities in England and the U.S.A., they acted like high-school delinquents. I knew I wouldn't be bored living with them in our military housing. Suat Altan, the most efficient and mysterious one, held diplomas in literature and computer science. While looking through the staff files I discovered he had been a technology consultant in New York. Like the old-time Indian chiefs, he said little but what he did say was meaningful. He had no trouble beating everybody else in chess and backgammon and sat in the corner reading tomes while the rest of the group sat around talking big. He seemed fragile, and maybe it was because of this and because of his mournful blue eyes that I felt sympathy for him. Twice I reprimanded the surly banking trainee, Mahmut, for harassing Suat; I even went so far as to dock his holidays when I caught him bullying the poor guy one day.

I ran into Suat once on a bus to Istanbul, and after that we started traveling there together the odd weekend.

On others, if we stayed in Ankara, I would take him to a concert or a play. His attitude seemed at once calculated and suspicious. Once, when I invited him to my usual kebab joint in Istanbul, he seemed startled and pretended he hadn't heard me. He reminded me of those mysterious priests in Westerns to whom the Mexicans readily confess their sins. Three weeks before his mustering-out I summoned up, without quite knowing why, my life story for him. He listened attentively with his head bowed.

As for him, I could tell all I knew in a few sentences. He was the son of a rich father and a Sephardic Jewish mother, and he'd obviously had a colorless but carefree childhood and youth. His superior intelligence ill-befitted his environment, and I was sure he bore a secret wound he was cavalierly disregarding.

When the time came to say goodbye I embraced everybody on the team except Suat. He shook my hand distractedly and practically ran away as he murmured something like an apology.

Later I heard that he beat the daylights out of Mahmut when they left our living quarters for the last time. According to the soldier who witnessed the incident, he used karate moves straight out of the movies to pound the big banking trainee into a condition fit for hospitalization.

*

My own monthly visits to the hospital nauseated me. Unable to deal with my deep-seated concentration problems,

I broke into a sweat during the stress tests. I didn't even bother mentioning my itching abdomen to my psychiatrist as I couldn't even make him believe in my "phantom" headaches.

I knew that I would be assigned more and more to less and less exciting jobs. For a while I tried to accept and understand this reality. Since I was without sin and a model individual, I believed that by God's grace I would in the end be rescued from my psychological problems. Still, I could see in my doctor's eyes that it wouldn't be easy for me to lose the traces of my trauma and I was slowly losing hope. I could even say that my passion for flying was beginning to diminish, though of course, as the hottest pilot in the Air Force, I couldn't stomach the idea of rotting away at a desk in some godforsaken corner of the country. I began looking for a way out. I had to find out, if I requested early retirement, if I could survive civilian life. I decided not to rush things, and meanwhile took comfort in Schoenberg's musical labyrinth.

As I was paying my check in a Kızılay restaurant one night, about to bolt from the place in exasperation, I realized that the cellphone ringing so insistently was my own. (Civilian life can be a real pain.) A confident voice said to me, "I'm Suat Altan's twin brother, Lieutenant. We need to talk about something important that concerns you." My head instantly began to throb. I couldn't remember Suat ever mentioning a brother, let alone a twin. The voice continued imperiously, directing me to be at the lobby of the Sheraton in half an hour. "You won't have a problem recognizing me."

This magnificent hotel was my favorite building in the capital and it was with some excitement that I started walking toward it. It was like a lighthouse on the city's horizon. I used to gaze at it from afar, wondering whether my feelings toward it would change if I saw the interior. Not until the moment I reached the grand entrance did it occur to me to wonder why I had been invited here. It had been a good while since I stopped thinking about myself in relation to God's chosen few. Now I remembered the expression "No good deed goes unpunished." I felt sure that some kind of chore awaited me thanks to that schizophrenic conscript I'd once helped out. I could have sworn, if the man who stepped out of a cloud of smoke and noise with an artificial smile on his face had not had a cigar in his hand, that he was Suat Altan himself.

"Welcome, Lieutenant," he said. "I told you you'd have no problem recognizing me. Aside from my being born twenty minutes before Suat, we're identical twins."

I had the feeling this wasn't the first time he'd made this clichéd introduction. Would I come up to his room, please, the better to chat? As we entered the elevator with a group of mustachioed civilians conversing in an accent I didn't recognize, my back began to itch. The elevator began its ascent to the top floor and I knew it was time to consider what my next dramatic surprise would be. Fuat led the way into the suite. I moved to the big window with the panoramic view. It was as if I were back in that peculiar funhouse world of mine in Z. If Fuat hadn't broken in on my thoughts by asking what I wanted to drink, I would have started categorizing the buildings spread out before me: the prettiest, the ugliest; governmental, private; and so on.

"Mineral water," I answered, and took a seat on the humblest chair in the room.

Fuat fished a half-empty bottle of cognac from a drawer and took a long sip as he walked to the elegant desk. I hadn't expected a CD player to be there. But he extracted a CD from a heap of newspapers and magazines and put it in the machine, then parked himself in the armchair opposite me. His face wore a sour expression, perhaps from the effort of executing an order that he hadn't been able to comprehend himself. While Vladimir Horowitz's magic fingers mastered a Chopin *mazurka*, I wondered how he would begin his speech. I didn't expect us to start with "May I call you by your first name?"

"Maybe in a few months, but not now," I replied. I knew I would be nervous and my right hand would shake.

Another sip from the bottle and the face turned sour again. It was if he were in the company of a person of inferior rank who habitually annoyed him. One more ill-mannered gesture and I would be on my way out.

But after a brief hesitation and an artificial laugh he said, "Listen to me, Lieutenant! I have a message for you from Suat. He told me about what you've been going through. I hope you'll overcome it in good style. Let me tell you straight off that I haven't come here to add another burden to those you've already got. If you can manage to hear me out patiently, you'll see that I might even have something that's good for you.

"My mother gave birth to us at San Francisco Hospital after a complicated labor. I was born at midnight on 21 May, and Suat twenty minutes later, on 22 May. This interval put us under two different zodiacal influences—me, Taurus; Suat, Gemini. My brother began to walk when he was ten months old; me, two months later. About this time my paternal grandfather died and we moved back to Istanbul to live with my grandmother.

"Though we were identical twins, Suat and I had diametrically opposing personalities. It looked as if the plusses and minuses of a whole had been parceled out to us indiscriminately. Maybe that was why we were so fond of each other. I was known as the calm, tolerant, decisive one, whereas he was distinguished by his aggressive intelligence and mysterious nature. He alternated between being an introvert and a social butterfly. I didn't take it amiss that I was overshadowed by his genius. In fact I got used to my grandfather's witticisms at my expense—like 'When God was handing out the brains, he gave a portion and a half to Suat, which left a half of a half for you.' My brother was a fragile child, and when necessary I acted as if I were twenty months, not twenty minutes, older than him to protect him.

"Whereas Suat was one of the top students to be accepted into the famous Robert College, I barely got into a French high school, and then only with his help. Our family was used to his shutting himself in his room to indulge his love for computers and mathematics, but it was really something else when he mastered financial and accounting terminology so that he could play the stock market. One episode I'll never forget. It was during one of those perennial economic crises in Turkey when the Istanbul stock market had fallen drastically. Suat told my father about a leading bank whose market value had dropped to $80 million while the buildings alone, he claimed, were worth $500 million. Not to hurt Suat's feelings, my father bought $10,000 worth of shares. My grandfather, on the other hand, who believed in Suat's genius, bought $500,000 worth. We learned all this two years later, when Suat made him sell. The bank's value was now more than $11 billion—one hundred and forty times what it had been. My father got $1.4 million for his $10,000, and my grandfather made $69 million on his $500,000.

"My twin was also fond of Uncle Izak Toledo, who was actually the twin brother of my mother. Uncle Izak was a professor of literature at the University of Jerusalem but spent his summers in Istanbul, in his dimly lit apartment in Balat, living like a recluse. It was under his influence that Suat took an interest in poetry. The intensity with which he became an Edgar Allan Poe fanatic scared even my uncle. My brother memorized every poem and short story of Poe and considered his every work of fiction to be a geometrical masterpiece of plot structure. We were astonished when he chose to attend the University of Virginia, Poe's hangout, in order to continue his education in computer engineering and English literature.

"We were all shocked by the painful news that my uncle had been killed by a suicide bomber on a bus. (As a pure Marxist he believed that owning a car was selfish.)

"Suat became more and more anti-social after that. He questioned every value and virtue. Though he had no interest in material possession, he became obsessed with making money. Now, in Virginia, he continued fearlessly to play the Istanbul Stock Market by pitting the fragile Turkish lira against the elite currencies of the world, and he made millions.

"My grandfather considered himself responsible for my uncle's death. This man of great strength, with a take-no-prisoners attitude, didn't give a damn about his health. After he died we discovered that he'd thrown his heart pills into the Iznik vase. Suat's behavior at the synagogue and cemetery turned our grief to panic. He started by weeping at the foot of the coffin, then began talking loudly to the corpse, and ended up giggling uncontrollably. I'll never forget the sight of his motionless silhouette in the cemetery. It was as if he were awaiting a command, his eyes focused on a ray of divine light nobody else could see. 'Go talk to your brother,' my father said to me. I approached him cautiously, knowing that he was reading my eyes for my intentions.

"'Don't worry, Fuat,' he said. 'I sometimes have these odd reactions at dramatic moments, but they always pass.'

"He invited me to visit him at Christmas. Suat, with his

cape-like overcoat, thin moustache, and long hair parted down the middle, was starting to look a bit like Poe. His house was in the city's wealthiest and loneliest district. A Doberman and a Siamese cat lived in uneasy harmony and made no attempt to get to know me. I must confess that Suat's study was appalling. His desk was a huge glass cube that I first took to be an aquarium. In fact there were four very small sharks swimming languidly around inside it. On New Year's Eve Suat's mysterious girlfriend was at the house. Maria, the daughter of a Mexican stable hand, was a waif who didn't look a day over thirteen, which was in fact Virginia's age when she married her twenty-seven-year-old cousin Edgar Allan.

"Suat was a sophomore and already considered one of the top software programmers in the U.S. He amused us by telling us how he worked with one of his professors on certain think-tank projects and made unspeakable sums of money.

"Toward the end of a holiday that we took in Miami, New Orleans, and Las Vegas I started feeling uneasy. Though we looked exactly alike, I was absorbing the reality that we were growing farther and farther apart. While flying back to Geneva I decided to keep better tabs on Suat, though not of course to disturb him.

"I knew that he'd signed contracts with international corporations even before graduating. As soon as he graduated he moved to New York. I settled down meanwhile in Geneva. I had all kinds of difficulties in reaching Suat; he, on the other hand, continually sent emails to me at odd times from places like El Paso and San Diego. This annoyed me. Still, when he invited me for the next New Year's, I flew to New York despite my heavy workload. As his African-American Moslem chauffeur drove me from the airport to Suat's Central Park duplex, I wondered which of the residents I would meet this time. I wasn't sorry to note that the fish were gone, but seeing Maria again upset me. She looked older now than thirteen, or even sixteen, but I was repulsed by the theatrical show of respect she paid my brother. As the housekeeper took me to my room she filled me in. The relationship was totally platonic. Her master was financing Maria's education and supervising her personal development to the point where her manners would meet with his approval. They would marry as soon as she graduated. I suspected that the housekeeper was passing on this philanthropic rubbish to me as part of a plan hatched by my brother. I made my excuses and headed back to Geneva the next day.

"Six months later, after I'd ignored two emotional messages, he resorted to our mother. She went to New York for a month and stopped in at Geneva on her way home. It seems that while visiting her uncle in Mexico City Maria had gone to a disco where there had been a terrible fire, and she had been among its victims. I was certain that Suat would be doubly tormented by his doubts regarding his beloved's fidelity. My mother, who was totally in denial, focused on talking about Suat's professional success. I was glad she hadn't realized that her genius son was living in the twenty-first century by day, and in the nineteenth by night.

"I never saw a more harmonious couple than my parents. We lost my father three years ago. A drunken taxi driver jumped the curb and ploughed into him while he stood reading a book at the bus stop. My mother sank into a severe depression. I took her to Geneva. On the day I thought she was finally about to pull herself together, she swallowed a bottle of sleeping pills ...

"It was interesting that Suat faced all these tragedies more stoically than I. He was calm and generous during the inheritance proceedings. We divided the money and the stocks equally. I visited Suat every three months, and I became quite familiar with the way he looked down on everything and everybody around him. I thought he looked like those fundamentalist bodyguards who stand around twirling their amber prayer beads and waiting for orders. Besides his chauffeur, there was now a Japanese assistant, toward whom Suat was most respectful. The three of them would often go out on secret excursions together.

"I don't know why he wanted to get his military service over with—he could have waited another three years. I was in Istanbul when he finished it. He barged into my office carrying a thick envelope that he said was to be opened two months later. He appeared more rested and energetic than I ever expected. Just after this I read in the papers that the taxi driver who murdered our father had been killed in a robbery. It seems he'd been let out of jail early.

"I never saw my twin brother again. His last words were, 'I've got my discharge papers and if I don't get out of here I'll go crazy.' For two weeks my messages went unanswered, then I flew to New York. There was a new tenant in his apartment. Suat had disappeared into thin air along with his pets and assistants. Nobody knew anything about where they might be. I had no idea if he was on another secret project or if he'd committed suicide, but I was perfectly aware that I was no closer than his cat was to his inner world. That night I didn't sleep a wink. At the last minute, however, I gave up the idea of going to the police and decided I should go back to Geneva and wait for a sign. Days full of nightmares went by, then suddenly I remembered the envelope in my safe. Hoping to find some kind of clue, I opened it five days ahead of time.

"The reason I told you about my family in such detail is because of the four items that came out of this envelope. It's debatable whether they constitute a will; what's not debatable is that you've hit the jackpot. This is what was in that envelope: a $2.4 million check made out to me, a notarized letter giving me power of attorney, written instructions on how to deal with the check, and a personal letter for you.

"What Suat wants is, firstly, for me to deposit the check in an account to be opened at our Geneva bank. Then, every month, $5,000 will be transferred to your bank account. This arrangement will start when you retire from military service and will continue for forty years. At the end of each year the accumulated interest will be added to your account as well. If you die before all this is finished, the fund will go to your heirs, or, if that doesn't work out, to the Foundation for Support of the Turkish Air Force.

"There's more. Suat meticulously restored the house he inherited in Balat, and always stayed there when he came to Istanbul. His directive states that I'm to transfer that property to you.

"Well, I suppose there's good reason for what my brother wants to do. But what I've been curious about ever since I opened the envelope is what's in that personal letter to you. If the clue I'm after happens to be in there, let's have it, Lieutenant, please."

*

I was exhausted by this tirade. All that stuff concerning me could easily be a trap, or a joke. I took the letter from the outstretched hand of the civilian whose other hand had gone to the bottle with every pause in his speech. I intended to read it quickly and hand it back to him. With so many of my own troubles, I was perfectly indifferent to the crises of these rich twins playing hide-and-seek. (Like a man developing a hunger at the wrong moment, I had the feeling I was missing Rachmaninoff's Piano Concerto No. 3.) A UNICEF card fell out of the envelope. On the front was a drawing of a violin surrounded by the words: "MOZART, ALLES GUTE." Inside was a thin piece of faded paper, which I guessed was a photocopy of the check that Fuat had mentioned. There were also two notes signed by Suat, which appealed to me because they were short. One of them said, in English, "It is hereby certified that Kemal

Kuray is to be the recipient of this check and the accrued interest." As I looked at the signature, which looked like Kufic script, those blue panic-stricken eyes came to mind.

Staring at the shaky handwriting on a postcard, my right hand began to tremble, and I turned my back to the civilian whose cigar had gone out again.

Commander,

When I was a child I used to think that great men were re-warded with death to increase the treasures of heaven. In high school I thought that the injustices blocking the paths of good people were entrance tests for heaven. In the end I believed that heaven and hell were wandering the earth arm in arm.

My twin brother Fuat, whose astrological sign is different from mine, blames my obsession with heaven and hell and night and day on my being a Gemini.

I don't remember who first said, "Incomplete praise is a stain on honor." But as you are a good person, I'm sure you won't refuse the check I left with my brother. My mother used to say that the house in Balat never brought any luck to my uncle. To me it was neither lucky nor unlucky. But now I think it's time real luck arrived, and that it's you who should benefit from this turn of events.

I think that the night is the true owner of the sky. From now on I will try to take refuge in the night, Commander...

S.A.

I read and reread these Tchaikovskyian lines. If he hadn't committed suicide, Suat had certainly left a mysterious trail.

I knew that the bewildered Fuat would be staring at me imploringly.

I turned to him and said, "Suat didn't leave a clue. He wants me to take the money and the property. If there were some kind of tragic situation here, there would surely be an indication in these lines."

He relaxed a bit. He deserved to know about the bond between his twin brother and myself, so I told him everything about me—except for the part about my father's choice of career. I couldn't accept Suat's offer without talking to my doctor and commanders, so I asked for twenty-four hours.

I announced to the authorities that I was prepared to request retirement if I was no longer able to fly. (Had there been even a glimmer of hope, I would have turned down all the mansions on the Bosphorus.) I received the lukewarm response I had expected and called Fuat to tell him I was retiring. He asked for my bank details, which I duly gave him, and we made an appointment to meet at the Pera Palace Hotel to arrange the transfer of the Balat house.

II

The hotel was hibernating its way through the last days of winter. I was given the Ernest Hemingway room, which had perhaps remained unchanged for ninety years. From my creaky window I had a bird's eye view of the Golden Horn. It looked like another country out there. I went downstairs and out to Istiklal Avenue to mull over the prospects of my new abode. While I was on Istiklal, whose winding course from Tünel to Taksim had always reminded me of the River Ganges, I decided to do some research.

I passed the old music store. I'd heard that it shut down when the boss's wife threw him out. Now a "Kebab and Pizza Palace" occupied its neglected premises. Just beyond it was a quiet bookstore. I ducked in to find out something about my new neighbourhood.

As I looked at the blurry photographs of mosques and

synagogues, it occurred to me that I had never been to Balat. But why would anyone go there when the Agora Tavern no longer existed? I hailed a cab in front of Galatasaray. How naked I felt in my civilian clothes when I ordered the unshaven driver to turn off the awful music pouring from his radio. He told me I was the first customer for Balat that he'd had in ten years. He made a terrifying right turn at the Unkapanı Bridge. Suddenly on our left appeared the old city walls, with a row of desolate buildings leaning against them. I was moved by the baroque sense of sorrow emanating from these abandoned houses. The driver dropped me at the mosque at the fork in the road.

"I went into that alley over there once and barely found my way out," he said and sped away.

I slipped through an opening between a kebab house and a tripe-soup restaurant and dove into the labyrinth of narrow streets. I felt like I was on a movie set depicting 1970s Anatolia. The names of every village in the Black Sea region could be seen on the signs attached to tiny coffeehouses and cafes. I couldn't believe my eyes when I saw shoe and stove repair shops. Was there only one doctor in the whole district? A "For Rent" sign hung on the glass door of a charming Internet café, and the windows of the famous Agora Tavern, which had opened in 1896, were boarded up.

But I felt close to these simple folk who spoke to each other in low voices and walked slowly along the two-foot-wide sidewalks flanking streets too narrow for even a single car. They all looked like they were getting ready to go back to the villages they'd left for temporary work. The only woman at the marketplace not wearing a headscarf was the middle-aged one who poked her head out the door of the synagogue to joke with the shopkeepers. I asked the sniffling boy selling lottery tickets which town near the Black Sea he was from.

"Cide," he said.

I bought two tickets from him.

"I'll give you a cut if I win," I said.

"Sure," he said. "Good luck."

I ducked into a nameless cafe for a bite to eat. The toast was bland. To avoid eating it I mentioned to the proprietor that I was thinking of moving to Balat. He asked where I hailed from. Figuring I'd need to be a Black Sea man to want to live there, I told him "Samsun."

These Black Sea folk had taken over Balat house by house, he claimed, but could neither adjust to the city nor give up their rural ways, and worked mostly in construction.

"If you really want to dig into Balat," he said, "turn south and follow the side of the hill."

I took his advice. In this, the second stage of my quest, the deserted shops seemed smaller. I'd seen hardly any trees since entering the neighborhood. I felt like I'd walked out of the bazaar and into a toy city—synagogues, mosques, and churches were all of a size that matched their diminutive surroundings.

On emerging from the arcade of shops, I found myself in

an area full of dilapidated Greek houses painted so that from a distance they looked like a watercolor. As I turned another corner, there were more and more abandoned houses, their bay windows still intact, jutting out onto the street. Just as I began to feel like I was wandering the back streets of Venice, the *ezan* rang out. I took it as a sign to begin my descent.

Meandering among the chador-cloaked women, it occurred to me that perhaps the reason why the Jews had never developed a distinctive architecture was that they never knew where and how long they would settle in a given place. The streets here, full of the high-pitched cries of children, took me back to my own childhood in L. I looked at the innocent faces looking back at me from the pavements and windows and said a prayer: Let them not have dreams, if those dreams are to be shattered in the midst of coming true. On the way back to my hotel I began to suspect that my inner voice might have been hiding my place of refuge from me.

I was hungry, so I made my way across the Golden Horn to Istiklal Avenue, thronged with young people. While wondering what I might do after a beef stroganoff at Rejans, I took a wrong turn and found myself in front of the Turkuaz secondhand bookstore. I went inside and, incrediby, staring out at me from one of the shelves was *Great Instrumentalists*, from Selçuk Ergene's renowned collection. I hugged it to my breast and continued on to Rejans, with its timeless charm. There were six tables set up for dinner, and all the diners looked relaxed. For coffee I returned to my hotel bar, which had seen so many artists and kings from around the world. Cheered by the carefree chatter of foreign journalists, I delved into my book, nostalgic for the grand virtuosos. My hand started shaking when I attempted to underline a staccato passage of Prokofiev. I hid it under the table, then jammed it into my pocket, running upstairs to my room. I considered the part played by the Rejans vodka in the absence of a headache and smiled. That was the night, I believe, when I abandoned the notion that I could best adapt to civilian life by keeping away from civilians.

I stood beneath the recalcitrant shower for half an hour before breakfast. I was lying on my bed listening to Boccherini when it started to rain. Scanning the ceiling for traces of the ninety-year-old tapping of Hemingway's typewriter keys, I told myself, "Don't turn into Suat, Kemal!" I decided to go to the little restaurant next to the English consulate for dinner because the impenetrable composure of the Pera's headwaiter annoyed me. I was about to find out for real whether having one door closed in your face meant another one opening.

*

Fuat and I met in the lobby. He was obviously impatient to get this business over with. In clipped sentences he informed me that he stayed at the Pera whenever he came to town from Geneva. When I replied that I'd been there for two days he muttered something in French that startled me. We went to the Deeds Registry in Fatih in the Jeep of a real estate agent whom he introduced as a childhood friend. Fuat handed me an envelope containing a receipt showing the first monthly transfer to my new bank account. While the real estate agent loquaciously explained to me the intricacies of deed transfers, Fuat whispered into his cellphone. After a while he turned to me, the gleam in his eye indicating that it was time for his last declamation.

"While my mother was working a woman named Akile looked after us. When we moved and she couldn't come with us we cried for two days. She was an introverted person for whom questions about the past were off-limits. But about the time we graduated from middle school we happened to learn her secret. And three days later she died of cancer.

"It turned out that Akile had had to flee her hometown because of an illicit relationship with a cousin, which had left her pregnant. Her widowed aunt took her in and the two of them raised the child, Sami, on their own. Somehow hearing this story made us feel a bit guilty. When Akile died, our grandmother assumed responsibility for young Sami, and Suat became the boy's guardian.

"In ten minutes you'll own the top floor of Balat's most fashionable building. Suat once owned the ground floor too, but he transferred the deed to it to Sami on our grandmother's death. Sami is now a graphic designer. He's apparently been operating a business as an art consultant and painting restorer out of his apartment.

"It was he who called a minute ago. He's waiting for us in his van in front of the building. He's a very straight fellow.

If you let him, he can become a real friend to you, not just a neighbor."

I took the title deed in my hand and felt a swirl of strange emotions, almost as if I were receiving a pass for a course I'd cheated in. We left the office and went outside. The diminutive stature of the man standing next to his van didn't alarm me, but as I got closer I was startled by the strangeness of his face. It was as if, instead of a nose, a wax block had been stuck between his eyes. As we shook hands I noticed that his right arm was longer than his left. But even the way he periodically rolled his eyes in panic and lowered his gaze was somehow appealing. Fuat was relieved to see that I wasn't disgusted.

"Sami's here to take you to your new home. He's got the keys. If you need me, you know my address."

I somehow knew that this was the last I would see of him. As he said goodbye, the gold ring on his left hand attracted my attention. Had I seen that lion's head with diamonds glued into its mouth and eyes on Suat rather than Fuat, I wouldn't have been surprised at all.

*

As we drove along in Sami's van, with its aroma of paint and varnish, he informed me that he had just turned thirty-one. "I was born almost noseless," he went on. "Thanks to the plastic surgeon's talent and three operations it's much less of an eyesore now.

"I've never seen the twins together. I never got to meet

their grandmother either, to thank her for her generosity."

We took a left in front of the Agora Tavern. Somehow I'd failed to notice earlier how the street widened where the bazaar petered out. We pulled up in front of a faded pink Greek house on A. Street and I fell in love with it at first sight. Across the street from my new apartment was a neglected building used as storage by a bank. The graffiti smeared across it, "Tear Me Down", didn't seem that unreasonable. Except for the girl eating sunflower seeds in the bay window of a dilapidated building, the street was deserted. I reverently followed, house by house, the *via dolorosa* of the exhausted buildings on either side of the street. Despite the inviting gestures of Sami, who stood waiting at our door, I found it difficult to pull myself away.

The three-story house that I now entered with a *Bismillah* could have graced a postcard. As I climbed the stone stairs I was greeted by the smell of damp walls and cheap soap. A card over the doorbell of the second-floor flat read "Prof. Dr. Ali Uzel." How pleasing, I thought, to have an academic as my only neighbor, as we continued upstairs to the door of the lottery prize whose deed I clutched in my hand. The raven-shaped door knocker was clue enough for me not to be surprised at what would greet me.

Or so I thought. In fact the three-bedroom flat seemed to lack nothing except a staff of personal servants. The imported kitchen cabinets and refrigerator were fully stocked, down to the pastrami and wholewheat bread. In response to my quizzical look, Sami murmured something about instructions he'd received months ago from Suat. I had a little trouble reconciling the geometrical designs of the rugs scattered tastefully on the expensive wooden floors with the grotesque paintings on the walls, but I was quite receptive to the *adagissimo* sessions in front of the wide windows framing a view of the Golden Horn.

I sat gingerly on the swivel chair at the antique desk in the study. I didn't care how many thousands of books might occupy the shelves that covered the wall on my right, but I leapt up when I saw the Bang & Olufsen stereo equipment. I counted about 3,000 classical CDs on the tiers of glass shelves beside the massive system.

"They were all brought over from New York." Sami smiled.

My hand went out to *Pachelbel's Greatest Hits: Canon*, performed by eight orchestras. I carefully positioned my headphones and focused on James Galway, my eyes closed in adoration of the melody spilling from his flute. I felt my soul glide from my body cell by cell as his *Affetuoso* soared into the room. Just before the finale I began to sense that I was being watched. I opened my eyes. I was surprised to see that I had apparently overlooked a mysterious portrait hanging over the stereo: EDGAR ALLAN POE (1809–1849). His large eyes stared out at me as if he were warning and challenging me at the same time.

I needed to bring these fits of suspicion to an end before my inner voice decided to speak to me again. If the recluse who was pleased to have my friendship had indeed committed suicide, I had no need to feel guilty over the inheritance he'd bequeathed me. And if I was about to be lured into some kind of schizoid trap, I didn't want to come out of it defeated. I remembered the sentence about the house in Suat's goodbye note—something like *Now I think it's time has come to bring some real luck, and the one who should benefit from this turn of events is you.*

*

I went back to the Pera Palace for the last time with Sami, to collect my luggage. He clenched the steering wheel more tightly when I suggested he come in to the hotel for a look at its historic rooms. It recalled another dramatic moment when he had inexplicably put his carnival-mask face up to mine and hurriedly pulled it away.

Maybe because I realized he'd seen that I felt sorry for him, I accepted his invitation to dinner that evening. His house was minimalist in design, and I didn't mind the duet between varnish and sorrow that I found there.

He had an apprentice, Mazlum, who had just completed his military service and who was spilling pieces of *pide* bread all over the place. In my sternest military voice I questioned him: "And just where in the Black Sea region do *you* come from?"

"Inebolu, Commander."

With my first beer Sami was to learn that his new neighbor had once been the ablest pilot in the Armed Forces, at least until that moment when his plane fell out of the sky.

52

"My army friend Suat decided to leave Istanbul and proposed to sell his apartment to me," I went on, "I gave him a deposit before his discharge, and paid the balance to Fuat at the Deeds Registry." I was pleased to see that my right hand declined to give me away. I had no doubt that the clumsy Mazlum would lose no time in spreading everything he'd heard at the table to the entire neighborhood. From here on it would be impossible for me not to be respected as a warrior hero throughout the district and to become everyone's honorary "Commander."

Following my first leisurely breakfast I stopped by my old bank on Istiklal. There wasn't a single employee left whom I knew. I withdrew half of my first transfer in Turkish lira. My request for a maximum-limit credit card was immediately honored, and I headed to the ritzy Akmerkez shopping mall to buy some respectable clothes. At a café frequented by rich women I called my mother to tell her that I was in town on a special assignment and would stop by after dinner.

I went back to L. whistling improvised gothic overtures. I knew I would find my aunt and uncle waiting for me in that soulless living room. I was explaining to them how I was "retired on the advice of my doctors and senior officers" when my father leapt up, his face close to mine.

"How could you do such a thing without my permission?" he said.

I grabbed him by the collar of the shirt he'd worn for the last ten years and sat him back down on the couch.

"Baba, I'm through listening to you," I said, glad to see

my right hand starting to tremble. "Otherwise you'll go on treating me like a robot for the rest of my life. You forced me to become a pilot just because it was something you wanted to do yourself. If you'd asked me even once, you'd have known that all I ever wanted to do was become a musician like you. Instead, you brainwashed me so completely that I hated even to come home on weekends because I couldn't handle civilian life.

"I knew, as I came down in that parachute, that I would never fly again. But I thought to myself, okay, now I can become the musician I always wanted to be. What an empty wish! Look at this right hand! The doctors can't fix it, Baba. I can't even use it to take a piss, never mind play an instrument. I never know when it will shake and when it won't, and sometimes I want to take an axe to it.

"I can't go to sleep without my pills. Then just when I think I'm relaxed, I'm struck down by a headache. You may be resigned to working at the cemetery, Baba, but I could never sit here pinned to a desk and rot just because I can't fly. I might as well be sixty retiring, I feel that exhausted. I'm going some place far away where nobody can find me. I'll work on getting used to civilian life and see if I can heal my wounds. Know this, Baba, I'm going to throw away my phone if you call me for any reason other than an emergency!"

As I finished speaking I looked over at my mother. It was the first time I'd ever seen her cry, but her eyes seemed to say, "I'm proud of you, son." The other three people in that room were in a state of near collapse.

*

I delegated the logistics of the house to Mazlum and his mother, Aunt Cevher. He took charge of supplies while she took care of the housework. Between intervals of wrestling with the furniture she would wonder aloud why I wasn't married. Professor Ali Uzel and I said hello when we ran into each other on the stairs. He appeared to be in his sixties and was always elegantly dressed. From the look in his weary blue eyes I gathered he bore a hurt of some kind. According to Sami, this university lecturer was always writing. The neighborhood shopkeepers knew little about him, but since nobody had seen him smile for twenty years they concluded that he had a secret which would probably do as the subject of a novel. Obviously the professor's discretion as well as his gentle manners entitled him to respectability.

I spent a number of mornings choosing pieces from the CD library and transferring them to my iPod. I experimented with the classical cookbooks in the kitchen and got up from the table half-full. I sallied forth to explore the Golden Horn. Fener, Balat and Ayvansaray were like three stepsisters living in the same waterside mansion. Fener, with its naturally dense and mosaic-like texture, seemed to be the most mysterious. The grand buildings on the east end of the Horn were poetic: the juxtaposition of the lonely and abandoned Greek lycée against the Vatican of Orthodoxy, the Patriarchate, was positively *Felliniesque*. The real monuments of the district were the ruined Greek houses. At every crossroads of those fairy-tale hillsides I gazed at their empty windows, wondering what they were seeing. Whenever a faint breeze wafted inland from the coast I hoped that it would bestow a bit of rain on this faded glory, but it was always denied me.

Every tiny church that popped up on my path seemed to be assembled from stones cut from the same bottomless quarry, and I was charmed by the mosques that bore witness to the pious deeds of Ottoman pashas. It seemed ironic that as you moved west the rural layers grew thicker: nook-like tea gardens, labyrinthine alleys, dried-up ancient fountains, weary streets, and so many tombs of holy men. I memorized their inscriptions and used them as landmarks. I still wonder whether Ayvansaray is the Golden Horn's most—or perhaps one and only—cheerful neighborhood.

I was usually home by the time of the evening *ezan*. If it wasn't the view of Beyoğlu from my window that lured me back, it was the symphonic sounds of traffic on the coast road. I was becoming increasingly fond of my house—how could I not?—but I wasn't sure whether it felt the same fondness for me.

I met Sami every week for dinner. He smelled of paint and didn't say much except to complain about how tired he was. I wished evening would come sooner so that I could transport myself to the city's concert halls: the music lovers at those obscure venues appeared to be retired civil servants and rich Jewish ladies, all in their sixties, who liked to pamper me. Or sometimes if a well-known director's film came to town, I would seek out a quiet Pera café and wait there for it to start. If these were the pleasures of the single civilian life, I was pleased to make their acquaintance.

*

I made plans to expand my exploration of the Golden Horn. I decided to walk the territory street by street, from Edirnekapı to Sarayburnu on the Sea of Marmara. I would gradually unveil my old friend Istanbul. Long live idleness!

The more I walked, the more rested I felt. I saw women standing as still as mummies behind their bay windows, steadily contemplating the street—their only other occupation when not immersing themselves in housework. I imagined that none of them had ever left their wooden houses, teetering on collapse after God knows how many earthquakes, to take a boat ride on the Bosphorus. I joked with the children who ran after me thinking I was a tourist because I had an iPod. My hunger was almost sated by the bland grilled cheese toast prepared for me by mediocre chefs at their less-than-hygienic buffets. I was welcomed with suspicion by old men sitting in their coffeehouses with nowhere else to go. My wanderings were finally over, I suppose, when I realized that the textures of sound and color which changed every three streets or so had begun to blur at the edges. Did I envy those people who sat simply waiting, resigned to their imprisonment in a melancholy time tunnel? I've forgotten the name of the philosopher who said, two thousand years ago, "Don't exaggerate the importance of life. Remember that your slaves, even your animals, have it too."

At the main artery of Eminönü, a strategic hub for Byzantines and Ottomans, I ran into weird-looking tourists, aggressive shopkeepers, and giant official monuments whose silhouettes adorned postcards. Delving further into the crossword-puzzle labyrinth of the side streets, I found noble stone buildings abandoned by owners who had fled to *nouveau riche* ghettos. I passed a row of spice shops where the locks on the shutters hadn't been changed since World War II.

And just at that point, why did I suddenly wonder why Suat had fled the scene?

*

I wandered into a bar where everybody, especially the waiters, appeared to be absorbed in the horse races on TV. A rich brew of swear words and slang thickened the smoky atmosphere. Special "waiters" went back and forth between the bar and a neighboring bookie where they put down bets for customers. The slim man drinking and belching across the table from me laughed to hear that this was the first time I'd laid eyes on a betting slip. He claimed that his name was Muhlis and that he was a sociology student at nearby Istanbul University. Then he leaned close and said, "I like you, brother," though I had barely said a word. "If you'll meet me tomorrow night with $300 in your pocket, there's a world-class babe who'll suck your ..."

I got to the Valide Mosque gate five minutes early. Muhlis arrived ten minutes later. When he saw how I was dressed he laughed and said, "Are you on your way to a wedding or what?" As we walked through the dark streets of Aksaray I learned the unwritten rules of the night. We descended to the basement floor of a ramshackle shopping center. Did the sign that blinked on when it was in the mood really say "Disco Eden"? A couple of dull-witted security men checked us out and escorted us down a stinking corridor and into a dimly lit hall where Turkish and Russian music clashed. About thirty Slavic women were undulating on a small raised dance floor. I was informed that I might choose my own filthy table between them and the damp wall. I had trouble deciding whether to turn my attention to the girls with milk-white legs on the floor, or to the women chewing cigarettes and imbibing *raki* at the neighboring tables. Muhlis, the honorable pimp, advised me to dispatch a waiter to invite the lady of my choice over to negotiate. If we struck an agreement, I would order champagne for the girl, and then we could proceed to her room at the adjacent hotel. It was amusing how Muhlis swaggered like a country lord when it was I who was financing his extravagant charade. He waved his prayer beads airily and a *zaftig* girl swaying on the dance floor came running to our table. I don't know why but the fact that they knew each other bothered me. She was swearing in Turkish that the most sportive of the exotic dancers was her roommate Anna, who had a degree in education from Minsk University. I felt like fleeing this

59

place that reeked of piss but my inner voice spoke up and said, "Don't spoil the game." So after surveying the field once more, I asked the head waiter to bring over a girl who looked like the actress Sandra Bullock.

As the girl in black shorts minced her way toward us, I thought about what Muhlis had told me: "No names, no phone numbers." So when the art historian from Odessa asked my name I blurted out, "Peter Ilyich Tchaikovsky." My imaginary name made the rounds of these university-connected sex slaves, raising a chorus of giggles. It was with these words, which were the last thing they expected to hear from a horny Turk, that I first entered their memories.

I became a regular at Disco Eden. I went alone, twice a week. I would drink lemon vodka to relax and then retire to a room at the Da-Da Hotel, each time with a new girl. As those lips redolent of vodka and menthol cigarettes started roaming over my body, I would wonder what Suat Altan—if he was still alive—was doing at that very moment.

*

I bought the most recent issue of *Andante* and dropped by the bank to withdraw every last dollar of the second month's transfer. I walked toward Tünel, planning to sit and read at a quiet café while I waited for the matinee of "Capote" to begin. Suddenly I was startled by somebody whistling Matia Bazar's "Vacanze Romane." It came from the side street next to the Swedish consulate, and it took me back fifteen years. Cautiously I approached the barefoot man in rags who was inspecting the contents of a large metal garbage bin.

"Is that you, Hayri Abi?" I asked.

Muttering to himself, the man turned a face toward me on which long hair and a beard were intermingled. One eye was shut; but the creature in front of me was indeed my music mentor and exploiter, Hayri Abi. The nails on his scarred hands had turned into claws. He began to stammer and then burst into tears, trying to back away, but he fell over. I saw the filthy underwear beneath his overcoat. He got up with difficulty and, dragging one foot, limped down the street and into nothingness.

I stood there expecting my right hand to start shaking, but instead my head began to ache. I turned and set out on foot toward Balat despite the autumnal nip in the air. Only when I reached home did I feel better. That was the night I stopped taking painkillers and sleeping pills. It was as if Hayri Abi had extracted a virus from my body as he had extracted himself from my life.

III

I'd spent the night with the philosopher Tanya, who was counting the days until she returned to Lvov.

"In two days I'm getting out of this meat market, Tchaikovsky," said the ballerina with VITA and BREVIS tattooed respectively on her left and right buttocks. "And don't you get bogged down in this life either. Go out and look for love even if you know it's going to end in disaster. It will help you mature spiritually."

"I hope you won't laugh if I tell you that the meaning of my name in Turkish is 'mature'," I told her as I was putting her fee together. "And as for your sound advice, Tanya, I have actually begun the search for 'self,' thank you."

From the ranks of battered taxis in front of the hotel I chose one with a bumper sticker that said, "Take me to Sivas, boss." I smiled to myself, thinking of my oblique response to

Tanya. It was probably justice for me to be banished from Aksaray for a while.

The ether-soaked cloth slapped over my face and the stone to the back of my head carried me back to my collision with the rocks and those days in the hospital. When I awoke, the sound of the *ezan* was battering my ears and my head was throbbing with pain, but I had no time for self-pity. I was curled in a fetal position and shivering on a couch in a stranger's living room. I tried to sit up, feeling queasy in this meticulously tidy environment. On the walls and end tables were a series of photographs depicting a couple in youth and middle age. With an effort I got to my feet. It was my neighbor, Ali Uzel, standing next to the pretty woman with shining eyes in every picture. While I waited for him to make his appearance, I checked my pockets. The mugger had taken $200, and my credit cards and house keys. I folded the flowery blanket that had covered me into a neat bundle and sat on the couch waiting to express my gratitude. At that moment Professor Uzel walked into the room, wearing elegant pajamas under a maroon dressing gown.

"Good morning, young man, and a speedy recovery to you."

"Thank you, sir. I must apologize for all the trouble I've caused you."

"The mugger must have followed you—a Balat person would never do anything so tactless as this. The doorbell started ringing like mad, at midnight. I looked out the window and there was a man calling to me in a shaky voice that my new neighbor was lying unconscious in front of my door. I came down but didn't see anybody on the street. I called for Sami to come and help, but for some reason he wasn't here even though he's usually home all day. I couldn't find any keys in your pockets, so I dragged you up here myself. It took a while. Come on, let's have breakfast. Later you can have your locks changed. And I'll expect you for dinner at 7.30. It will give us a chance to get to know each other."

Thanking the good professor, I asked to be excused. I got the spare key from Aunt Cevher and rushed back to my apartment, where I immediately cancelled my credit cards. After a long hot shower I called the locksmith and watched while he changed the locks. Then I slept for two hours listening to Mozart sonatas. I got up and went to Le Cave in Cihangir, where I bought two bottles of good imported wine. The professor welcomed me in his red apron. His living room was filled with the music of Nat King Cole and the aroma of fresh warm butter. The professor set a good table. He smiled at the two bottles of wine and I felt a bit embarrassed. The food was perfect and the service impeccable, yet I sensed he wasn't fond of praise. My respect for my neighbor was growing with every sip I took. Summarizing my life story for him—with the exception of being underwritten by Suat— released a good deal of my negative energy.

"May I ask whether the lovely lady in these photographs was your … wife?" I said while opening the second bottle.

"You can decide for yourself what she was to me," he replied, staring for a while at the picture on the wall furthest from him. "I went to the Robert College School of Engineering in 1959. That was the year the engineering school first accepted girls, as I was to learn from Esther Ventura, who was standing behind me in the registration line.

"'Let me buy you lunch,' she said. 'Just to be nice.'

"From that moment we became, like the poet said, two halves of one apple. We were hardly apart until the day we graduated. Since there was no girls' dormitory on campus in those days, she lived in a wooden house in neighboring Hisar with her friend Suna. It was a thrill for me to walk her home in the cool of the night after a long study session at the library.

"She was a spirited girl with a great sense of humor. Maybe she wasn't the most beautiful girl at the college, but she was the most popular. As she was a chemistry major, we didn't have all that many classes together. At class breaks I would meet her in front of Hamlin Hall. She would spot me from 300 yards away and start running toward me, yelling 'Aaa-liii,' and it would feel like a curtain of fog was lifting from my eyes. But it was also a little embarrassing because I imagined the eyes of the whole campus on us as she threw her arms around my neck. We were considered a model couple by the other students. They knew what time we'd be going to which canteen and would save our favorite table for us. Esther always had a greeting for everybody and a joke for the waiters.

"We never fought, and only once did I have to lay down the law to her. It was after our first-year finals. She made a proposal that shocked me—she wanted us to show up in swimsuits and dive into the Bosphorus in front of the Bebek gate of the campus. Of course I was angry when I realized she wasn't joking.

"'Then I'll do it on my own,' she said.

"'Look,' I said. 'If you go swimming in a place where even the drunks don't dare to fall in, you'll not only cause a traffic jam, but you'll be known as the crazy lady of the school. I can't let you go down in Bosphorus history like that.' I walked away and left her sitting on the bench.

"Next day, at the time of the morning *ezan*, the windows on the tennis-court side of the men's dormitory were full of boys craning their necks to see what was going on. It was Esther. She was at the front door yelling my name at the top of her lungs. I knew she wouldn't stop until I went down.

"'What's all this?' I said.

"'I couldn't sleep. What would you have done if I'd dived in?' she said.

"'I don't know, I might have transferred to Middle East Technical in Ankara,' I said.

"Quick as a shot she hooked her foot behind my leg and flipped me onto my back, then jumped on me and started pinching my cheeks.

"'What! So you think I wouldn't follow you?' she shouted, whereupon the crowd of spectators burst into a round of clapping and cheering.

"During summer vacations I worked as a so-called intern at my sister's company. I'd send Esther flowery letters signed

'Aliye,' the feminine version of my name, and she would secretly send me postcards from the magical European cities that she toured with her mother. I read them five times a day.

"For three years, we lived a dream-like existence. Then, in the summer before our senior year, we decided to get married, as we intended to go to America for Master's degrees. Esther knew it wouldn't be easy to get permission from her pious Jewish mother to marry a Muslim boy, but we were prepared to spend a while in İzmir softening her up. We waited until the end of finals to bring up the subject. I didn't worry about my sister—she was carrying on with a company manager who was married, after all. As for my father, his response was, 'Well, if you think you've found the woman of your life, what can I say?'

"So the mission of tearing us apart was left to Esther's mother. In our farewell scene Esther said, 'I couldn't care less about her threats to disown me, but she vows that if I marry a Muslim she'll commit suicide. She never really recovered from my father's death, you know. She's dependent on me. You'd be appalled if you saw her. She curses me and weeps, weeps and curses me. You're the only man I can ever love, Ali. But …'

"And that was it."

*

"More because it was in New York than because of the scholarship they gave me, I chose Columbia for a Master's in industrial engineering. I believed my wound would heal

67

in that great city, and I wasn't wrong. Still, as I struggled with the city and the school, Esther remained like a clot in my blood. The following year I ran into her old housemate Suna on a flight to Istanbul. She hadn't been all that sorry to hear that Esther and I had broken up. Anyway, this dumpy, disagreeable woman was nattering on about Esther marrying a Jewish fellow and emigrating to Buenos Aires. I said, 'If you're passing on this gossip to make me feel bad, you needn't bother—it won't work,' which shut her up.

"During the three years it took to complete my degree my sister Oya's lover divorced his wife, married Oya, and was divorced by Oya. I taught in New York for two years and then returned to Turkey for my military service. My sister by then was living with my father in his new Maçka apartment with the Bosphorus view. I was assigned to a military translation project at General Headquarters in Ankara. My father, in a burst of delayed affection, wanted me to visit every weekend. I decided not to return to the States when I learned from my sister that he had cancer. I finished my military duties and took a job at my old school, which by now had been nationalized as Boğaziçi University. Oya had risen to director of one of her company's divisions. On hearing how much I was earning, she arranged some consulting work for me. That New Year's Eve my father passed away. It never crossed my mind to think about matters of inheritance.

"In the 1970s the ideology wars hit Boğaziçi like every other Turkish university. Maybe I should have gone back to

Columbia. Anyway, I was tidying my desk in preparation for summer vacation one day, when who should walk into my office but Esther? I acted as if I wasn't shocked. We said our hellos like distant friends; she smiled a guilty smile. She was still attractive and elegantly dressed. The weight she'd put on had only added to her sexiness. It was odd to feel so horny after all that time. She heard me tell the secretary to cancel any further appointments and asked if we could meet next evening in the Hilton Hotel lobby.

"'I'll die if you don't come,' she said.

"I didn't expect a miracle, but of course I was curious about what she would say, so I went. She'd made reservations for dinner on the terrace and it wasn't long before she was telling me everything. Her mother had tried to marry her off but she wasn't having any of it. She met a man called Eli Arditti who whisked her away to Buenos Aires. She was glad to go, thought it would get her out from under her mother's thumb.

"First he tried to go into partnership with his cousin in Buenos Aires, and when that didn't work out, he set up an export business. He lost a fortune. Yet when they returned to İzmir he managed to sweet-talk Esther's mother into another loan. She sold her apartment building to fund a jewelry business with an Istanbul Armenian. Esther was expecting that to fail too.

"She felt trapped, she said. She couldn't divorce him because of her daughter Stella, who was seven at the time and adored her ridiculous father. She couldn't take the money she inherited from her mother's rental properties out of the country for regulatory reasons. So she holidayed in Istanbul each year, then bought rugs at the Grand Bazaar with what was left and sent them back to Buenos Aires to sell.

"She told me all this like it was some kind of joke. It reminded me of her goodbye speech nine years earlier. I couldn't get a word in edgeways, not even to offer my condolences for her mother who had passed away. I asked the odd questions alright, and nodded when I was supposed to. To be honest, I was surprised that she wasn't offended by my diffidence. She dragged me up to her room with a view of the Bosphorus to show me Stella's picture. Reluctantly I took it in my hands. It really irked me to see how handsome her husband was. There was something of Alexander the Great about him. Stella seemed to have inherited her father's looks. She was as pretty as a china doll. I felt a sudden urge to flee. I reached out to stroke Esther's cheek goodbye and she grabbed my hand.

"The next morning we left for Cappadocia. It surprised us to discover that we were as passionate about each other as if we'd been separated for nine days rather than nine years.

*

"Every June for thirteen years she came to Istanbul. Every year I waited for her. We went on dream holidays, as carefree as two university students in love. We never brought up our problems—we lived in the moment and never thought about how it might end. By then I was a professor and my sister was nagging me to marry. I somehow found out that Esther had had to sell her last property. She mentioned once that Eli had gone into the used-car business. However naïve her husband might be, I never believed that he completely bought Esther's story about having to visit Istanbul every year to collect the rent from her apartment.

"On her last two trips Esther stayed at three-star hotels. She was happy for me to pay for everything. She was having trouble hiding her uneasiness. On that last trip, as though it were something to brood about, she told me that her daughter had become Miss Argentina. That night I had a dream. Her husband was speeding along in his sports car, crashed and died. As soon as the funeral was over Esther and I would get married …

"She'd never given me her address or telephone number, for fear that I might call her. When she didn't show up in June of 1987 I was almost in tears. Early in July—which is 'Tammuz' in Hebrew and means the month of tragedies—I ran into her childhood friend Luna, whom Esther visited whenever she was in town. She had bad news for me: Esther and Eli had been killed in a car crash.

"I collapsed on the spot. From that moment on I could be little more than a zombie. Esther was the vital half of my body and soul. The inner paralysis that lay in wait for me was too horrible to contemplate.

"My sister ignored my depression. As far as she was concerned I had brought dishonor to the family because

I had turned forty-five and was still unmarried. I couldn't bear it. I decided to move out and asked for my share of our inheritance. She swore that our father had left no cash and when I found out for myself that she wasn't lying I felt sick. I also learned that the law prevented me from forcing the sale of the apartment. I left on bad terms and moved in with a widower colleague of mine who lived in university housing. Your apartment's former owner, Izak, had been a school friend of Esther's and mine. When he told me that the flat beneath his old place was up for sale I bought it, heedless of the debt it would saddle me with. I moved here about twenty years ago.

"The pain of losing Esther eased little by little. I couldn't mourn for her because she'd locked herself within me. We fell asleep in each other's arms at night; in the morning she was the first thing I saw in the mirror. It made me feel good when I heard her voice in my ear or noticed her smile across the table at a restaurant. If I heaved a sigh, I murmured her name along with it. If the music was anything other than her favorite Nat King Cole I didn't listen to it. Whenever I heard the *ezan* I turned my face toward the city walls and stared. If I went out, my legs would involuntarily take me to our old hangouts. Esther was no longer my illegitimate wife for a month each June, she was my beloved who lived and breathed with me twenty-four hours a day. She might leave the room when I was lecturing or reading the papers or watching TV, but then she would re-enter and passionately embrace the whole of my existence.

"I'm sure I haven't expressed myself very well. But to make a long story short, my dear neighbor, my beloved's death turned the flame of love in my heart into an eternally glowing ember. To honour her memory, I retired and went into seclusion here. Now I teach part-time and translate romantic novels under a pseudonym, though it does worry me that I might discover a deeper passion than my own …"

*

The professor's words had left me moved. Under that mask of melancholy was a philosophical heart, and what he wanted to convey to me was that I shouldn't dwell on my sufferings but, like Tanya from Lvov, persist in the search for true love, regardless of the outcome. Who was it said, "Ah, how sad they were, the happiest days of my life"? Well anyway, those words were on my mind as I returned to my study and put on Brahms' Sonata No. 2.

A book fell from one of the library shelves. It was *The Complete Tales and Poems of Edgar Allan Poe*. Inside it was an envelope containing six photographs stuck together with Scotch tape. On the front of the first three were question marks; on the other three were "X's". The pretty girl smiling at the camera must have been Suat's girlfriend, the one who died in the fire. On the back of each picture someone had written, pressing hard with a red pencil, a different stanza of Poe's mysterious poem.

I felt compelled to read it twice:

Annabel Lee

It was many and many a year ago,
In a kingdom by the sea,
That a maiden there lived whom you may know
By the name of Annabel Lee;
And this maiden she lived with no other thought
Than to love and be loved by me.

I was a child and *she* was a child,
In this kingdom by the sea,
But we loved with a love that was more than love—
I and my Annabel Lee—
With a love that the winged seraphs of heaven
Coveted her and me.

And this was the reason that, long ago,
In this kingdom by the sea,
A wind blew out of a cloud, chilling
My beautiful Annabel Lee;
So that her highborn kinsmen came
And bore her away from me
To shut her up in a sepulcher
In this kingdom by the sea.

The angels, not half so happy in heaven,
Went envying her and me—
Yes!—that was the reason (as all men know,

In this kingdom by the sea)
That the wind came out of the cloud by night,
Chilling and killing my Annabel Lee.

But our love it was stronger by far than the love
Of those who were older than we—
Of many far wiser than we—
And neither the angels in heaven above,
Nor the demons down under the sea,
Can ever dissever my soul from the soul
Of the beautiful Annabel Lee:

For the moon never beams, without bringing me dreams
Of the beautiful Annabel Lee;
And the stars never rise, but I feel the bright eyes
Of the beautiful Annabel Lee:
And so, all the night-tide, I lie down by the side
Of my darling—my darling—my life and my bride,
In the sepulcher there by the sea—
In her tomb by the sounding sea.

IV

Next morning I woke abruptly from a restless sleep. My head felt as if it was encased in a ball of thick fog. I found myself before the stereo with an urgent need to purge my soul of that story of shattered love. I sought solace in *Tristan und Isolde* ...

*

The professor and I began meeting every other day. Did this fact escape the sharp eyes of Sami, who surely noticed that I'd been drawn into Ali's melancholy orbit? Ali's invitations were actually a source of relief to me. I felt relaxed and reassured in his apartment. He would sometimes criticize my idleness while giving me cooking lessons, but I was honored even by this. And I wasn't at all curious about whether he knew Suat. And when his eyes became fixed on a faraway point I knew it was time for him to be alone with Esther.

*

I'd done my weekly shopping at the Balıkpazarı gourmet grocers like a jolly retiree. My good mood was ruined when I got home to find a gray-suited man with a briefcase at the front door. This small middle-aged man appeared annoyed at being kept waiting. He was obviously foreign. When he told me he was a lawyer from New York, I invited him in. I was excited, thinking he would have news of Suat.

"I want to tell you why I'm here," he said, stirring the warm milk he'd requested into his tea. "When the Red Army took over Russia, among the first refugees to seek asylum in the Ottoman Empire were First Lieutenant Vladimir—Vlad—Nadolsky and his brother, Lieutenant Maxim Nadolsky. We have to assume that they had with them a bag full of English pounds and precious jewelry. Their father, after all, was a wealthy count. The brothers' aim was to settle in America as soon as possible. Maxim never imagined that he would have to go to the States alone when their visas finally came through after two and a half years. But Vlad had taken a job teaching French at a private school and had fallen in love with the married vice-principal. Zoe, as she was called, was unwilling to go with him to New York since it would mean leaving her paralyzed husband behind, so Vlad had to stay too. To be close to her, he rented the apartment that is now yours. Maxim was an ambitious but honest man; he made his brother a fifty percent partner in the import-export business he founded in his adopted country and, when the business flourished, sent Vlad enough money to live on comfortably. During the Second World War Vlad became foster father to an orphan named Haluk Batumlu. He loved him as a son, yet when the boy was expelled from university as a communist sympathizer, Vlad was quick to disown him. Meanwhile he continued to wait for Zoe's husband to die so that he could marry her. But his beloved preceded him in death. So on his seventy-fifth birthday Vlad flew to New York to be near his brother. Maxim died in 1984 and his son Alex took over the company. Vlad died in his bed in 1999, aged 105. Except for the day on which the collapse of communism was announced, nobody had ever seen him smile.

"Vlad left his entire inheritance, apart from his $1.3 million savings, to his nephew Alex. Other than an old telegram Vlad carried with him, we had no clue at all as to the whereabouts of Haluk, who had inherited that $1.3 million. I ran ads in two popular Turkish newspapers. We waited six months but heard nothing. At that point Alex founded an investment fund in his uncle Vlad's name. For the last seven years the profits on the money that never found its way into the luckless Haluk's hands have been donated to Vlad's favorite church. Last month, when his uncle showed up in Alex's dream scolding him for not trying hard enough to find Haluk, I was dispatched immediately to Istanbul.

"I knew that an ordinary interpreter would get me nowhere. So when one of the locals mentioned a brave English-speaking pilot who'd just moved in, I wanted to meet you. Firstly, Lieutenant Kuray, I have a proposition for you: use this telegram Haluk sent to Vlad fifty years ago to trace him. I'll give you $10,000 in advance. If you find him or his heirs in ten days I'll give you $20,000 more. Here's a card with a phone number. I'm available twenty-four hours a day. If I don't hear from you in ten days I'll assume that Alex's dreams will no longer be disturbed by his uncle …"

I thought this would be foolish to turn down. I was curious about what the half-century-old telegram said, more than about where it came from. And even if the whole thing ended up being a fruitless Anatolian goose chase, it might at least be a good opportunity for me to adapt to civilian life. The lawyer was already taking a yellowing envelope out of his briefcase. It pleased me to see the anxious look that fell across his face when I ignored his card and failed to open the envelope, but I said "Okay" anyway.

He whistled as he left the apartment.

Then I remembered Professor Ali, to whom I had promised some specially wrapped fish and a bottle of hot pepper sauce. I went down to him and told him what I'd just learned. From the way he drew in his lower lip and arched his eyebrows, I gathered that he had no reservations about my trying to track down this Haluk Batumlu.

I counted the dollars—I don't know why—that poured out of the A4 envelope, and read the telegram twice through its protective plastic. It was dated 5 June 1956:

> *Vlad Baba,*
> *I have one last favor to ask of you. If you could send 400 liras*
> *to me, care of my friend below, you could change my life. The*
> *address:*
> *c/o Hasan Gezgin,*
> *Ziraat Bank,*
> *Mahmudiye,*
> *Eskişehir*
>
> *I kiss your hand,*
> *Haluk Batumlu*

I went to the Internet to find out about this town whose name was probably bigger than itself. I liked what I saw, mainly because it had a population of less than 5,000. The reason why this tiny spot on the map had been named after Mahmut the Second was that the sultan, for some reason, had set up a stud farm there in 1815 to breed Arabian horses.

I caught the Başkent Express to Eskişehir the next morning. I was agitated throughout that four-hour journey, reliving those days I spent in the hospital after my plane crash. My hand started shaking as we approached Eskişehir station. I hid it behind my back, hoping the anxiety would pass.

I took a taxi to Mahmudiye. The slant-eyed driver asked me enthusiastically whether I was a horse dealer. I don't know with what tone of "No" I answered, but he seemed a little peeved.

"Sorry, sir," he said. "It's just that I've never seen anyone come to Mahmudiye who's not a horse dealer or owner."

Long before we reached our destination I grew weary of the bleak thirty-mile stretch of road. I disembarked at a gas station, marvelling at this town which appeared to live in the slow lane. The men I saw wandering the half-deserted main street were all moustache-free, well mannered and slant-eyed. I plunged into side streets where buildings with even two floors stood out like high-rise eyesores. I didn't see a single cigarette butt on the ground; nor could I find a single blind alley with wild dogs and walls disfigured by graffiti. As I roamed about accompanied by a soft breeze, I heard a melody from a distant accordion and stopped to listen.

I headed back out to the main street where I saw a green hearse looking quite at home among the John Deere tractors and farm machinery. I noticed that the shopkeepers had all gone home for lunch. Looking for a coffeehouse where I could pick up some information, I realized that if Haluk Batumlu had been in secondary school at the end of World War II he would be in his seventies by now—assuming he was still alive. I reckoned that Hasan Gezgin, the man in the letter, would be about the same age. And no doubt every old man in town would have his regular table at the Friendship Tea House that stood before me. I approached a bearded old man dozing in the sun outside the door. I must have greeted him rather abruptly because he leapt up and began quickly straightening his clothes. I introduced myself. He gestured to the chair next to him and ordered me a tea. When he heard that I was looking for Hasan Gezgin he closed his eyes to aid his thinking, then spoke as if he were reciting a quiet prayer.

"I moved from Mesudiye to Mahmudiye thirty-four years ago, sir, and I've never heard of a Hasan Gezgin. But before you ask that bunch of old liars in the teahouse, let's call someone here with the same surname—Talat Gezgin. He may be a relative ..."

He stood and took a cellphone from his pocket, then went over to a bald man and spoke to him in a foreign language. I expected to be assailed with curious looks from the small knots of students ambling past the teahouse, but I was surprised at their politeness. Watching this quiet parade of children, I felt like I was on the set of a Fellini movie. The man returned looking satisfied with his homework.

"I spoke with Talat, Lieutenant; Hasan Gezgin is his cousin. He's had an accident at work and is staying home. The teahouse boy will take you there."

Talat Gezgin met me at the door. He had a dramatic patch over his right eye and appeared to be in his sixties. It seemed to me that he wore his beige jockey pants to emphasize his bowed legs. The living room smelled like detergent and was so clean and tidy that I felt bad about keeping my shoes on. His wife offered me tea and pastries. Her face beamed kindly as if she were trying to atone for past misdeeds. I sipped the aromatic tea and thrilled to the horses surrounding us in photographs and mementos. Talat, on disability retirement after thirty years at the Anatolian Agriculture Association's stables, was in a dejected mood, not merely because of losing his right eye but because of being kicked by a puny colt. The old groom leapt out of his chair when he heard that I was looking for Hasan Gezgin in order to find Batumlu, a man unaware of his inheritance in America.

"Is it always the world's way to shower gifts on charlatans?" he thundered. "That Istanbul commie first caused Hasan to be thrown out of university, then came here and took advantage of him as if nothing had happened. By the time he left Mahmudiye he had turned the lives of two families upside-down ..."

"Sir, please, calm down," I began, not knowing how I was going to finish, and went on with something like, "If we can join forces to find this rogue, Batumlu, maybe it will help heal old wounds."

I paused hopefully.

"Just a second," said Talat, and left the room. When he came back minutes later he looked more relaxed. Flourishing the old cellphone in his hand, he went on. "You can meet with Hasan tomorrow morning at nine at his shop in Eskişehir. Patience Stone Carvers is in the old *caravanserai* next to the Sefa Hotel."

The Sefa Hotel's gracious hospitality bored me. I chose a Tartar restaurant for dinner. After that I went to a bar with a trendy name and sat with my iPod in my ears while I watched the men watching a football game on TV. By the time I put on my pajamas I was tired of the hotel. At the last minute I'd thrown *Tales of Detective Dupin* into my travel bag, but it too failed to interest me. I turned an ear to the rhythm of the traffic on the street below. The receptionist, who persisted in mispronouncing the name of the hotel, had said that Patience Stone Carvers was one of the "strangest" meerschaum shops in the city. I nodded off finally while absorbed in what seemed to be a map on the ceiling.

The basement of the Yediveren Caravanserai, which apparently hadn't been painted since its opening, was full of small shops selling forms of meerschaum. The display windows, choked with ornate pipes and gaudy souvenirs, were dazzling. Patience Stone Carvers, however, did not have a window. The apprentice who let me in whispered that his boss was on the phone in the back office. I looked over the items on the shelves while I waited. I'd never seen anything like these human and animal figurines, these grotesque objects and delicate masks, anywhere, not even in the Grand Bazaar of Istanbul. Perhaps the craftsman's intention was to reflect the honor of pain. Even I could grasp the patience required in their execution. They were bursting with details like the lines and cross-hatchings in a bleak graphic novel (though perhaps I was reading too much into them to see regret in the mask-like faces).

With a wide smile Hasan Gezgin welcomed me into his spacious studio. He reminded me of those old portraits of Genghis Khan. He treated his tools like his children. It was disturbing to reflect that he'd spent his entire life in this shadowy hermit's cave. Clearly he had already thought about what he was going to say. I suppose the reason why he focused on the meerschaum snake on his table as he spoke was to try to minimize the tension he felt. When ginger tea was brought in, he began, carefully, to speak.

"My father was the foreman at the Yelkovan Horse Farm, the first privately owned stud farm in the area. The owner was Nabi Tabur. He was the richest man in Eskişehir; and his wife Safiye Hanım, the daughter of a Tartar chief, was said to be the most beautiful woman.

"The Tabur family would spend weekends and entire summers at their villa on the farm. They had a daughter, Nalan, who was as pretty as a picture. She was a year and a half younger than I and we used to play together, but I never dared to look into her beautiful blue eyes. Still, because I could make her laugh I believed she was in love with me as I was with her. I had a large head and pudgy body and when Nabi Tabur called me 'Fatso,' my father would laugh behind his hand. I think he was disappointed I wasn't going to be a jockey.

"Nabi Tabur took over my education after I finished primary school at the top of my class. On the advice of his Istanbul attorney I entered middle school at Galatasaray Lycée in the city.

"Haluk Batumlu was the most charismatic kid in our class. He was smart and daring and he took it upon himself to protect the outlandish Anatolian students from the Istanbul bullies. Nobody had the guts to ask him why his father was in prison.

"By the time we were in seventh grade Haluk, myself, and

a boy called Halit Mesutoğlu from Tirebolu had become inseparable. I was proud to be one of the '3 H's,' as we were known at school. Haluk was our leader; thanks to him our school days were a happy time. His mother, Aunt Selma, seemed to be generally dissatisfied with life. She'd taken on housekeeping chores for a White Russian refugee by the name of Count Vladimir Nadolsky who was stuck in Balat because of a hopeless love affair. The count was more than a kindly benefactor to Haluk: he treated him like his own son. He coached him for two hours every weekend in fencing.

"In my opinion Haluk was the most handsome guy around, yet he had little interest in the girls who chased after him. We all thought his newfound interest in Nazım Hikmet in our last year at school was a passing fad. In those days—1950s Turkey—just quoting from a Hikmet poem could make you a traitor to your country.

"We were together again in the Political Science department at Ankara University. I wanted to become a district official. By that time I'd awoken from the dream that Nabi Tabur would allow me to marry Nalan after I finished school. Vlad wanted Haluk to become a diplomat; and Halit planned to work with his father, a hazelnut grower, after getting a degree in finance. We lived together in a gray apartment in Cebeci—the doors, the windows, even the courtyard was gray. There was nothing by Nazım Hikmet that Haluk hadn't read, and he'd started in on a few other banned left-wing books as well. At the bottom of his dresser drawers you could find a Stalin poster or two. Of course we didn't abandon our leader in his new enthusiasm. We pretended to be interested in the books he brought home, and I managed to familiarize myself with those Hikmet poems that were like three-dimensional paintings. Haluk's mother passed away during our first year. The next year the police arrested us and kept us in over night because of those illegal publications. We were expelled from school even though the case never went to trial, and this, I think, shattered Haluk's dreams.

"Back at the farm, I didn't meet with the reception I'd hoped for. Nabi Tabur and my father thought my friend had victimized me. They decided I should do my military service and then come back to work at Tabur's flour factory. Haluk came to Mahmudiye in May 1956; Vlad had thrown him out of the house when he learned why he'd been expelled. Haluk decided to run off to Moscow but wanted first to say goodbye and to apologize to my family for what had happened. My father was touched by this gesture and invited him to stay with us. That invitation was to be a turning point in the lives of many people.

"Nalan and Haluk fell in love at first sight. The Tartar beauty easily vanquished Haluk's notion of love being a bourgeois fantasy. I took a perverse pleasure in assisting their exchange of love letters and observing their love play on the riverbank. When her sneaky brother caught them together, I hid Haluk at a friend's place in Mesudiye. They wouldn't let Nalan out of the house after that. The family was on at her to marry a pharmacist, so the lovers decided to elope. Haluk asked Count Nadolsky for money but he never got a reply. So the lovers pooled their pocket money to try to make their way to Halit's. How Nalan jumped from a second-floor window to meet Haluk ... it's a long story. Anyway, they went off to Tirebolu while I caught the first bus to İzmir to go live with my sister. Halit and I parted without a chance to say goodbye properly. It's been fifty-odd years now and I've had no news of any of them ...

"The passion between Nalan and Haluk was too cinematic to last. Once they got through the money they'd borrowed from Halit, Haluk probably joined up with his comrades; and Nalan was, no doubt, taken back into the bosom of her family after a tearful apology.

"Perhaps I can show you my permanent collection, Lieutenant? Let me explain why you won't see any nudes or horses in it ..."

But I didn't let him finish. I didn't need to see his collection. I'd seen enough of the self-pitying expressions on the pieces I'd studied while he talked.

*

I ducked into the first Internet café I found and was annoyed to find there were no free terminals. I commandeered a computer from the only youngster who wasn't surfing porn sites. My plan was to get some information on Tirebolu, famous for its hazelnuts, and clear out of this tired town.

I took the last train to Ankara and spent the night at the Sheraton, where I'd met Fuat. I ate at the old establishments—kebab at Hacibey, rosewater *lokum* at Ali Uzun's. Next morning I couldn't face traveling by plane, so I boarded the Trabzon bus with tickets in my hand for adjacent seats, thus saving myself from the interminable questions of a fellow passenger, but unfortunately not from the sighs of the prayer-bead-twirling man behind me. Luckily I slept until we got to Samsun. I was enjoying the lovely villages between Ünye and Tirebolu when the man interrupted my reverie.

"Ah can see yew ain't ever seen Çayeli before," he declared in a thick Laz accent.

The ticket booths at the Tirebolu bus terminal looked like beach cabins in a black-and-white movie. Once I collected my bag, which was handed to me as if it were a sacred relic, I raised my head, excited to form my first impressions of the town. The small bridge between me and a hill covered with handsome buildings divided the town in two. With good will I approached the venerable taxi waiting at the roadside sporting a bumper sticker, "Hurşit from Harşit."

"I'm looking for Halit Mesutoğlu," I said hesitantly.

I could have kissed the driver's slicked-back hair when he said, "Get in, brother, I'll take you to his house."

We climbed the hill somewhat laboriously, zigzagging up the narrow deserted streets. The driver was quick to declare that he was a student at the Open University, and then asked if I was a magazine journalist.

"No, no," I said. "I have the happy task of asking Mesutoğlu for a friend's address."

"Sorry," he said. "It's just that the finest old Greek mansion still standing in Tirebolu belongs to Professor Mesutoğlu and the Istanbul magazines come here to take pictures by the hundred, so I thought …"

We wound our way through a silent neighborhood of decrepit houses and stopped on Terzili Street at the top of the hill, in front of an imposing pink and gray piece of history. Before ringing the bell I turned, at the taxi driver's suggestion, to regard Tirebolu as it lay spread out below us. The panorama struck my eyes, then my soul.

The door opened and I was greeted by a man of otherworldly ugliness.

"The professor's gone to Giresun," he said. "He may be back in an hour. Write down your number and the reason for your visit and he'll call you if he wishes." The way he stared and muttered as I scribbled a hasty note brought to mind the hunchback of Notre Dame.

I thought I might as well explore this mysterious town while I waited for Halit Mesutoğlu's call. On the taxi driver's advice I set out walking along Terzili Street. In one of the many ramshackle gardens with mossy stone walls I thought I saw a small flock of sheep that had somehow escaped the butcher's blade. Where the street went over the top of the hill I could see the crowns of a group of ancient pines. I shivered to think how far their roots must descend, down to the base of the cliff. At the other end of the street clusters of pink and well-scrubbed schoolchildren were walking home as proudly as the self-conscious sons and daughters of exiled aristocrats.

Mid-afternoon seemed interminable here and the people on the street appeared neither happy nor sad, content with the swinging pendulum of their moods. I left the center of town in search of a restaurant that served the local delicacy, *pide*, with Trabzon cheese, and saw a hearse sitting at the side of the road, out of gas.

I was finishing my *pide* when the call came. On our way back to Terzili Street I learned that Aleko, the man who'd met me at the door, was the last Greek in Tirebolu and that the confirmed bachelor Halit Mesutoğlu was a professor at a French university. Every summer without exception he came back to his hometown; he was early this summer because of the death of a close friend.

The professor was standing waiting for me as I stepped out of the lift on the third floor. His white hair was combed back from his forehead and his eyes were deeply set. He wore a purple cotton shirt and white denim jeans. His hands were clasped behind his back, as if I might readily be dismissed. I greeted him with military courtesy, looking him in the eye and nodding my head. The great hall into which I was escorted looked like an antiques warehouse. I skirted the silk carpet on the floor. It was a good thing that he sat me down in the armchair at his desk, as the view from the balcony would have distracted me too much. Professor Mesutoğlu called Aleko and issued orders in a melodic language spoken probably by only a hundred people on earth. I knew enough to keep quiet until the grotesque servant reappeared. Soon he did so, grumbling and pushing a cart on which were a bottle of cognac, two glasses, a plate of cornbread, and some chunks of bitter chocolate.

Halit listened to me with apparent disinterest. On learning that Haluk Batumlu was due an inheritance in the U.S., he simply said, "That son of a bitch." He was amused to hear that Hasan had become a master of meerschaum. When the cornbread was finished he refilled our glasses, lit a menthol cigarette, and frowned. I sank further down in the old armchair.

"For three days after I started school I cried secretly in the restrooms," he said. "The Istanbul kids always picked on the few Anatolians in their classes, and I was no extrovert. Haluk took me under his wing. He was the charismatic and rebellious class leader. I, in turn, loaned him money. Hasan, who that unruly bunch nicknamed 'Fatso,' joined us at the price of becoming the Sancho Panza of the trio. Though Haluk was the one who introduced us to brothels and bars, I continued to associate him with dreamy Hollywood stars. What I understood about him was limited to the knowledge that he never knew his real father, for whose imprisonment he made up noble reasons; and that his mother, a proud Kurdish beauty, entertained a platonic love for Count Nadolsky. I saw for myself, with a certain sadistic pleasure, the nature of the love-hate relationship between Haluk and the count, who swaggered as if he'd never taken off his gilded uniform and who didn't refrain from beating our leader with the riding crop he'd brought from Russia.

"Hasan withheld from you a critical detail of our

detention in Ankara. The plainclothes cop who arrested us threatened us with torture and imprisonment if we didn't give him the names of every communist who'd ever come to our house. When we walked free without so much as a slap in the face, I assumed that Hasan had sung like a canary. As we left the police station I spat in his face. The poor guy just bowed his head.

"Haluk showed up in Tirebolu in the summer of '56 with this Tartar beauty. As he stammered out an apology my father stood staring, mesmerized, at the lovely girl with the apple-red cheeks. Not only did he instantly lend the money Haluk requested to keep them afloat for two years, but he also sent the fugitives to Trabzon the next morning in his own car. While Haluk's lady friend was settling herself in the car, he and I had an interesting conversation. We were walking arm-in-arm when he turned to me and said, 'I was the one who talked.' I was stunned. The heroism of the friend whom I'd idealized for nine years melted into nothing. I grabbed him by his dirty shirt collar and said, 'You sorry bastard. I won't spit in your face because I respect my own spit too much, but by God, that god you don't believe in will damn you to hell.' I'll never forget the disgusting smirk on his face as he turned back to the naïve girl he would abandon at the first opportunity.

"Back in Ankara that jerk used to bring in books and broadsides hidden under his coat and say, 'If you read these well, you'll be a communist; if not, you'll be an anti-communist.' Well, I've become a realistic socialist.

"I never really left Tirebolu. I spend summers here with my childhood friends. I've spent too many mornings gazing at French menus and longing for nothing more than a Black Sea *pide* with white sheep cheese. The vision of chef Hayri's meatballs and hunchback Halide's ice cream never leaves me.

"The year I completed my PhD thesis—1965—my father told me that Haluk had paid off his debt with interest in two transfers, six months apart, from Ziraat Bank in Ayvalık. I don't know how much this will help you. I imagine Count Nadolsky wanted to ease his conscience a bit. Who knows, maybe the inheritance will prove a turning point in the lives of Haluk's innocent children—if he has any.

"I sent an apologetic letter to Hasan but it came back marked, 'No forwarding address. Return to sender.' Before I go back to Grenoble this time, maybe I should drop by Eskişehir …"

The professor invited me to view the nude male sculptures he'd brought back from France along with the Fikret Mualla drawings he'd purchased from the artist for the price of a glass of wine. I delicately declined.

On the drive back to Trabzon the delicate filigree of mist before our eyes slowly lifted and I felt like a Byzantine choir was rising to a crescendo in the hush after the afternoon *ezan*. To the right of the highway a sequence of heavy buildings hunkered between the sea and the mountains. We soon found ourselves in Trabzon again. As we said goodbye in front of the Zorlu Grand Hotel, the cab driver said, "For the love of Allah, brother, don't hide your talent under a bushel. You're a detective!"

*

I couldn't book a decent seat on the Ankara-İzmir bus, so I convinced myself to fly. As I boarded the plane I was sure I would hear my inner voice announce, "Welcome aboard the ox-cart of the skies. Have a nice flight." The bumper sticker on the taxi I took from İzmir to Ayvalık sported a rhyme, "This super taka / Made in Karşıyaka." It was Greek to me. The swarthy driver, Sadi, pointed out twice that he was a middle-school teacher who had taken up driving to pay his credit card debts. On hearing that it was my first visit to Ayvalık, he automatically began, "Neighbor to the Mount Ida of Homeric myth, Ayvalık is a paradise of sea, forest, and fresh air. One of the world's premier olive-oil centers for the last two hundred ..." I closed my eyes; I wanted to play Brahms' 'Hungarian Dance No. 1' to myself. We stopped for a snack at a gas station and Sadi asked what I did. I told him I was a detective. I vowed there and then, amidst the smell of gasoline and piss, to go home on the first bus if I failed to find Haluk Batumlu.

The city lights appeared in the distance as Sadi—not such a great driver, judging from his death grip on the steering wheel—was explaining, "Ayvalık, boss, is actually a holiday resort favored by anti-high society Istanbulites and Ankara bureaucrats." He sounded like a collaborator trying to suck up to the invading army commander by giving him a reason to like the place.

The pungent smell that affronted my nostrils at the Ayvalık Palace Hotel, located between the bazaar and the sea, was annoying, but it would grow on me. It was a fragrance secreted by olive oil factories on their night shift, and it followed me to my room like a friendly street dog. I asked the receptionist, who greeted me in English, if he knew Haluk Batumlu though I knew all too well what the answer would be. Bored by the view of the Martı Restaurant and the murky sea from my third-floor room, I wandered out to the bazaar. The olive-oil aroma, sadly, had gone. But I knew that strolling along these quiet dark streets would relax me. As I entered a café with a TV blaring, an analogy between myself and a dung-beetle rose to mind. The only customers were two old men practically glued to their table, gawking and grinning at the TV with the night-shift waiter.

"Ayvalık only wakes up after the schools shut down for the summer," said the horse-headed waiter when he brought me my sage tea. The old codgers stirred slightly during the commercials.

"If anybody knew this fellow—at least if he had a government job—it would be Muhtar Celal. He'll be dropping by the coffeehouse next to the Port Authority as soon as he finishes his breakfast," said the swarthier of the two men, who gave a sniff of his nose after each round of his prayer beads.

I stopped for breakfast at a café under an arbor of

grapevines and was surprised by the friendly reaction of the waiter when I ordered a toasted cheese and tomato sandwich. The people meandering along the labyrinthine streets seemed to be moving two beats slower than normal. I wondered whether they would speed up when the tourist season began. Muhtar Celal appeared to be in his seventies and wore a woolen vest over his short-sleeved shirt. I had a fleeting urge to ask how he filled his days once he finished his morning newspaper. He observed that people had been calling him "Muhtar" ever since the day he ran for the councillor's office and lost. No, he wasn't aware of the existence of a person called Haluk Batumlu. There was, however, someone called Haluk Erçelik the French teacher, who had lived on Marshal Çakmak Avenue. But he didn't know where this Haluk came from exactly, nor where he went when he left.

I stood up with the pleasant feeling of having done my best, and walked happily off to buy a bus ticket to Istanbul. But as I neared the station, which looked more like a rodeo arena, my inner voice, that devil's advocate, whispered: Is it possible that Haluk Batumlu changed his last name to cut his ties with the past?

The pounding in my head intensified as I called Ali Uzel.

"Professor, if a fanatic Stalinist wanted to change his last name, what would you advise him?"

"In Russian, Stalin means 'made of steel'," he said. "Permit me to call to your attention the resemblance between 'Stalin' and 'steel' in English. If I were a Turkish Stalinist, I think I would choose a surname like 'Çelik' or 'Özçelik.' You know, 'steel' or 'real steel.'"

Or "Erçelik"—"true steel."

"Are you okay?" he asked, as I hung up. I was up to my neck again in the Haluk Batumlu case. I chuckled nervously to myself as, instead of asking for a ticket at the window, I requested directions to Marshal Çakmak Avenue.

The streets that ran up the hill past a store selling books, stationery and real estate to the old Greek neighborhood had various sacred and epic names attached to them. The mortar smeared on the limestone buildings looked like poorly applied suntan lotion. The zigzag streets designed for bicycles and horse carts reminded me of Balat, except for the lack of screaming children. I was happily distracted from my search by the pleasant sight of bougainvillea vines and pomegranate branches draped over the stone walls. As for the women sulking at their windows, it was as if they had all turned down their radios so as not to miss the command, "Come on, get up, we're going back!", when it came.

At the ground-floor window of a ruined building on Marshal Çakmak Avenue sat a smiling middle-aged man whose body, below his chest and shoulders, remained hidden. When I told him I had some business with Haluk Erçelik he became effusive.

"Haluk the French teacher, God knows, was the Rock Hudson of Ayvalık society. He lived on the top floor of Number 19b, just behind you. The women and girls, young and old, used to dress to the nines and parade in front of his door. I think it was the year Tony Shumacher transferred to the Fenerbahçe football team—wow, that's nearly twenty years ago—that his wife finally put her foot down and they moved away overnight. He told me that they'd bought an olive grove near C. village. Maybe ..."

Suddenly a very large white-haired woman appeared behind him, screeching, "Eh, Mahmut, enjoying ourselves with the passers-by again, are we? Don't you know God will strike you down, Mahmut? Eh?" She swooped down on the smiling man and snatched him up, whereupon I saw that he indeed had no limbs.

I had no better idea than to head down to the Clock Tower Mosque and watch the boys play football in the courtyard. My attention focused on a left-footed blond kid who ran circles around the opposing players and just grinned at his teammates whenever he lost the ball. When they got it back they passed it to him again. I soon wearied of watching this dramatic but repetitious circling. The match ended abruptly when a mosque official came out and planted himself in the middle of the courtyard. The sweaty boys scattered and in the wake of the cats and pigeons I also took my leave. It occurred to me while watching that blond ball-wizard that Hasan Gezgin and Halit Mesutoğlu could have been hiding something—a suspicion all the more reasonable if you looked at their stories side by side. The hope arose in me that if I bequeathed to Haluk Erçelik the happy news of his inheritance, he might reward me by spilling some dramatic secrets.

Trusting that Mahmut the Fenerbahçe fan hadn't been pulling my leg, I approached a *dolmuş* minibus idling beneath an acacia tree. I didn't warm to the mustachioed driver, but I did enjoy the olive-oil fragrance that enveloped the vehicle.

"You'll be there in ten minutes," said Bilal from Harput, who opened the door and gave me the seat beside him. As we slalomed through the olive groves in the direction of Edremit, I followed the parade of patient trees with amazement. "The youngest of those trees is two hundred years old," Bilal said, "and the oldest is six hundred."

I was surprised too at the enormous mosque that appeared at the point where the tranquil village met the sea. The mosque looked like a blueprint for a town of 20,000 rather than the small village that it was. Not a person was in sight to ask directions. "Are they all at a meeting in the mosque?" Bilal asked, then hurried toward a man who finally appeared on the horizon. I waited on the bus. I understood that we'd found Haluk when I saw the grizzled villager pointing at a spot up in the hills. A mixture of curiosity and petulance swept over me and my right hand began to shake. I felt like praying for a flat tire.

The hill we climbed was silent and covered with olive groves. A bashful boy who was studiously flicking a cigarette lighter showed us which house belonged to Haluk. Ancient stone walls protected the garden, and a green mailbox hung next to the main gate. With a silent *Bismillah* I pushed the doorbell. A middle-aged man who looked like a bodyguard emerged and said with some surliness, "What d'ya want?" I told him I was bringing news of his boss's old-time pals Halit and Hasan. He barked a command—it sounded like Kurdish—and threw his cellphone to a little girl in a bright red dress who came running up. She pushed a couple of buttons—trying hard not to laugh—and handed the phone back to her father. I knew the exchange between this neatly mustachioed fellow and his boss would be short.

Immediately on entering the rectangular garden, I had to let myself be sniffed by a large Kangal mastiff named Arrow. "Otherwise, God forbid, he might tear you to pieces," said Haluk's long-time factotum. The man was Zakir by name, and hailed from Bitlis in the east. Having mentioned in passing that he could hit the eye of a blackbird from 300 yards but, alas, was incapable of mastering a cellphone, he said, "If ya don't mind me askin', sir, what is it ya do for a livin'?" When I said that I was a retired Air Force officer and pilot he declared, "Allah be praised!" and fell in two steps behind me until we came to his boss.

Each fine old olive tree that caught my eye looked at first like a unique grotesque; taken as a group, however, I saw that they all moved in harmony like figures in a melancholy painting. About the time the underappreciated baroque composer Viotti popped into my mind, I came face to face with Haluk Erçelik, who stood waiting for me in the doorway of the two-story stone house.

He was tall and fit. I tried to associate this handsome

101

man with the name of a particular movie star, but couldn't. Then it came to me why. It was because, with his long silvery hair gathered at the nape of his neck and the perfect features of his proud face, he resembled nothing so much as a statue of Apollo.

Actually those piercing green eyes might not have been so benevolent a gift from God. His tone was peremptory. He tried to reduce the tension of my surprise visit by donning a mock sincerity. The walls of the study we entered were covered with books. Bereket—Zakir's wife, I assumed—offered home-made lemonade, her sidelong glances meanwhile betraying the fact that this was a house not used to lavish hospitality. I found myself suddenly missing Balat.

When I disclosed to him the news about the $1.3 million something about the way he chuckled, like a person responding courteously to a clumsy anecdote, struck me. I tried to provoke a response by repeating word for word what his once-close friends had said.

When he saw that I'd uttered my last sentence he put two fingers to his mouth and whistled. He didn't open his mouth until Bereket appeared with a small bottle of *raki*, a glass of the turnip juice they drink with it in the south, and a bowl of nuts. As I awaited his next move the oil painting behind him caught my eye. Had that young, beautiful, and seemingly blind girl been eavesdropping on me? Was she now looking at me sympathetically?

I relaxed as Haluk shut his eyes and took a long sip of *raki*. I guessed I was going to hear more than I'd bargained for.

"When my father, a sailor from Hopa, on the Black Sea, married my mother, whom he'd met during his military service in Diyarbakir, they were disowned by both families. Their penniless friends took turns hosting them until eventually they found shelter in a rented flat in Balat. My father's lifelong dream was to work with his cousin on long-haul cargo ships until he was thirty, and then open a fancy fish restaurant in Salacak on the Asian side of Istanbul. I was just five when the news arrived that he'd been killed in an accident at a South Asian port.

"As a boy I was the mascot of the Balat streets. The lord of the district, Count Nadolsky, showed his affection for me by calling me *belka*—'squirrel' in Russian. His offer to become our benefactor shocked us at first. But my mother took over running his house, and slowly became attached to this White Russian who had saved us from going to live with my dictatorial grandfather.

"His exiled majesty, who ordered me to call him Vlad Baba, was forty-six when he came into our life. He was a charming vagabond, energetic but also fickle. He looked after me well, yet on occasion would order me around like a lowly conscript. When he acquired Turkish citizenship after twenty years of sanctuary in Istanbul, he drew himself up as if he'd done us a favor. Once he was complimented on his Turkish by his favorite author, Peyami Safa, to which he replied, 'You should hear my English and French.' He was close to Istanbul's consulate circles. He gave fencing and chess lessons to a few diplomats and taught foreign languages in the minority schools.

"As for his brother Maxim, whatever you've heard about him is a lie, except for the fact that he went to America alone. He took the Fabergé jewelry they'd smuggled out of Russia to New York with him. There he sold it all and put Vlad's share in the Bank of New York. The count had a London account too. He never had financial problems. Maxim taught Russian at several second-rate universities and sometimes worked as a museum consultant. He married three times, I believe, but never had children. We received the news of his death in 1980 just as the 12 September coup was declared.

"What *is* correct in the accounts you heard is the reason why Vlad Baba stayed in Istanbul and lived in Balat. Yes: it was to be close to Zoe Zervudaki, who looked much like Virginia Woolf. The person most irritated by the pretentious but mysterious Zoe was my mother. It was no secret to anyone in the Fener–Balat district that Zoe would keep the count in reserve as long as her paralyzed husband was alive. I myself saw how this honorable behavior only caused his respect for the hoarse-voiced Zoe to grow. Her husband Nico Zervudaki, however, was unhappy with the situation. Rumor had it that the Byzantine historian repeatedly urged his wife, who was his former student, to 'put me in the Balikli Greek Hospital for good and then let's get a divorce.' It was Vlad who looked after Professor Zervudaki when Zoe died. Today all three of them lie side by side in the Greek Orthodox Cemetery at Şişli.

"The month I started university my mother had a stroke and died. I knew very well that the count, whose house I'd moved into, was a hard-core anti-communist. In fact he confessed to me, when I was telling him the reason for my expulsion from school, that he was an Anglo-American spy. I sought help from my stuttering cousin Bayram, an organizer and the main reason for my involvement in the leftist movement. It blew his mind when I told him I wanted to escape to Moscow to be near Nazım Hikmet. My intention was to sneak into the U.S.S.R. from the Georgian border, stopping off on the way to say goodbye to Hasan and Halit.

"If you were to ask about my romantic adventures before the age of twenty-one ... well, I made the count laugh once when I complained about the freckled girl in grade school who wrote a poem for me. I never went to movies or read romantic novels. I believed that the real theme of Nazım Hikmet's love poetry was freedom. I learned from the stuttering Bayram to open my heart to no other love than the communist ideal.

"When I looked into Nalan's eyes at the Mahmudiye ranch I was speechless. Petrified. It felt like water, fire, and air were all mingling in my soul at the same time as an earthquake was erupting. My whole past unrolled before my eyes like a blank film. At that moment I decided that she was the woman of my life. I didn't know who she was, nor was I even curious about her name. It never occurred to me that to reach out to her was an impossible fantasy. I saw the invitation in her green eyes and I thought my heart would stop. We took two days to get acquainted, and two weeks to decide to marry, come what may.

"As soon as I sent that panicked telegram to the count I was overcome with regret. I knew, really, that if I went to Halit for help I wouldn't be refused. His father, who had had to accept his own arranged marriage, was impressed by my boldness in eloping with a factory owner's daughter whom I'd known for just two weeks. I never forgot how generously he gave us the money to see us through those two years. But in Tirebolu I felt queasy when I divined the riddle of Halit's insinuating glances. Actually, when we were freshmen at university I sensed a sort of strangeness about him. Besides his clinging ways, he would sniff my underwear and roll around in my bed. I wouldn't have shared a house with him any longer even if we hadn't been kicked out of school. The person who spilled his guts at the police station was Hasan, not me. It was while I was saying goodbye to Halit for good that I decided to assume the role of stool pigeon. I preferred being a surprise traitor in his memory to being the subject of his erotic fantasies.

"Nalan and I managed to get from Trabzon to Ankara. We married as soon as I changed my last name. She became a student of Turkish literature at Ankara University, and I entered the French department. In the fall of 1957, when our son was born, my mother-in-law relented and we began to visit the family again. My father-in-law supported us financially until we finished school. When Yusuf was two years old, however, my wife came down with chronic bronchitis. It was clear that to prevent her lungs from collapsing she would have to live and work where the air was better. As it happened, on the very day we were appointed to teach at a high school in oxygen-rich Ayvalık, her father died. We paid our debt to Halit's father—with interest—with Nalan's inheritance, and put the remainder in the bank for Yusuf's education.

"My wife was a proud, reserved woman. She always had her head in a book. I took great care not to hurt her. Yusuf was four before she realized that I'd named our son after Joseph Stalin—which was the first time I saw her angry with me. Yusuf greatly resembled his mother. They were very close. Yusuf went off to England to study. But he fell into the clutches of a so-called neo-Islamic group, and he fell in love with a German girl three years older than himself. Despite his mother's opposition he married Magda, who converted to Islam and took the name Miriam—Meryem in Turkish. He didn't visit us that year. On the night of 31 December 1981, their daughter Sim was born. Her name means 'silver' in Persian. Six weeks later Yusuf came home with his child in his arms and strands of gray in his hair. His tired face reminded me of my father's just before he set out on his last voyage. He handed the baby to her grandmother and collapsed in wild heartbroken sobs: a traffic accident had killed his wife. When he finally regained his breath and launched into a half-English, half-Arabic exhortation, I doubted his sanity. He drank a glass of water and left the house and I never saw him again. He called at odd times and talked to his mother, and apparently told her that he was working in America for some sort of scientific organization. He said he would come back to Ayvalık when he had pulled himself together. After that his calls fell off to once a year or so, and when he did call he never spoke to his daughter. The truth is, my wife never really gave me the opportunity to get close to my son. I haven't heard from him since she died.

"I knew Nalan would never recover. She took early retirement to raise Sim. The closer she became to her grandchild, the further she pushed me away. Back then I didn't suppose that she was aware of my little romantic escapades, or that they would make any difference to her if she was.

"Vlad and I made peace with each other after Yusuf was born. During his sixty-eight years in Turkey he rarely left Istanbul. He said, when he came to Ayvalık for the first time, 'I've been nowhere but Ankara, and I thought I would die without seeing the Aegean.' He lived to be ninety-five and saw the breakup of the Soviet empire before he died. Since I'd always taken the daily struggle to make ends meet as a desirable thing, I have very little sense of money. It surprised people, naturally, when I refused to get excited about inheriting $1.3 million. When the money went into my account Nalan said, without looking me in the eye, 'Haluk, why don't we move to a place where men don't chase after easy women?' I was ashamed to the core.

"My wife loved this olive grove. She brought workmen

from Mount Ida and had this abandoned stone house rebuilt almost from scratch. I retired at fifty-five so that we could move here. Nalan was the caretaker of 1,200 trees on two adjacent plots of land. Some of them she gave names to, and she would carry on conversations with them. When Sim went off to high school in İzmir, Nalan took to looking after the trees individually. Me, I never could feel close to any of these thankless plants … each one a unique study in ugliness … posed like a tragic sculpture … calling down incurable diseases … Olives demand constant attention, you know. They bear fruit only every other year, and the profit margins are slim. Under the terms of my wife's will I can't sell the olive groves; but I leave the job of tending them to sharecroppers.

"Sim made her decision to become a painter when she was only ten. Her grandmother always said, 'That girl was a color fanatic from the day she took her first step.' She never missed an exhibition. She collected art books. She always had her nose in painters' biographies. During her childhood we took her to see every major art museum in Europe. It didn't bother me when her grandmother said, 'Even this girl's sweat smells like paint.' It was as if her passion had developed into a philosophical position. With her professors' support she decided on an academic career. Then, in the second year of her doctoral studies, she had a traffic accident and completely lost her eyesight. Nalan's joy of life withered away after that and she stopped taking her medication. The following year she passed away. I buried my angelic wife in the village cemetery up the hill and dug a grave for me beside her. The best compliment I've had in the last six months was to be called a dead man walking.

"Sim's portrait—the one you see behind me—was painted by a lady named Banu, whom Sim used to visit often in her studio. They say it's not impossible that my grandchild could see again if she could just find the will to recover. After her grandmother died she gave herself over to music. Whenever she's not playing the *ney*, she's dozing off in the middle of listening to melancholy compositions.

"I think, now that you've heard about the 'three H's', you'll agree that the saddest story is the leader's. You must understand that you've been the target of an elaborate and expensive practical joke. Vlad always kept the telegram I sent him from Mahmudiye in his diary. I imagine some idiot got his hands on that thick notebook and used a few things he found in it to send you on a fool's tour of Anatolia."

"One minute, sir," I said. I fished out Stuart Fugato's card and dialed the "Available 24 Hours A Day" number. A metallic female voice scolded me three times in English: "The number you have dialled is not in service. Please hang up and try again."

With the calm of someone who knows he's right, Haluk said, "Don't be discouraged, Kemal. There's a rule at play here: a practical joker lies low for a while, and then will come to the surface if you don't find him. In fact, tracking me down like you did wasn't a bad piece of detective work ..."

As I retraced my steps through the olive grove I struggled

not with the question "Who?" but "Why?" I walked faster so that the hunchbacked trees couldn't sneak up behind me shouting, "Idiot! Idiot!" And all the while I couldn't remove the image of Sim from my mind.

V

I slunk back to Istanbul feeling like a marathon winner whose medal has been revoked. I was too tired even to grumble at the burned-out driver of the taxi I grabbed at the bus station. We pulled into the Balat neighborhood with me slumped down on the tattered back seat. It was the first time I'd ever run up my stairs. I didn't treat myself to a hot shower, I didn't even feel like listening to Bach. I felt more like an exile than someone coming home. I thought my right hand would distract me by starting to shake, but it didn't. I took two sleeping pills and went to bed as the late afternoon *ezan* rose up from the 3,000 mosques.

It was midnight when I stirred sluggishly and pulled myself out of bed. I ate the last two candy bars in the fridge, then put on and took off my shoes twice, choosing not to go to Disco Eden in the end. Professor Ali must be up translating Madeleine Bourdouxhe's *Marie*, I thought. At the risk of being turned away, I knocked on his door, thinking I might feel better if I told him what I'd been through. He finally opened the door and for the first time I saw him unshaven. I suspected he'd been watching a documentary on great white sharks.

"I've been expecting you," he said.

I launched into a passionate diatribe, but his interest seemed gradually to fade, to my surprise. He sensed my uncertainty.

"You accomplished more than I thought you would," he said. "But not every story you play a part in is going to have a prosaic ending. Don't you think that as a classical music fan you should react more calmly to surprise developments? Besides, the last act of this drama may be still to come ..."

He looked satisfied to see that I was more confused. Putting a glass of wine in my hand, he said, "I have things to tell you too, Kemal. While you were gone my sister Oya passed away. I thought of you as I was burying her at Z. She left the Maçka apartment and enough money to rescue me from teaching snobbish rich kids. When the university closes in two weeks for summer vacation I'll be on my way to the States. And you're coming with me! We'll be hitting the New York-San Francisco-Santa Fe-Juneau circuit."

Stunned, I was still shaping a refusal when he went on.

"I know you don't exactly deserve a prize. But it would be painful for me to be alone on a trip like this, so you'll be my traveling companion."

Two days later I saw him as he was leaving the building. His face was such a mask I didn't approach him. I decided to wait for him to call after he got over whatever it was was troubling him. I attended the Istanbul Classical Music Festival, hopping from venue to venue with my eighty-year-old friends. On the day I renewed my passport he invited me to dinner. He looked considerably more relaxed. Luckily I didn't ask him why we were having Argentinean wine with our rocket salad, artichokes in olive oil, risotto with mushrooms, and profiterole with ice cream. When he rose and turned down Nat King Cole, I expected an announcement. He came back with an envelope. The piece of paper that fell out of it read:

TO FIND ESTHER:
CALLE 3 DE FEBRERO, NO. 2035-B
B E L G R A N O

"For four days I've been grappling with the riddle that came out of this envelope," he said. "It was mailed from Taksim with no return address. Once I found out from the Internet that Manuel Belgrano was an eighteenth-century Argentinean national hero, I bought a guide to Buenos Aires. There I discovered that Belgrano is also a neighborhood favored by wealthy Jews. Esther always kept her address and phone number to herself. But the address on this piece of paper might refer only to her first address there. I can't check with our friend Luna because after her husband died she moved to Israel and lost touch with everybody. I commissioned one of my former students from İzmir to do a little investigation, but he came up empty-handed as well. The Ardittis and Venturas apparently either died off or have been scattered throughout the world. But one of Eli's close friends, a bridge teacher, said that she'd heard nothing about Esther dying in the accident.

"This could be a trick somebody's playing on your eccentric neighbor, but I'll never rest if I don't go to Belgrano, Kemal. I'm ready to run the risk of playing the goat in somebody's expensive joke, if that's what it is.

"I can't help feeling that your Anatolian wild goose chase was preparing you for this Argentinean chapter. We'll have to modify our travel plans a bit. Let's first fly to Buenos Aires for a five-day reconnaissance. We don't need visas. Winter is about to start there, but they say the temperature never falls below fifteen degrees. You'd better pack your fall clothes ..."

*

The next evening we were on a flight headed to London and then Buenos Aires. As I buckled my seat belt I felt like the reluctant driver of a garishly decorated horse cart. Professor Ali, who was afraid of flying, closed his eyes. To my left sat a green-eyed young man. He was trying to get his hands on the single-malt whisky reserved for first class passengers by touching the stewardess's arm and whispering in her ear.

That first flight from Istanbul to London that I'd taken fifteen years ago to study English was what, to a certain extent, had awakened my passion for flying. But now, as this BA 677 set down at Heathrow, it was a deserted café in Beyoğlu named Londracula that was on my mind. Slogging from Terminal One to Terminal Four gave me the feeling of having landed in two foreign countries simultaneously. We grabbed something to eat then stopped in at an adjacent bookstore. While Professor Ali was browsing through the magazines I found a copy of *Love in the Time of Cholera* on the shelf and read the blurb: *Fifty-one years, nine months and four days have passed since Fermina Daza rebuffed hopeless romantic Florentino Arizorsquo's impassioned advances and married Dr. Juvenal Urbino instead ...* As we boarded the clunky aircraft that would take us to Buenos Aires via São Paolo, I asked Professor Ali if he thought it was the greatest romantic novel of all.

"It's not how many years you've had to wait for your darling, but what you've had to endure while you were waiting," he said.

We hopped like a kangaroo on the deserted São Paulo runway shining in the early morning light. The numbed São Paulo passengers filed out of the plane, and the uniformed mulattos of the janitorial crew filed in. Bored, I regarded the shy women at their chores. Without taking their eyes off the floor they were somehow managing to check out the male passengers. It was only two more hours to our final destination. I began to calculate how in how many minutes—ten, maybe—I could cover the distance in an F-16, but it was depressing. I resolved not to say a word beyond "Good morning" to my next neighbor.

The stewardess was announcing take-off when an attractive young woman came toward me with confident steps. I concentrated on her snow-white trousers as though I'd been assigned to find a spot on them. I was devastated when she sank into the seat beside me without so much as a "Good morning." Even *I* couldn't miss the pleasing symmetry of her turned-up nose, wide brow, and ponytail. It didn't surprise me when she immediately produced a book from her purse to hide behind. I inhaled her intense perfume and bent closer to the "Buenos Aires Statistics" section of my guidebook.

I skimmed through her book while she was in the restroom. For me to weary of a novel, it's enough to glance at the plot summary. I was a bit alarmed, however, by the synopsis of *The Tango Singer* by Tomás E. Martinez: *Bruno Cadogan has flown from New York to Buenos Aires in search of the elusive and legendary Julio Martel, a tango singer whose voice has never been recorded yet is said to be so beautiful it is almost supernatural* was too close to the probable parameters of our own mission. The title page bore a dedication: "To Sheila-Lucy, fugitive from Gemini." The fountain pen that wrote one word in green and the next in black apparently belonged to one E.S. As Sheila-Lucy came crisply back to her seat, it struck me that she knew very well how her sulky countenance contributed to her mystery. She disappeared again into her book and I feared she would realize, with the intuition of her astrological sign, that I had riffled through it. Every now and again she would raise her head and narrow her eyes to focus on some unknown point, and it looked as if she were posing patiently for a portrait painter.

Whose profile did Sheila-Lucy's remind me of? This idle question quickly grew into an obsession that made me forget my apprehension.

*

Our stewardess gave us two forms to be filled out and turned in to passport control.

"It's like entering the U.S.A.," Professor Ali said.

Had I not been so engrossed in this Sheila-Lucy woman, I might have been more acutely aware of his rising anxiety.

"If a terrorist suddenly changed this plane's destination to Istanbul, I wouldn't mind at all," he confessed as I was filling out his form.

On the descent to Ezeiza Airport I had the crazy idea that the sky would fill suddenly with bandoneon tunes and our clunky vehicle, trying to cut a couple of simple tango figures, would miss the landing strip.

At last, Buenos Aires.

Professor Ali didn't approve of the party atmosphere in Arrivals. I appreciated that he at least managed not to scold the assistant at the exchange bureau who insisted on seeing his passport. To get a taxi we first had to queue up in front of a cash payment booth, then, with receipt in hand, join another queue.

"Kemal, have we been thrown into an Iron Curtain

country of twenty years ago?" the professor grumbled.

The undernourished porter said to follow him and picked up the lightest suitcase, thus letting us know what kind of tips he expected. Ali, to my surprise, didn't say something like, "After all that, we damned well better get a limousine." We crammed ourselves into a Renault-9 and I felt as nervous as if we were passing into Turkey through an eastern border gate. But as we neared what looked like the city center, I began to appreciate it in the manner of somebody leaping from Anatolia to Istanbul. The wide streets of Buenos Aires, a city established on flat ground thirteen centuries later than Constantinople, looked like a scrap yard for old cars.

I amused myself by saying, "Has every thirty-year-old Peugeot 504 on earth decided to retire to this backwater?"

I was thinking that Argentina and Turkey were like two cousins who couldn't shake off their chronic illnesses long enough to get together, when the taxi driver broke into an old folk song.

*

The huge Buenos Aires Sheraton put me in mind of the elegant "Mediterranean Statue" stuck in a hidden corner of Istanbul. I handed my bag to the bellboy but Professor Ali, following me, insisted on carrying his own heavy suitcase, stumbling and falling flat on his face. He limped to reception on his own, refusing to take my arm, but ten minutes after we'd retired to our rooms he knocked on the door. I opened it to find him sinking to the floor, groaning in pain. The ankle was swollen; he couldn't stand on it. We had to put him on a stretcher for the trip by ambulance to Arrivadavia Hospital. The receptionist Ricardo accompanied us, trying to make up for his lack of English by grinning perpetually.

After the ordeal of registration we were ushered into the presence of a dark-haired doctor whose nametag read "Armando Kaltakian."

He saw me smiling as I read it and said, in perfect Turkish, "If you're smiling at my surname rather than my face, you're amused by your own limited vocabulary." I was taken aback. "Maybe it's true that the word *kaltak* has been abused as 'whore' in street slang, but what it really means is the wooden part of a saddle. My forefathers were the most respectable saddle-makers in Malatya. They were the major suppliers for Ottoman sultans and pashas."

It was like reliving the embarrassment of the time I got caught cheating on an exam. Kaltakian saw my face fall and leaned over to whisper, "Come on, let's get this old coot back on his feet." As he listened to Ali he patted his head and took his pulse like a virtuoso tuning his instrument. Tenderly he probed his right ankle. Watching the physician nimbly apply his cure I could easily visualize his ancestors in Malatya working on those saddles. Giving the professor some rehydration pills and painkillers, he said, "Keep your ankle bandaged for five days, Professor. Except for bathroom calls, don't let that foot touch the floor. Rest as much as you can. On the fourth day the swelling should go down and you can try walking, though without putting too much pressure on your ankle. *Geçmiş olsun* as we say in Turkish. Get well soon."

I knew that Professor Ali, now that his pain was lessening, wouldn't let this mysterious doctor off so easily. The self-proclaimed Armando was backed into a corner by his patient's questions.

"My real name is Armenak," he admitted, "and I'm from Pangaltı—thank God—in Istanbul. My father, believing that 'Turkey was finished' after the 1980 coup, sent me to Argentina—the land of military coups. The financial situation here is no better than in Turkey. I work extra jobs so that I can see the city I was born in every two years."

Armenak of Pangaltı seated his whining patient in a wheelchair and pushed him to the ambulance. He never asked what we were doing in Buenos Aires. He handed me his card and kissed the professor's hand farewell. Ricardo, who now thought we were friends, grew frustrated with me on the way back to the hotel when I didn't know the Argentinean player on Istanbul's Fenerbahçe football team. In an attempt to distract him I asked the number of rooms in the hotel.

It was comical how my companion settled himself into bed, groaning in pain but enjoying himself all the same. I waited expectantly for him to evaluate the latest events and double the chores for me on his list.

"Look, my dear Kemal," he said. "It's obvious that I haven't come here with romantic expectations. My intention was only to visit Esther's grave and arrange a meeting with her daughter Stella if possible. As Armenak was bandaging

121

my ankle it occurred to me that this little accident might be a sign. It looks as if Esther doesn't want me to visit her grave. I'm sure, one way or another, she'll eventually explain why.

"I want you to go to that address we have. An unexpected clue might surface and direct us to Stella. Why not? I worry about her. I don't know why but I believe she needs help. Ask the hotel to get you a private guide and try to enjoy Buenos Aires while you're at it. We can have breakfast together and meet in the evenings to discuss our progress. Fortunately I brought the novel I'm about to start translating with me. I may as well get started on a draft. And please, don't forget that we're only booked in here for five days."

He gave me $5,000 in cash for expenses. As I left his room I realized that I hadn't communicated with my inner voice for a long time. This new wave of excitement, I thought, might provide an opportunity to see if my hand was getting any better.

To set out on a quest for two ghosts in a metropolis I'd set foot in only hours before, a quest moreover colored by Professor Ali's skepticism, did not inspire confidence. If he hadn't brought along his translation work it might not have crossed my mind that the professor had planned all along to take himself out of the search by staging an accident.

Since Buenos Aires was experiencing the mild beginnings of winter, the most popular guides were either on holiday or already booked. So as soon as I heard that Ariel Gluckman, an eccentric but intelligent guide, was available, I arranged to meet him immediately. He said he could be at the hotel in two hours so I went out to the nearby high street, Florida, to kill some time. What revealed the country's dire economic straits better than the quantity or quality of goods in the modest window displays was their prices, which were convenient even for a Turkish tourist's budget. Worried-looking men in tired suits and old women in fake fur coats stood in front of their shops, desperately offering fliers to passersby. It was fascinating to watch the stream of pedestrians flowing over sidewalks and disappearing down the street in tango steps, dancing to tunes that, possibly, only they could hear. I liked the way they looked, anti-*lumpen* in their tired but chic clothes, and I felt that I could sit and drink coffee with almost anyone walking down this street. Music shops breathed life into semi-deserted arcades. I couldn't tear myself away from a rhythmical *milonga* seeping out at the corner of Florida and Tucuman. From that hoarse but smooth female voice I breathed in the sorrow that permeated the city. When the song ended I barged into the shop and discovered that the mysterious voice belonged to Adriana Varela. I walked back to the hotel with her CD containing "Milonga de pelo largo" in hand. In the cover picture the singer looked as provocative as a Buenos Aires billboard and as glorious as a beauty queen. I wanted to yell, "Stella Arditti, I'm going to find you sooner or later," but by a slip of the tongue I pronounced the name of her dead mother instead.

*

123

The bar's single customer, forced to watch football on TV, had to be Ariel Gluckman. I admired his concentration on reading a pocket book-sized tome despite his thick smoke-colored glasses. With each page he turned he buried his nose deeper in the book, and yes, he was sniffing the print. It looked as if the last tuft of hair on his elliptical head would fly away with the first gust of wind. I would have laughed at the joke he made about my fifteen-minute delay if I'd understood it. (I couldn't tell him about the ten-minute surveillance he'd been under.) His tone was feminine but assertive and his English was fluent. I felt too weary to refuse this tiny young man who looked like the ever-youthful Tintin. When he became emotional on hearing the reason why we'd come to Buenos Aires, it was good enough for me. Tucking his book into his backpack, he said, "My fee is $80 a day. If we use my car I charge fifteen pesos per hour and 300 pesos—$100 dollars—in advance for expenses."

The 1992 Citroen in which we immediately hit the streets was the youngest vehicle I'd seen there. The deserted districts on the Retiro-Belgrano axis seemed about to go into hibernation. Even though the rows of photogenic *gomero* trees, which I'd never seen before, were doing a slow striptease, they hardly spoiled the sorrow-laden panorama of the city. Once upon a time old and wealthy Jews used to live in quiet Belgrano.

"I'll be testing the advantages of my religion in this job, looking for my fellow Jews from Turkey," said my guide, himself a Hungarian Jew.

Ariel hesitantly entrusted the Citroen to a car park on February the Third Avenue, but I couldn't get him to tell me the significance of the street's name. I didn't feel estranged by the surroundings. For me the architectural chaos created by heaps of apartment buildings besieging the calm streets was normal. After all, when property owners plucked from various European subcultures exercise their taste in architecture, the result will naturally be a mosaic of gaudiness.

The handsomest building on the street might have been 2035B, before which I stood somewhat quizzically. I could have sworn that I'd seen its dirty white façade in İzmir, on the Kordon. I stepped back cautiously as Ariel rang the bell marked "Encargado." First we heard a girl's high-pitched voice, then the weary one of a man, emanating from the intercom. I was feeling fatigued as my guide spoke slowly and distinctly to them. Finally the concierge, who appeared to be in his fifties, climbed the steps from the basement. I was embarrassed to see Ariel tucking a fifty-peso note into the recalcitrant man's shirt pocket. I left them talking at the door and went out to the street. I was deciding which direction I should take to find the ugliest façade in the district when Ariel emerged with a smile on his face.

I was expecting an apology for keeping me waiting but none was offered. Tintin managed the situation with simplicity: "We're lucky. In Buenos Aires the job of concierge, like lighthouse-keeping, is passed from father to son. Forty years ago, when the Ardittis moved to the seventh floor here, the concierge was Juan Gomez's father. And five years later, when Esther was packing up to move to another part of town, it was Gomez who looked after baby Stella. Nobody from that period remains in the building, and no one has seen the Ardittis since then. The talkative Gomez also tells us that Eli, said to be a husband better looking than the wife, was Izak Roditi's relative. This is an important clue.

"Roditi was a man of prominence in Argentina's Jewish community, and today might well be the richest businessman in South America. Last month the newspaper *Clarin* ran an interview with him in honor of his eightieth birthday. If it's true that he feels a special affinity for Jews of Turkish origin, why shouldn't we be able to meet with him?"

As we passed the Museo Hombre on the way back to the car park, Professor Ali's Esther speech came to mind. Izak Roditi must have been the cousin with whom Eli broke off relations after he came to town. Therefore, even if we made it into Roditi's august presence, I wasn't sure he would give us the time of day. So as not to demotivate Ariel, however, I didn't mention the Roditi-Arditti conflict to him. We climbed into the car after opening the door on the fourth try, and I consoled myself with the thought that at least the address which came out of the mysterious envelope was real.

On that late winter afternoon, the city traffic that I'd earlier found as calm as that of Eskişehir was now more like that of Istanbul. But on witnessing the furious drivers of the World War II relics used as city buses here, I understood that I'd been unfair to Istanbul's bus drivers. At the hotel we got stuck for nearly half an hour, with a quartet of tourists, in its pernicious revolving door. As I stood behind an old couple locked hand in hand, a strategy for finding out who had sent the Belgrano address suddenly came to me.

We were supposed to meet Ariel in the lobby two hours later and go to a local club. I impressed my guide by suggesting we abandon the idea of going to a dance show if there were none better than the Tango Passion, which I'd seen in Istanbul. In the elevator a wave of sleepiness came over me, reminding me of the six-hour time difference between Argentina and Turkey. I was eager to present my first report to Professor Ali, but when I got to his door I didn't have the heart to knock. I retired to my room and put on Adriana Verala and tried to remember who it was that I'd compared the girl on the plane to. I knew I'd be sound asleep by the time the woman with the face of Buenos Aires was crying, "Mano á Mano."

I felt an irrational craving for a kebab at the Club del Vino, even as I was eating a steak you could cut with a spoon. But after tasting the red wine I felt bitter about Istanbul's imported varieties.

"I have to revisit the memory of my accursed grandfather before I can begin my own story," were Ariel's promising opening words when I asked him how he had come to be a book dealer in Buenos Aires. "In 1937 the poor and unemployed journalist Israel Gluckman migrated from Warsaw to Buenos Aires with the money his fiancée Aviva had saved. There he moved in with his cousin Saul

Rosenfeld, a supervisor at a textile wholesalers. He began giving private religious and language lessons, with the goal of saving enough money to bring his fiancée over from Warsaw at the earliest opportunity. Saul was surprised to see the anarchist Israel, known for his conflicts with his rabbi father, whose teachings he rejected back in Krakow, seeking refuge in the Talmud now that he was abroad. Israel began a flirtation with Sarah, the daughter of the wealthy Moshe Grossman, who owned a chain of kosher restaurants. The news that Israel's fiancée, to whom he had been sending deceitful letters, was among the first victims of the Nazi invasion of Warsaw, seems to have been the opportunity he has been waiting for. On New Year's Eve of 1940 he married Sarah. To appeal to his fundamentalist father-in-law he continued to teach religion and joined the Templo Libertad synagogue. In 1942, an hour after their son was born, Sarah passed away. What would later come to light was how he had forced his wife, who suffered from a rheumatic heart, to go ahead with the delivery despite the risks.

"Their son David was blind in one eye and missing a finger on his right hand. His maternal grandmother took him in, and Israel became lost in dissipation with Gentiles. His Argentinean adventure came to an end, though, when his gambling companions, who had loaned him money, went to his father-in-law to collect. Moshe Grossman gave him enough money to flee to the U.S. in return for custody of his grandson. Israel reached New York on the day after Hitler commited suicide, and the first people to cold-shoulder him were his comrades at the *Jewish Daily Forward*. One of them was said to be Isaac Bashevis Singer, winner of the 1978 Nobel Prize for Literature.

"One day, in the middle of a battle to get a meal on credit at the delicatessen of someone he knew in Warsaw, who should walk into the place but Aviva. After the first moment of shock, he managed to convince his former fiancée to buy him lunch at the nearest cafeteria. Aviva had miraculously survived the first street massacre organized by the Nazis but had lost her entire family. With their neighbor, a close friend of her father, she had managed to escape to Czernowitz, a town in the Ukraine. There Rudi Seinfeld, a widower and the neighbor's cousin, took them in. When things got out of hand there too the three fled together to Southampton, where they took a ship to New York. She now lived in Brooklyn and had a peaceful marriage with old Seinfeld, who had become a timber merchant.

"By the time Aviva finished her tale, Israel had his life story ready: he'd been imprisoned for six years for seriously wounding a Gentile in a fight that broke out when the Gentile insulted the Jewish race. All he could do while he was in prison was think of Aviva. Forty-eight hours after his release, he had been expelled from the country and now he was in New York, penniless, homeless, etc ...

"Israel not only managed to charm Aviva once more, but also to get himself taken under Rudi's wing, who was led to believe he was Aviva's childhood friend. He couldn't hold down either of the two jobs Rudi found for him. He neglected the many people from whom he had borrowed money. By the time Aviva caught him with a young Irish immigrant nanny, she'd already heard about his shady career in Buenos Aires. Three months later Israel's body was found in a hotel room. According to police reports, it was suicide by a bullet to the brain, but his homeboys weren't convinced.

"David was the name chosen for the son born prematurely to Aviva two days before the death of Israel, whose last name meant 'man of luck.' At sixty, Rudi had become a father for the first name. As soon as David began to walk Rudi took his family away; he didn't want people noticing that David, with his green eyes, was growing up to look just like Israel.

"Actually I learned the story of Israel, or Serpiente—the Snake—as he was known, from Saul, who is 103 years old and supposedly the oldest immigrant in Argentina. The rest of it is part of my family's oral history. It was feared for a while that the motherless David would grow up as fragile as his mother and as cunning as his backsliding father. When he finished elementary school David received private tutoring, particularly in English and Yiddish. By the time he'd memorized the Old Testament and the Talmud he was the darling of the family and his grandmother's confidant. After his bar mitzvah his physiological progress came almost to a halt. He stopped going out during the day except for trips to the synagogue. And if he did go out at night without leaving a note nobody dared ask him what he'd been doing.

"David was thirty when his grandmother married him off to the childless Runya Korn. Runya was a lonely Hungarian immigrant seven inches taller and four years older than her husband. Five years after their marriage I was born. We had a spacious house that looked onto my father's favorite synagogue. He was a cold and silent man who spent much of his time in his study. I couldn't understand why he kept telling me to read everything I could and to always love my mother. She was a simple person who was keen on housekeeping and treated my father like a saint. I assumed we were moving when he sold all but 200 of his book collection to a New York dealer. But four months later he died of heart failure, just as we were about to celebrate my ninth birthday. Though she knew how feeble my father's health was, my mother had never prepared herself for this eventuality; and for the last twenty years she's made mourning for him a way of life. Marcel, the youngest of my three uncles, once said to me, 'David knew that he would never see fifty. The reason you were born was to take care of your mother.'

"Thanks to the economic crises Argentina kept passing in and out of, my great-grandfather lost much of his wealth and had to shut down all but two of his restaurants. When he lost his favorite grandson too, he lost his will to live. Forty days later my eldest aunt would swear that she saw him smiling for the first time when she found him dead in his bed.

"At the reading of the will Marcel and my mother received two apartments and enough money to last a good ten years; the other uncles divided the money equally and got the two restaurants. Marcel is a bachelor and teaches chemistry at Buenos Aires University. Under his watchful eye, I completed my education at the same institution, in the Department of English Literature, where I was an honors student. My father had entrusted the money from the sale of his library to my uncle for my education."

He paused.

"And now you'll see why I could not avoid becoming the bibliophile that he intended me to become all along."

Draining his wine glass, he scanned the room before removing his glasses. His face looked like a tragic mask cobbled together by an amateur shaman. The leafy-green eyes two sizes too big for his face were like snake's eyes. He put his glasses back on, sighing with the relief of completing an onerous task, and ordered more wine.

"After primary school I began taking off my glasses only when I went to bed," he continued. "If the other kids called me 'Snake-eyes' on the street I would run home and cry in front of the mirror. I found solace in books. According to Uncle Marcel my father became absorbed in the secular Jewish authors, starting with Kafka, just after noticing the peculiarity of my eyes. I found notes in Yiddish between the pages of two of the books he'd bequeathed to me. On the copyright page of *The Metamorphosis* was written, 'Protection from the curse of Gluckman I: Books'; and in *The Trial*, 'To live longer than Kafka: Punishment.'

"I did more than use books as a prophylactic to prevent the birth of a grotesque child. By becoming a secondhand book dealer I surprised my teachers. And I think that because I've come to prefer the pleasure of bringing to light a book hidden for eighty years to that of sex, my father's soul can rest in peace.

"Buenos Aires is the world's most bookish city. There are twelve million people in the suburbs and three million in the city center, and more than a thousand bookstores. To survive this kind of competition I started working also as a tourist guide three years ago. The hotels don't call me for the average naïve tourist, and I prefer working with travelers from surprise places. I would never reveal my face, like a strip tease artist, to someone with whom I didn't feel a connection. You're the second Turk who has looked into my eyes.'

I couldn't help but think that Ariel's family history had all the makings of a gothic Poe story.

I liked the Club del Vino's wedding-hall atmosphere and the clientele's stylish vintage clothes. They looked like they were on a movie set waiting for the director's call. I began losing interest in the trio on stage, though, because after each piece the other two members bowed long and repeatedly to the old pianist. In fact I was having trouble keeping my eyes open. Ariel took my arm to help me up. The soft winter wind revived me somewhat as we waited for a taxi at the door.

When I came to Professor Ali's room I heard the radio murmuring softly, so I knocked, but there was no answer. I opened it with my spare key. I knew I would find him with his hardcover notebook on his lap, jotting away with his pencil. The cynical expression on his face as he listened to my Belgrano report didn't surprise me—because it was a lie that Esther Arditti's original Buenos Aires address had been sent to Ali Uzel by a mysterious stranger. Why would my cunning and sneaky neighbor want to hide the fact that he'd had the address of his beloved in his possession all along? It struck me then that, yes, the good professor *was* quite capable of spraining his ankle on purpose to keep himself out of the investigation. But if that was true, could I solve the Ali Uzel mystery by reaching one of the Ardittis?

I paced up and down my room. I listened to Italian songs on the radio. I looked at the ads in the *Buenos Aires Herald*, as if there might be clues in the advertisements. I laughed at my futile efforts to find "Arditti" in the phone book. As consolation I surveyed the letter "T" in the mosaic-like list of names. I counted fifty-eight "Turco"s: Turchi … Turci … Turck … as I came to Turcoff, I dropped off to sleep.

*

A warm winter morning, earth and sky all dressed in the same tone of gray …

"Target: Recoleta," said Ariel, abruptly pulling me back from my reverie. Then I remembered: the reason Recoleta was the only name from the guidebook that stuck in my mind was the presence there of Cemeterio de la Recoleta and its funerary monuments.

Ariel was euphoric, smiling like someone enjoying the pleasure of taking a kitten he'd found on the street home to its owner. He'd showed up in his most flamboyant clothes on the assumption that he would be ushered into the presence of Izak Roditi. He looked like a cartoon character, but I was too exhausted to laugh.

Of course I knew he would tell his mother that we were in Buenos Aires, and why, but I didn't expect her to be inspired to conduct a preliminary investigation of her own. According to what Señora Gluckman had unearthed since dawn, Esther had never succeeded in getting along with her middle-class compatriots. Señora G's sources couldn't agree on the number of Ardittis who'd lost their lives in the notorious traffic accident, and they had no idea what had become of the beauty queen, Stella, whose picture they occasionally saw in magazines. By the time the Citroen turned into the elite Avenida Alvear, I'd decided that if I failed to see Roditi I would make a final search for Esther in the Jewish cemeteries and then head back to Istanbul. Walking past those rows of highrise apartment buildings, I felt like I was strolling through the Alsancak district of İzmir. We approached the outer gate to number 1866C and at once encountered a large man in uniform who stood like an Inca warrior and produced his careful sentences in a deep clear voice. He softened as words like "Turco" and "Estambul" poured out of Ariel's mouth. After a few words on the phone he escorted us to the main entrance. It was as ostentatious as the building was unimposing. Once inside, we were led to an area walled off by glass and guarded by another uniformed giant. After quietly making his own phone call, he allowed us to sit on the couch facing him like detainees before a judge. Under the terms of a response that arrived ten minutes later I was to record my first name, surname, and precise Istanbul address. Nervously I wrote "Balat" on the letterhead stationery. The guard seemed as tense as an anti-aircraft gunner as he committed my three-word message to a fax machine. The machine was still whirring when a small thin woman with glasses materialized. The burly guard jumped to his feet like a soldier, but kept his eyes to the ground.

"My name is Astrid Radzymin," said the woman in stilted English. "Welcome to Buenos Aires, Mr. Kuray. Izak Roditi is expecting you." As she led the way to a private elevator, Ariel said to my back, "I'll wait for you across the street at the Alvear Palace Hotel."

The old elevator was rising toward the eighth floor when it suddenly fell under the sway of a high-pitched male voice. I seemed to be listening to a sad Spanish *ghazal*. Noting my startled look, Astrid smirked a little; I felt as though I was being dragged into a *film noir*.

"You have half an hour," she warned as she took me through a black door.

The far wall of the spacious salon was taken up from top to bottom by an aquarium in which two black fish about a foot long swam proudly. A man in a gray suit sitting at the black glass table in front of the aquarium like some kind of swashbuckling captain said, in Turkish, "Come on over, my countryman." The very fit Izak Roditi, silver-gray hair combed straight back, looked like the actor Stewart Granger. Not only did he shake my hand warmly, but he caressed my cheeks and his eyes filled with tears.

"I can hardly believe that after fifty years in Argentina I finally have a Turkish guest from Balat," he said, on the verge of breaking down.

The phone rang. As he scolded the caller I surveyed his headquarters, object by object, from my armchair. Hanging on the walls were a world map on which colored pins marked a few remote islands, and a number of family pictures in heavy frames. Though I could think of no Latin actresses as charming as the wife whom Izak Roditi embraced in each picture, I didn't much care for the buck-toothed daughter or the snobbish-looking son. In glass cases arranged symmetrically around the room were fossilized sea shells and beads that looked like black pearls.

Two cups of Turkish coffee sat on the porcelain tray that Astrid brought in just as Roditi hung up. Eyes glittering, he said, "If I didn't get a cup of Turkish coffee every two hours I'd go crazy." He went on. "I'm pleased to say that the only thing I inherited from my father was this addiction. He asked, "What do you want from this poor Roditi, my countryman?"

I recalled those dim Balat coffeehouses. As I related the story of Esther and Ali, I decided that his drooping countenance was not the result of my accomplished narrative abilities.

"Forget Astrid's half-hour time limit." Downing the

thick coffee, he launched into a speech in mixed Turkish and English.

"I was born at the Or-Ahayim Hospital in Balat on the day the Turkish republic was declared. I was never sure whether to be happy or sad when the neighborhood called me 'Cumhur' for 'Republic.' My father Henri Roditi taught history and religion at the Jewish schools. He was an ambitious man. After school he kept accounts for Jewish businessmen, swearing under his breath. He seemed angry at the fact that his careless father had lost a fortune in Europe. My mother Alma worked part-time at the Jewish orphanage in Galata; she was a soft-hearted woman with the soul of an artist. We led a modest life on the ground floor of a two-storey house behind the Yanbol Synagogue.

"We moved to İzmir when I was seven. A relative of my father had found him a job with an exporter of dried fruits. Within two years my father became foreman, then manager, then chief financial advisor of the company. But despite his new status and our new flat on the top floor of a modern building in Alsancak, he wasn't satisfied. The year I became a third-grader the whole family began taking Italian lessons from a coquettish old Levantine lady who had never been to Italy in her life. I didn't know why. I started to cry when they told me we were moving to Milan. It had been tough enough adapting to İzmir. According to my father, however, the young Turkish republic, except for a handful of established merchants, held no promise for brilliant young Jews.

"Our downstairs neighbor Sophia had a cousin who was

a jeweler in Milan, and Baruch Shapiro was looking for an honest assistant. I remember my father shouting, 'Alma! I think I believe in God now!' after he'd been promised a partnership with Shapiro. It didn't take the widower Shapiro long to feel close to our family, which had always lived by Ottoman values. He secured for us the furnished apartment below his own, taking it over from his cousin who had lived there with his Gentile wife when they were working together and whom Shapiro had evicted when the cousin tried to swindle him. A quiet and mysterious man in his sixties, Shapiro wanted me to call him Grandpa. Not only did he send me to a school for rich Jewish kids, but he hired a private teacher to help with my Italian. He respected the memory of his wife who had died in childbirth. I heard once that he tolerated no objects in his plainly furnished flat that would overshadow the pictures of his Rita in their silver frames.

"The treasure of Ali Baba and the forty thieves was always what I thought of when I went to Il Rubino, Grandpa's shop on Via Montenapoleone. I hid my obsession with the beauty of the precious stones I found there even from my mother for fear that somebody might think me unbalanced. I could hardly wait for summer vacations and the pleasure of working as an apprentice at Il Rubino. It was always interesting to observe our customers, some of whom came all the way from Switzerland for our rubies. By the end of our second year I was starting to feel at home in Milan. But in the winter of 1936 I wasn't surprised to learn that we were moving to

Paris with my honorary grandpa: the prime minister, Benito Mussolini, had entered Adolf Hitler's orbit and the country's Jews were becoming increasingly agitated. When encounters in town turned physical, valuable properties and expensive moveable items sold fast and cheap. In Paris we moved into a duplex apartment at Quai de Jemappes, where I learned that the most exquisite diamonds and rubies had been sent ahead and put in the safe of a private bank.

"It then emerged that Shapiro, who was again residing on the floor above us, was the senior partner in a store called Le Rubis on Rue de la Paix; I was as angry as if I'd caught him cheating at cards. Sometimes when I became distracted during my French lessons with Madame Nemirovsky of Odessa, I would calculate how many months we could last in Paris. As worry-free Parisians were celebrating Christmas of 1938, Shapiro made a guess: 'By next Christmas Hitler will invade Paris, and London by the one after that.' I was aware of the bottleneck that the jewelry business was becoming. What we needed immediately was somewhere where Hitler could not follow us. New York? My father wept when the U.S. embassy, despite pressure, refused us a visa because Baruch, a staunch anti-communist, was born in Belgrade. I was amazed to hear that our Plan B was Havana, that notorious center of intemperance. A diplomat whose mistress was our customer had little difficulty in persuading us that we could escape from there to New York when the war was over. My father took a ship to Havana in the fall of 1939 and I'm sure he had the rarest gems with him. By the new year he had opened bank accounts and made the other necessary arrangements to gradually transfer Shapiro's holdings to Havana from his Paris and London banks. The remaining inventory at Le Rubis was disposed of by February 1940. In April we boarded an old steamer at Le Havre and sailed for Havana by way of Martinique. In June the Nazi army invaded Paris ...

"At first sight Havana looks like an eternal holiday resort. I was apprehensive on hearing that we would have a maid and driver at our villa in Vedado. Turkish was our family's favorite language, though we would resort to Ladino—Sephardic Spanish—for really important matters. I had to take lessons in modern Spanish for six months to go to high school. When I took a shine to my so-called poet-teacher's mulatto daughter Ramona, I was surprised to see that my parents agreed on something for the first time—opposing me. If I was the least visible student at the exclusive Belen College, the most charismatic one was Fidel Castro. It amused both of us that people had trouble understanding our affinity. It so happened that Fidel's maternal grandfather was an Istanbul Jew who had changed his religion and last name (from Ruso to Ruz) when he married. The official name of Mr. Cuba, who was, by the way, devoted to his ailing mother, was Fidel Alejandro Castro Ruz. Castro Ruz graduated from high school a year behind me, but he and I met up once more at Havana University's law school. I watched him in action during student elections and other incidents and said, 'If they don't assasinate him before he turns thirty, he'll take over everything.' The year we'd landed in Havana the retired officer Fulgencia Batista had become president after a shady election, causing unrest in the country. My family decided not to open a shop in that atmosphere, and so we wandered around like Anatolian village women with bags in our hands, trying to sell jewelry to tourists' wives and rich businessmen.

"After a heart attack in 1942, Grandpa Baruch turned to religion. When synagogue services were over he would drop in at cafés frequented by European Jews and lose himself in nostalgic conversation. (There were 20,000 Jews in the city at the time.) Although we had no real financial problems, my father continued to import semi-precious stones as if to prove to his benefactor that he was not an idler. The day Hitler committed suicide, Baruch Shapiro died in his sleep. Just before they took him down to the hospital morgue I sneaked into his room out of curiosity. What I saw was an expression of great peace and accomplishment on his face. I still can't believe that I kissed him on both cheeks and stroked his hair.

"Neither my mother nor I were surprised to learn that the sneaky Shapiro had left 90 per cent of his fortune to the Zionist organization that was lobbying for the founding of Israel in 1947. The remainder of the inheritance was to be shared between us and the city's three synagogues. There were some interesting provisions in the will. Although we could receive interest on the United States government bonds, we were not allowed to sell them before their date of maturity. The proceeds were earmarked for three things: the purchase of an apartment in New York, the establishment of a business, and the completion of my Master's degree. Later I understood that these were precautions to keep my father, an ambitious man, from endangering our future.

"We moved to New York in 1946 as soon as I graduated from law school, which I entered on my father's insistence. Judging from the money he bequeathed us, Grandpa Shapiro thought that an apartment in Brooklyn would be sufficient. At the end of the summer I signed up for English-language courses at New York University. The next year I took my second undergraduate degree. My father still hadn't found a job, but we didn't complain. The precious-stone market was in the hands of a few ruthless Jewish merchants, and the mood of pessimism the war had left behind hadn't yet dissipated. The month I started an M.B.A. at N.Y.U., my father founded an import-export business with the wishy-washy son-in-law of an antique dealer he'd met at the synagogue. At first they imported glass souvenirs from Venice and watches from Switzerland. They made money selling the watches wholesale to institutional buyers. The week I took my third and last degree the pair had a falling-out. My father had put in an order at a very low price but without having lined up customers for the goods, though apparently he had received certain assurances. When the customers failed to materialize he was left holding the bag. He made drastic efforts to save his reputation. We managed to unload a third of the shipment at home and in Canada.

For the rest of the stock my father chose a strange target – Tokyo. And I was the one to go there, alone …

"All this time during which he was struggling to bring me up flawlessly, he also seemed to be blaming me for the suffering he had had to endure in his own childhood. Now, at least, he could have the pleasure of disparaging the diplomas I'd earned if I came home empty-handed. My savior was the mysterious Jake Mifune, who occupied the seat on my left on the plane to Tokyo. This middle-aged man with part-Japanese blood spoke only once in the course of the entire flight.

"Discovering that I was Turkish, he said, 'I visited your city twice when my uncle worked at the American consulate in Istanbul.'

"I spent the week in Tokyo stressed out. Japan's war wounds were only beginning to heal. Among the companies I talked to there were none that did not have cash problems. Still, they seemed to be interested in the watches as long as they could pay for them in installments on fixed terms. That night as I sat pondering darkly in the deserted lobby of my hotel, Jake Mifune walked past. I could hardly believe my eyes. He was quietly scolding a group of men in suits treading carefully behind him. I thought he hadn't seen me but just as I stood up there he was, asking 'What's the problem?' in the sweet-and-sour tone of the neighborhood tough guy, and I proceeded to tell him.

"'If I were in New York, I'd give your father a good thumping,' he said. 'But in Tokyo my cousin Taro may be able to help you.'

"The nosy bellboy who led me to the restaurant at Ginza told me that Taro was the most famous eel chef in the city. I had first to prove to this cousin who reeked of fish that I was not a pure-blooded American. After that test he gave me the address of his customer Shizoku Nasu, whom he described as 'quite honest despite being a gourmet'. I met the francophone Nasu at his tiny office, permeated with *chansons*, in the strategic Shinjuku district. Nasu proposed to take the watches in exchange for necklaces of black pearl. As if I wasn't already dazzled by these gems worthy of a pharaoh's treasury, he said, 'They're twice as valuable as the white ones, but if you lose money on a sale I can make up for it by supplying you with extras.' Since I was flying back the next day I had no opportunity to verify his claim. I showed up in New York with a bag full of black pearls in exchange for 30,000 watches. The pearls proved to be worth four times as much as the white ones, and I ended up making two more trips to Tokyo that year.

"Well, it was a bit awkward for me to ask Shizoku, who lived with his sick mother, about the source of those necklaces. But it was obvious that in the U.S. and Europe, whose post-war economies were booming, these gems were desirable objects. And they could only be produced by the Japanese. We invited Shizoku to New York for Christmas of 1950. Apparently unimpressed by the Waldorf-Astoria where we'd put him, he wandered out to discover the city by himself. On his last night he wanted to go to an Argentinean steak house and listen to music. I took him to Cabaña las Violetas. I was a bit diffident when the waiter told me there would also be a dance show – I was prejudiced against tangos by my father, who always said, 'Tangos are like *kemençe* tunes. You hear one, you've heard them all.' But when the blind Argentinean musician laid hands on his bandoneon I felt a tingle. The melody pouring out of that old instrument was a flame to kindle a new day. Twenty minutes later three casually dressed couples took to the stage. I focused my attention on the olive-skinned girl with a turned-up nose and an inviting smile on her face. The way she wrinkled her brow during the dramatic passes was completely charming, and the way she frowned when she embraced her partner made me shiver with pleasure. When Julio the headwaiter saw me sitting in the same place at the foot of the stage for the third time, he grasped the situation and helped me out. A generous tip brought forth the happy news that, no, Rosalba Martinez was not in a relationship with her dance partner. He then conveyed to her the notes that we wrote together in Spanish and attached to bouquets of flowers and boxes of chocolate. Finally I was able to meet the skittish girl on a gloomy Sunday at a café next to the restaurant.

"We walked toward Broadway, which was flowing like the Amazon, and I considered stretching out my hand for the forbidden fruit. We went into a café named Artwin and I remember praying, 'Please let her turn out to be stupid so that I can just drink a cup of coffee and get away.' But I was already under her spell. Born twenty-two years earlier in Buenos Aires, Rosalba Anna-Graziella Martinez was unpretentious and enchanting. She had a sense of humor. About Istanbul she said, 'Isn't that where they made Aladdin's carpet?' She exuded self-confidence and wore simple but chic clothes. I can still describe what she had on that day, down to the buttons on her blouse. She was perfectly aware that she was shaking me to the core with her straightforward language and the twinkle in her eye.

"On our second date we watched a romantic movie at a musty theater in Spanish Harlem. By the third date, as I kissed her goodnight on the cheek, I was sure I'd found the love of my life. We began meeting like high-school kids smitten with puppy love. Sundays always meant the movies. We walked the back streets hand in hand, and if she felt like whistling a tune I felt like I was floating in the air. Twice a week or more I was at Cabaña las Violetas. If I said to her, 'Don't raise your left leg so high, people can see your underwear,' she would raise it higher with a coy look. I can still see it.

"She had had to break off her training in ballet to look after her twin siblings when her father died of a heart attack. I was twenty-seven and my family was already tense with the effort of finding me a suitable Jewish bride with a satisfactory dowry. About the time my mother wanted me to meet the daughter of a diamond wholesaler on 47th Street, Rosalba's troupe was on the point of leaving for Chicago. Telling my mother I had a lover was a relief to me, even though she cried and beat her thighs like a Muslim woman.

When my father got the news, he wasn't slow to deliver an ultimatum: leave the girl or leave home immediately! Next morning as I packed my belongings I felt like a prisoner who's received the surprising news that he's been freed.

"I moved in with my pal Bernie Jacobsen, who worked at the Chemical Bank. My mother's efforts as a go-between proved futile, and my father disowned me. As an undergraduate at N.Y.U. I'd been a scholarship student, so I still had some of the money left that Baruch Shapiro had earmarked for my education. When my father's secretary brought it to me, she informed me in tears that I was no longer welcome in my father's presence, even at his funeral. Rosalba, who spent the spring working in Chicago and Detroit, was amazed at my ordeal. If I was job-hunting in New York two days a week, I was running after her the rest of the time. We planned to get married as soon as I found a decent job. If I wanted my future wife to stop dancing in front of those haughty young men, my salary would have to support her family in Buenos Aires.

"I founded a go-between company called Black Beauty Ltd. and became Nasu's New York representative. Puerto Rican Julio, who played matchmaker to Rosalba and me, said on his first day as my employee, 'I'll bring luck to you.' We did good business in a market where certain unscrupulous Japanese organizations were passing off painted stones as black pearls. We multiplied our profits by living up to our promises about quality and quantity. When I married Rosalba in 1952, I had an apartment on Park Avenue and the latest Dodge sedan. But my wife didn't feel completely at home in the richest district of New York, and her first pregnancy resulted in miscarriage. Just as she was starting to pull herself together she was devastated by the news that one of her twin brothers had drowned in the Río Plata. We traveled to Buenos Aires; she couldn't leave her depressed mother for months. The next three years of traveling between New York and Buenos Aires left her exhausted. In her absences I followed Shizoku's advice and went to South Asia in search of precious stones. For a while, at least, the profits I made were embarrassing to me, especially those I made at the expense of distressed maharajahs. I was thirty-two and rich when our son Salvador was born in our Buenos Aires house. My travel on the United States–South Asia–Argentina triangle intensified when my wife finally decided that she could no longer bear to leave Buenos Aires. Rosalba attributed the lack of friction in our marriage to these continual separations. Her capacity for compromise and her unassuming attitude enabled her to manage me and her problematic mother for years.

"Our daughter Daniela was forty days old when my father died in the summer of 1958. In keeping with his will, my mother refused to see me. She was ninety by the time I managed to get admitted to her presence, and then she confused me with Musa, the son of the *imam* who was our neighbor in Balat.

"'Musa,' my mother said to me on her hundredth birthday, 'if you see Gerda, tell her I'm tired of waiting for a letter.'

"She never spoke again, but turned into a kind of radiant statue. I've come to like her saintly disposition. I enjoy sitting at her side once every three months when I visit her in New York. She strokes my cheek and whispers Old Testament verses to me, and I recall the *ezans* I used to hear in Balat.

"In the summer of 1960 I went to French Polynesia, where they'd begun the experimental production of black pearls. They told me that black pearls were troublesome to produce but that the start-up cost was not terribly prohibitive. I took special note of two critical steps in the process: the injecting of 'seeds' into the oysters that were then lowered into the ocean with special nets, and the impeccable care lavished on them for more than eighteen months underwater. So first I founded a company called 'Noir Est Noir', then I set up a processing plant on Mangareva Island. I brought in Japanese professionals but couldn't put together a competent local team to take care of the underwater maintenance. Only when I had a synagogue built on the island to attract Ethiopian Jewish divers was my destiny realized of becoming the world's leading black pearl producer. The cost of a single large and flawless Type A black pearl starts at a $1,000, and there will never be a lack of women willing to pay $30,000 to get on a two-year waiting list for a small pearl necklace. I was nudging the billionaire level by the age of fifty-four, the year of the heart attack that I concealed from my wife. I gradually reduced my work load, and when Salvador came onto the scene I gave up all the routine chores.

"Rosalba and I went to Europe after her mother died,

and I returned to the country of my birth after forty years. Most of my relatives were dead and the rest were scattered to the four corners of the earth.

"Rosalba really liked hearing the *ezan* and seeing Arnavutköy and the Mihrimah Sultan mosque at Edirnekapı in Istanbul, and meeting the İzmir people who called her 'Auntie.' She never interfered with my work. I began to fear for her psychological health, though, because she never wanted to change her style or her philosophy even though she was married to perhaps the richest man in Argentina. I almost grew used to the way her uneasiness rose in proportion to the rise in my wealth. The last two things that brought her happiness, I suppose, were Daniela's graduation as an honors student from the Düsseldorf College of Music and her subsequent appointment to a cellist's chair on the Boston Symphony Orchestra. My wife didn't see her seventieth birthday. I was on a business trip to Tahiti with my son when we lost her. They said she'd been struggling with an incurable ovarian tumor. Apparently she'd mentioned this to her daughter six months earlier but to nobody else, because she didn't want to spoil the happiness the family had enjoyed for ten years.

"I thought it would ease my pain if I threw myself into my work again, but it was useless. I never forgave myself for spending all those days without her for the sake of my financial ambitions. My respect for my wife increased with her death, yet I was immersed in guilt. In her honor I shut myself up in this soulless building. I've never succeeded even in throwing away her handkerchiefs. Some days I go twice to visit her grave at the Recoleta Cemetery. She used to be frightened by thunder; now whenever I hear thunder I get goose bumps. Now that she's gone, my secret paradise Mangareva just annoys me. I never leave Recoleta except to visit my mother. She made me laugh the last time I saw her, after I'd completed my wife's mausoleum. 'Musa,' she whispered in my ear, 'have you been circumcised?'

"Yesterday was the anniversary of Rosalba's death. I've confessed to you what I haven't been able to tell my insensitive fifty-year-old son. Your face eases the heart and your eyes do not judge. If you've brought news from heaven, tell me. What do you want from this poor Roditi, my countryman?"

Moved by his story, I related the story of Esther and Ali.

"Eli's grandmother and mine were cousins," he said. "People used to call Eli, who had nothing going for him except his good looks, 'the actor.' It was a bit of a joke to me when he approached me on my fortieth birthday with a proposal to become my business partner. He wouldn't listen to reason, and he took serious offense when I said no. I hardly knew him! We would nod to each other from a distance if we happened to see each other, but that was all. It wasn't difficult to see that he and his elegant wife were a poor match. Losing money would have been avoidable if he hadn't mixed with the wrong people. It was said that he was the most handsome and the least talented Jew in Argentina's long immigration history.

"It took seven years for him to cross my path again. One

evening as I was getting into my car to go home, he opened the door and sat down in the front seat and started crying. That was when I learned that he was in partnership with an Armenian jeweler from Istanbul. He begged for a loan to replace what he'd taken secretly from the safe and lost on the stock market. I knew he'd never keep his promise, and he didn't, but two years later he got me again with a note he sent to my table at a business lunch. This time it was his daughter. If he failed to pay her tuition immediately she was going to be expelled from her private school. I gave him the money and told him, 'From now on, the only help you can expect from me is paying for your funeral expenses.' He didn't even feign embarrassment.

"I felt sympathetic toward Stella, who looked like her paternal grandmother. She had a little temper and a lot of attractiveness. I hired her to work in my public relations office, where she stayed until she became Miss Argentina. She always took her father's side when her parents argued and so eventually became distanced from her mother. Her second marriage was to an Australian diplomat, and when she came to say goodbye, she vowed never to set foot in this town again.

"I kept my promise to Eli when I took care of his funeral expenses after the accident twenty years ago. Esther appeared more grief-stricken during the funeral than I'd expected. Nobody saw her after that; but if she'd died, I would have heard about it. If it's any help, you can take it to the bank that that headstrong İzmir woman would never chase after her daughter. Once I met Eli's old partner, Dikran Gumushian, and remembered that my father never let me play with the Armenian kids. He told me that Eli had suffered a psychological breakdown and was dealing in used cars. Dikran is a likeable man. If he's still alive he would be about seventy-five. You might find out more about Esther if you ask around among the jewelers at Libertad. Interestingly, Dikran and Esther behaved as if they were quite close friends at Eli's funeral ..."

After a brief but adequate silence I thanked him and politely requested permission to take my leave. He insisted on giving me a brooch of black pearls in a glittering box. "This ruinous object will be locked up eventually in some woman's jewelry box," he said. "And for you, my countryman, I have a message: A man who has never had an unforgettable woman in his life has not lived, but merely existed on this earth."

We were both surprised when I kissed the weary hand that he stretched out and laid on my forehead. His eyes filled with tears and I quickly took refuge in the elevator.

Ariel was sitting at the bar in the lobby of the Alvear Palace reading Samuel Beckett's *Ill Seen, Ill Said*. It seemed to me that he disapproved of my seeing Izak Roditi without him.

"Did you know that this is the year of Beckett's one hundredth birthday?" he said.

"Did you know that 'Godot' was coined from 'God' and 'idiot'?" I said.

We visited the Recoleta Cemetery before commencing our search for Dikran the jeweler. I felt no nostalgia for Z.

when I beheld the *tableau vivante* created by the marble tombs of Recoleta. Avoiding the commotion caused by tourists trying to get their pictures taken next to Evita's monument, we came to Roditi's wife's place of eternal rest. It was a jet-black pyramid. Her effigy was inscribed on each side. Ariel translated the lines on the side facing the street; I was sure they were borrowed from a Turkish poet:

> Your absence is the other name of hell.
> I'm cold, I'm shivering. Don't close your eyes.

Libertad had lost its old dynamism; the perpetual economic crisis had caused links in the caravan of jewelers to be broken. The obstinate middle-aged Armenian caretaker we spoke to said he'd never heard of a Dikran Gumushian. Then I remembered Dr. Kaltakian. We rushed to Ariel's office and bookstore to call him. The bookstore was as tightly organized as a military archive and smelled strangely of hay. I reached Dr. Armando Kaltakian on the fourth attempt. He sounded glad to hear that I needed his help. "If I can't call you with the information you want in two hours, I'll fax it to your hotel this evening," he said. I decided to take a stroll along Corrientes.

As I emerged onto the spacious avenue I felt the same sense of relief I used to feel when math classes were over. I wandered along accompanied by gentle gusts of wind. Was this a mirage, or was I seeing in this faraway land shops that I knew window by window? Were these the cinemas and theaters that were etched into my memory by years of movie-going? Like Anatolia, the streets were saturated with people walking as if they were playing parts in a pantomime behind a giant lace curtain. I walked to the head of the street, where a musician in an orange velvet jacket had situated himself. His legs were amputated below the knees and, if you ask me, he was willfully murdering the melody of "Over the Rainbow" with his harmonica. I poured all the coins in my pocket into the tango hat in front of him, and he thanked me by winking at me twice. I entered the desolate café behind him and sobered up on bad coffee brought to me by a waitress who thought that Istanbul was the capital of Egypt.

I went back to the bookstore, but gazing at the shelves of tired books was making me sleepy. I selected *Las Poemas de Edgar Poe* and felt satisfied to have filled a gap in the library I never touched. I wasn't surprised when Ariel didn't give me a discount. As I was imagining a competition for the most attractive cover among the complete works of Nobel Prize-winning Jews, a fax message arrived:

> *Brother Kemal,*
> *Master Dikran will be at a café called Confitería Ideal tomorrow morning at eleven o'clock. I tried describing your features to him but he said there was no need. He is from Istanbul and can spot a young Turkish fellow by the way he walks into a room.*
>
> *Good luck.*
> *Dr. A.K.*

As Ariel was dropping me off at the hotel, he told me how

he had met a Turkish bibliophile.

"I didn't think he would know about the rare book dealers here. Anyway, he was middle-aged and looked like an Italian, though with a surly face. He said he wrote novels and essays under a pseudonym. His Spanish was more satisfactory than that of the Boca Juniors football players. He told me, 'Whenever the name Borges is pronounced, I think of Dali.' He'd been to a town in Patagonia whose name he wouldn't tell me. But he didn't mind telling me why he was here: he had bought the first volume of Aulus Gellius's *Attic Nights*, translated into English in 1795, from an Istanbul dealer last year. This book was actually, as the naïve dealer arrogantly confided, a $3 acquisition from the nephew of a White Russian who died at the age of 105. According to an inscription dated 19 September 1908 on the title page, the book belonged to a Constance Radcliffe who worked at the British embassy in Istanbul. It contained numerous passages underlined in Indian ink. When these were combined, they formed a message:

> *I can no longer tolerate the burden of the sin laid on me. I want to shake off the curse of this secret that will change the history books.*
>
> *If Markham and Unsworth at Burlington Arcade (London) still stands, you are not too late.*
>
> *Take this book there. You will be rewarded with the second volume.*

"So he goes to London. Markham and Unsworth at Piccadilly is now a fountain-pen boutique. The owner of the shop, who's in his eighties, says, 'I suppose I don't have the right to ask you why you are so late?' and hands him the second volume, which he has removed from a wall safe. The original title of this cultural touchstone, which comprises three volumes in English, is *Noctes Atticae*. Aulus Gellius wrote it in the second century A.D. while living in Athens. It was obvious that he, who did not care to say any more, was set to go to Patagonia with the fresh clue. I didn't ask him about his pseudonym. But in my latest dream—about as long as an MTV video—I saw you escaping from a novel that he wrote and trying to take shelter in the novel he was about to write ..."

I managed to extricate myself from the paranoid book dealer and went back to the hotel and fell into a deep sleep after drinking two beers I found in the mini-bar. Later, as we had dinner in his room, Professor Ali complained about how his enthusiasm for translation had diminished along with his pain. It was a great surprise to me that he bewailed his beloved's disappearance instead of rejoicing at the good news that she was still alive somewhere.

"If she's gone back to İzmir and kept it from me, I couldn't bear it," he moaned.

"Sir," I pointed out, "we still have three days to find her. I would prefer to hear such a lamentation from an acknowledged translator of romantic novels when he has to board the plane empty-handed."

I went back to my room and out onto the balcony, realizing that I had yet to enjoy the view. The haunting darkness that rose up when rush-hour traffic died down grew on me. Between the hotel and the desolate port were the Retiro train station, which was fast approaching retirement, a bus station resembling a dumpster and, the last figure in the frame, a colonial clock tower rearing up like an agitated Trojan horse.

I took it as an omen when the light rain let up. Starting with Leandro Alem, I walked the half-deserted streets interlocked like lines on a chess board. Converting prices on the goods in those dimly lit windows to New Turkish Lira was somehow therapeutic. I observed dignified groups of people rummaging through garbage bins and greeted weary men out walking their dogs. When I got cold while counting the buildings with only one lighted window, I ducked into a bar with lively music. My drinking companions were a retired sailor and a trade unionist who confused Turkey with Estonia. At my next bar a gay antique dealer's invitation to San Telmo was enough to send me scampering home.

*

In view of the average age of the walking monuments on the morning shift in the crumbling Confitería Ideal I wondered whether it was okay to put in an order. It seemed clear that the hawk-nosed man talking to the eighty-year-old waiter was Dikran the jeweler. As an extra hint, I assumed, he wiggled his shoulder. The way he used his right hand to signal for coffee for the two of us took me back to my days at the Huzur Coffeehouse at L.

"I felt close to this quiet man from İzmir, although they told me that a partnership between a Jew and an Armenian was unheard of even in Ottoman times. But Eli looked like Robert Taylor, and this of course was an advantage when it came to attracting female customers. So I put him downstairs at the cash register. It took only two days to realize that he had the mind of an eighteen-year-old. This lost soul couldn't focus on life, let alone the cash register. If he wasn't diving into youth magazines at his desk, he was doodling sports-car designs. He was well mannered and helpless, so for the sake of his innocent face I never said much. I even accepted the three hours in the middle of the day when he regularly disappeared. I was thankful that he was not a meddlesome guy who put his nose in his partner's business.

"One day I caught him pilfering from the cash register and he grasped my hand and begged me not to say anything about this shameful act to his wife. We took our salaries out of the company profits, and our families didn't socialize with each other, so I didn't find out for a long time that for an eighteen-month stretch they lived solely on his wife's bank account. He convinced her that there were no profits and therefore no salary, so that he could use the money for installments on the sports car he had secretly bought. At that I returned his capital and fired my so-called partner of seven years. Esther, whom any man would consider a prize, was probably sent to Eli as divine retribution. For a while I thought this mismatched couple were victims of love at first sight. If only the fault-finding Stella hadn't been so devoted to her father, Esther might have said to hell with her inheritance and kicked her foolish husband out straightaway.

"She was a woman full of life who radiated joy wherever she went. Chic, intelligent, and well educated, of course she found it easy to make friends with men. Two years after I got rid of Eli she paid a surprise visit to the store, looking as exhausted as a firefighter. She asked what I thought of her husband going into the used-car business. 'If he has to work, let him do what he knows and likes,' I said, feeling somewhat regretful. The last time I saw her was at Eli's funeral. She still carried herself like a queen though she was on the far side of fifty. I have to be honest—God knows the truth anyway—during the whole funeral I was only thinking about how I would woo her if I were a widower. The only clue I have for you is this old address, and I doubt that it's much use. When we last met she told me they were about to move again; and from the way she sighed it was obvious that it would not be to a more delightful home …"

Seeing me consult my watch, Dikran summoned the waiter, whom I felt like strangling for sneering at him as he asked for the check in Grand Bazaar Spanish. He extracted a yellowing card from his exhausted briefcase, put on his glasses, and flourished his antique fountain pen. He wrote down Esther Arditti's address and blew on it twice. I knew as he handed me the note that he was going to invite me to dinner. I dealt with it by accepting, provided we met in Istanbul at the Taksim monument on Christmas Eve. I walked to the door aware of being followed by the restless gaze of everyone in the establishment.

On the dim street my feet started to lose their feeling and I felt a piercing ache in my forehead. I closed my eyes and tried to grip the earth with my toes. When I opened them again everything around me seemed turned into a scene from a graphic novel. I could hear nothing but the casual fluttering of the puny pigeons' wings. I set my feet in motion along a trail of withered leaves fallen from the tall rickety trees. At precisely the moment when I pulled myself together and began to crush them under my feet I understood that my inner voice had deserted me. My real worry was that it had taken my passion for classical music with it. It occurred to me that I hadn't even so much as hummed Pachelbel's Canon to myself since the day I started chasing after Esther.

I took another taxi to Ariel's bookstore. There I met Sebastiano Valido cracking jokes in his high voice. The old book collector was wearing a cape. "I never set foot outside Argentina, but I can describe Haghia Sophia to you down to the last stone," he said. Ariel looked at the address I was holding and bestowed on me the honor of pronouncing the word "once", meaning eleven, correctly as "onsey." I felt the urge to pull out the last tuft of hair remaining on his head.

We made it to "eleven" in a taxi driven by Rita, an ex-dancer who'd become a driver after breaking her leg. They informed me that this district where middle-class Jews once lived hadn't been able to withstand the vicious cycle of inflation and deflation, a remark that brought to mind the sorrowful back streets of Fatih. In fact, when I saw those miniature synagogues I could hardly convince myself that I wasn't in Balat. It was equally difficult to believe that I was not in Mahmutpaşa when I saw the clumsily scattered rolls of fabric in the lifeless shop windows. We reached the soulless building at 721E Larrea after leaving several gray or beige worn-out and deserted streets behind. Ariel reached for the bell next to "Portería (Jorge S. Perez)" and I stepped back. The salmon-faced doorman seemed to diminish in size as Ariel tucked a fifty-peso bill into his shirt pocket. The Ardittis had lived first on the top and then on the ground floor. According to Perez, who had helped them move to their new place in Paso in the fall of 1980, they were a respectable couple who even during their endless quarrels avoided disturbing the neighbors.

As the doorman muttered and scribbled the Ardittis' new address on an old lottery ticket, I felt weary to the bone. After a ten-minute tour around the block we pulled into a street parallel to Larrea. Paso seemed wrapped in a coal-black veil, but despite this it didn't feel threatening. The balconies of the houses on the street where we looked for number 184F were fenced off by net-like metal screens to keep children from falling off, which created the feel of a grotesque open-air exhibition. I noted a rare number plate that looked like a fighter pilot's ID tag. The building had collapsed after a fire brought part of it down. It disturbed me to think that it was perhaps a depressed Esther who had lashed out at it. I followed my guide to the café next door. The drowsy old men sitting shoulder to shoulder in the dim interior seemed to be fighting the angel of death to a draw. We seated ourselves next to the old-time jukebox playing Engelbert Humperdinck's "Too Beautiful to Last."

My book-dealer guide learned the following from the plump waitress: the same week her husband died, Esther Arditti disappeared; the Adonis-like Eli used to escape to this very café after quarreling with his wife and he was a partner in a used-dealership called "Sí, Sí Usados Autos"; and as for the fire, that transsexual dancer who lived on the middle floor last year ...

I wouldn't have believed the waitress—clearly an Eli fan—except that I'd seen the company's name, "Yes, Yes Used Cars," in the hotel's telephone directory. My head swam with "Too Beautiful to Last" all the way back, reminding me of my childhood. The retired principal Selahattin at L. came to mind. He would raise his walking stick and yell, "Evening, once more evening, evening once more," but we could never tell whether it was a sad song or a happy one.

I hurried to Professor Ali's room. His reaction to my report was disappointing—at first quizzical, then cynical. I turned down his offer of a drink and went to bed. The sound of an *ezan* booming from the north soon had me up again.

I went down to the Retiro train station. When I'd had enough of that lethargy-inducing place I strolled along a few

streets with melodious names—Arroyo, Junkal, Arenales—
and felt more relaxed. A whistling cab driver drove me in his
rattle-trap vehicle to San Telmo. Suddenly I was surrounded
by a tourist trap of orange, pink, and cerulean blue buildings.
I walked until Brasil cut across my path at Defensa. The
city was handing me a slice of time that was a fusion of
afternoon-evening and fall-winter. I followed the crowd and
turned left. A brick-colored bar in the same row of buildings
as the Russian Orthodox church caught my attention. It
stood on the corner with its arms seductively wide open.
I went inside. The spacious saloon seemed to be savoring
the lull before the storm. I took a table far from the door.
The old man at the table next to mine who tried to help me
order a bottle of Malbec from the fussy waiter just made
things worse. In his neat but old suit he might have been
part of the furniture. As my bottle of wine arrived he asked
sternly in English, "Are you a Turk?" Forty years earlier he
had been a diplomat in Ankara. I thought he wanted to have
a chat about the old times, but I was wrong. He was content
to hear me answer "No" to his next and last question, "Have
you ever seen Genoa?"

"Then," he said, stretching, "you've probably declared
Buenos Aires and Istanbul cousins."

I was on the point of warming to the topic when an old
woman in a fake fur with a disapproving eye stepped in and
made him get up. (She must have been his long-suffering
wife.)

If I took my eyes off the label of the bottle in front of me, it would break the spell. Humming Humperdinck songs, I drank until I could see the bottom of the bottle. As my head cleared itself of thought, a fine maroon veil of tulle tried to interpose itself between me and the world. I could have had a second bottle if the bar hadn't begun filling up. I called Ariel on the cell phone he'd borrowed from his cousin. I knew that for $20 an hour he would be at my side in thirty minutes. When he saw that I couldn't even whistle in my condition he took my arm and helped me to his car. I remember vaguely that we followed an ambulance to Corrientes Boulevard and a huge building with a neon sign that blinked "Empuje" on and off.

In the unpretentious restaurant on the first floor where people spoke in whispers, I was cautioned not to ask for salt, pepper, or ketchup when ordering a steak, as it was considered improper. The man eating alone at the next table was an oncology professor and bibliophile who had precisely 1,000 books in his collection; whenever he wished to add a new one, he ritually burned an old one. Ariel was happy to see that he had surprised me with this revelation. We went down to the music salon as he rattled off the eccentrics who collect books with exactly 200 or 300 pages, or whose protagonists' names all start with "A," or whose narrators turn out to be the murderers in the end. I felt sorry for the authors of those books.

We shared a table with a honeymooning Austin dentist and his new wife who was his daughter's age. The waiter collected $100 from each person, checking the bills with the aid of a torch. He then put two bottles of wine on the table and disappeared. An old clown came on first, prancing airily on stage to the tune from a sharp whistle. I loved this artist, who cried on one side of his face and laughed on the other. "My name is Alberto Bernardo Cesare Diego Ernesto Fabio Guillermo ... but you can call me Evita," he said in accented English and began his show ...

My guide gave me fair warning about the next performer as the microphone was being lowered to a height of three feet. Juanito, nicknamed Señor Ruiseñor (Mr. Nightingale), was a twenty-year-old dwarf with a hunchback. Anyone who heard his voice cascading like a waterfall was grateful that the good Lord had compensated him for his physical deficiencies. The club manager, a retired pimp, had discovered him busking on the street. He went onstage only at Empuje and refused to make recordings because he considered them akin to "frozen meat." With the first notes from of his mouth a sacred hush fell over the room. Ariel removed his glasses and closed his eyes. The crystal voice of Juanito, who looked like a mischievous schoolboy, enthralled us body and soul. I felt somewhat ambivalent about the fact that not even Bach or Vivaldi had moved me as Señor Ruiseñor had.

The Lunapar Trio consisted of an Inca woman on contrabass and two thin men with bandoneons who inflated themselves along with their instruments. They deserved to be paid extra for the difficult task of following Juanito. (Listening to Mr. Nightingale had shattered my old standards for music; after that the cello was merely a noisemaker.) The trio would give a short recital and then accompany the Sevilla-Silvyo tango twins. Seeing my eyelids droop, Ariel leaned over and informed me that Sevilla, the blind one, was a world-class beauty.

I beat a speedy retreat from the room after the refrain-loving trio's third piece—the wine that I'd consumed beyond the pleasure-giving stage was about to take effect. Outside the club entrance I held my face to the soft wind and dropped to my knees under the buzzing neon sign. Just as I was about to fade away, Ariel picked me up and hustled me into the restroom reeking of vinegar, where he doused my face with cold water. We hurried back to our seats just as the Sevilla-Silvyo twins were making their appearance. I studied the charming face of Sevilla, who was injecting ballet and gymnastics instead of passion into her dancing. I focused on her wide brow to avoid her eyes. Then I remembered who it was that the arrogant young woman who sat beside me on the São Paolo-Buenos Aires flight reminded me of. It was Haluk Erçelik's blind granddaughter Sim, whom I'd seen in one of his paintings! This simple trick of memory relaxed me as thoroughly as though I'd found Esther. I was ready to go back to the hotel. There I closed my eyes, still suffused with the pleasurable lightness I'd felt on the way back. A vision of Miss Buenos Aires, wearing a gray cape and an anxious face, appeared before me. It looked as though she was trying to warn me.

*

I caught Professor Ali in front of the TV watching a porn movie. He said that he would get breakfast with Dr. Armenak, who was going to drop by to change his bandage. "We've got forty-eight hours left before heading back to Istanbul and I miss even the mold in Balat," he said. "My one consolation is that at least you haven't been bored to death on this wild goose chase." Aggravated somewhat, I replied, "Well, sir, maybe I won't come back empty-handed tonight."

"Avenida Cordoba, 3684H!" The four-digit number of Eli Arditti's last address aroused the anticipatory joy of following yet another trail down yet another infinite boulevard. Cordoba Avenue was as dignified as a river marking the border between two hostile countries. It was as if I were not seeing for the first time the calm landscape flashing by the Citroen's cracked windshield. I was telling myself that this might actually be a talent when we came to "Sí, Sí Usados Autos." The place doubled as a parking lot and used-car dealership and looked like the junkyards you see in American movies. We approached an emaciated lad washing a clunky old Jeep with a patched hose at a faucet in front of the office. Without raising his head, the half-naked Inca pointed to a giant of a man who appeared to be some sort of guard, in answer to Ariel's question. He was deeply absorbed by a lottery bulletin on the radio. He glanced up only briefly when Ariel spoke, but the fifty-peso note tucked into his shirt pocket soon loosened his tongue. We learned that the business had been taken over from Fernando Ruibial, Eli's surviving partner, and that Ruibial resided in San Antonio de Areco, 113 kilometers north of Buenos Aires.

Once more we hit the road; Fernando Ruibial was our last hope. We were still on the nearly deserted six-lane highway when a white Cadillac passed us and cut back, almost scraping the side of our car. Ariel reacted with wild hand gestures. The driver, who was wearing a uniform, stopped us in front of an abandoned warehouse. This was funny: the guy had cut us off and *he* was insulted! When he pulled Ariel out of the car and started shaking him, I saw red. I jumped out and head-butted him, then clipped him with two karate punches just above the belt. He staggered and I brought my right knee up between his legs. He moaned as he hit the ground. He had a handsome face and I supposed but for lack of talent he would have been a tango performer. My assumption that he would get up and leave was wrong. As Ariel climbed back into the car, the man attacked me from behind. This spurred me to renew my kicking and punching. Motorists passing by speeded up when they saw us—except for taxi drivers, who honked encouragingly to see me beating up a man in uniform.

"Hey, countryman, hold up," I suddenly heard in Turkish. A dark-haired man in his sixties with prayer beads in hand and a smile on his face was approaching. "Even if I hadn't heard your curses I would have known you were Turkish from your fighting style," he said. I told him I came from Balat and he asked me about the Agora Tavern; he wasn't happy to hear that it had closed down long ago. Mardig had left Feriköy thirty years previously and was now running a *milonga* bar on the boulevard. I politely declined his invitation to come back for a drink, pleading lack of time. He said, "Okay, disappear, and I'll see this sack of guts to the hospital."

Back on the road, the shock and relief of surviving an accident unscathed filled the car. "I saw the fury of a blind man trying to protect his seeing-eye dog in the way you attacked that Cadillac chauffeur," Ariel said. I attempted a humorous retort, saying I wouldn't like to lose my chauffeur. "Once I was the best fighter pilot in Europe, but unfortunately I don't know how to drive."

I couldn't decide which road was more boring—Buenos Aires-San Antonio de Areco or Eskişehir-Mahmudiye. I listened to Astor Piazzolla in between Ariel's anecdotes about customers who collected dictionaries, atlases, and books on incest. I tried getting acquainted with Fernando Ruibial's town by studying the guidebook Ariel kept in his car. San Antonio de Areco, with a population of 20,000, was in the land of gauchos, cowboys. The writer Ricardo Güiraldes had glorified the place in his book, *Don Segundo Sombra*, published in 1926.

The town, whose name evoked the knights of the Middle Ages, was occupied by the small homes of farm workers. We parked near where some sleepy horses, a spotted type that I recognized from cowboy movies, were grazing. The few people on the street were quiet, probably out of respect for the others having their siesta. The sound of a squirrel family in the old trees or a distant tractor was enough to puncture the silence. To find out where the Ruibial mansion was, I bought a primitive souvenir box at the gift shop that looked more like a hardware store.

We walked down Segundo Sombra (Second Shadow) under rows of dwarf trees unacquainted with autumn. Hollyhocks adorned the iron gate of 462I. The gatekeeper, probably a retired gaucho, called his boss when told him I'd come all the way from Istanbul. I was amazed at being immediately let in, and felt that I was getting closer to Esther. The gatekeeper led me through the garden that was like a colorful rug to the front door of the three-story villa, where we were met by an archetypal majordomo, Luis. Luis called the master on his cell phone as soon as we mentioned Señora Arditti. Ruibial was on his way in from the farm twenty-five miles away, so we were sent to the neighboring café to wait.

The high-ceilinged La Esquinada de Marti was like a monumental joke in this miniature town. It had more waitresses than customers. Still, the new-age music that filled it wasn't repellent. We were just finishing the vegetable omelettes we'd ordered with difficulty when Fernando Ruibial walked in with an artificial smile on his face. He was thin, of medium height, and looked about forty-five. Clearly he wanted to benefit from the mystery radiating from his deep-set eyes. His impeccable style and self-confidence were a bit unsettling. I took it as a good sign that he paid our check and invited us to his house. His accent revealed a slight American twang.

On the way to his house I was aware that he was making fun of his troubles at work and testing me at the same time. The two of us entered an old elevator while Ariel, gliding into the ground-floor library, said, "Don't come back for two hours." The third-floor study was choked with bronze statuettes of horses, glass cow figurines, and similar kitsch. It looked like a toy farm. I sat across from Fernando at the saddle-shaped table. I knew I had to explain the reason for my visit down to the last detail. While he listened he opened a bottle of red wine with a yellow label. I took a sip and dared to hope that it was something he was saving for a special occasion. He smiled good-humoredly when I uttered Professor Ali's name, but on learning that he was waiting, crippled, in a Buenos Aires hotel room his face changed. I took it as a compliment that he could hardly believe I was an ex-fighter pilot now retired because of an accident. His eyes settled on the giant map across the room.

"I used to drop by the Café Velocidad when I was at university. That's where I met Eli Arditti. He was a handsome devil. He wore old-fashioned but elegant clothes, and he was always modest and courteous. There was nobody who didn't like him. His nickname was Profeta, the Prophet. He was the best friend of every waitress.

"One Friday evening I was waiting for my girlfriend at Velocidad when Eli came in and sat down at my table. He was shaking, and he quickly offered me a partnership in his car business. His face was as sad as a saint's. I couldn't bring myself to hurt him.

"But the real reason I put up with 'Sí, Sí Usados Autos' was Esther. She was a smart and charming woman who knew how to befriend men. I was bewitched immediately. We had dinner twice a month at my house or at Café Tortoni. I could hardly wait to be mesmerized by her conversations. At these dinner parties, attended also by her husband, I saw the constantly widening gap between them. I was aware that they tried to conceal the real reason for their antagonism. In my opinion, love had never been a part of their relationship. After her third glass of wine one evening Esther said, 'By losing my money in every business venture of his, Eli is trying to make me pay the price,' and fell silent.

"I was content to subsidize the company. Yet I knew that every two months Eli would come up with some ridiculous excuse to borrow money to meet his personal debts.

"I finished my degree and before going back home to San Antonio de Areco, I signed over my share of the business to Eli and wrote off his accumulated debt.

"Four months later came the news of his death. Eli had collided with a garbage truck in the gray Jaguar that he could never bring himself to sell. The official report listed the cause of the accident as 'dangerous driving by the deceased.' At the funeral I saw his daughter Stella, the former Miss Argentina, for the first time. Despite her beautiful features she was most unattractive. She was boasting about how she had come from the other side of the world with her diplomat husband for the funeral. It was said that she whispered to a childhood friend that she believed her father had committed suicide because of her mother's constant and relentless pressure. Esther couldn't cope with these rumors and fell into a depression, so I put her in a private clinic. When she got out two weeks later she didn't want to go back home, so I agreed to take her to San Antonio de Areco. We went to her house to collect her belongings. It looked like a gang of burglars had broken into the apartment in that run-down building and made off even with the coffee table. 'This is why I couldn't invite you here,' she said. 'In the end we had to sell the furniture to buy food. What's left not even the flea market would take.' She was crying. I paid the landlord the back rent and told him to distribute the remaining furniture to the poor. He smiled cynically.

"As Esther told me the story of her life on the way home I waited in vain for her to curse the mother who had darkened her destiny. Eli assumed she was visiting old childhood friend in Istanbul all those years. Just before he died, Esther received a letter from Ali's sister, pleading with her to set her brother free; she said that he was considering marriage to another academic. Esther believed the story—which now, after talking with you, I understand to be completely fictional—so, while passing on the news of her husband's death to her friend in Istanbul, she included her own.

"Esther stayed at the villa for two months. Even though she wasn't in her best form, she managed to captivate the whole neighborhood. It's still difficult for me to believe that my own grandfather confided in her, 'If I were a widower I would never let you go.' Another strange thing occurred during her stay with us. A letter came to my Buenos Aires house from Eli Arditti; it was sent on the day of his accident, but arrived six weeks late because of a mistake in the address. Poor Eli! I couldn't help laughing—my old partner couldn't even get my address right. Really! Anyway, when I opened it a small piece of cardboard fell out of the envelope. On one side was the drawing of a coffin-like car and on the other was a flawless note:

> Dear F.,
> *This time I will not fail. I know you won't abandon Esther. For the last time: Sorry.*
>
> *The Graceless Prophet,*
> *Eli(as)*

"Which is to say, the ungrateful Stella was correct in her assessment. I had a hard time tearing up Eli's last and perfectly realized design. Esther insisted on my finding a government nursing home for her. I never told her about Eli's note, but it seemed to me that she herself had reached the conclusion that her daughter wasn't completely mistaken. I had her admitted to a private rest home that was like a four-star hotel. I doubt she believed my lie that her share of the proceeds from the company's sale would cover the cost. I steeled myself to witness her gradual decline because of a guilty conscience. Over the next eighteen years she moved three times, and took to spending summers at our villa. We watched as she came to terms with the past and learned to forgive herself. She grew more relaxed after shedding her 'mysterious woman' identity, and even my grandmother had to confess that she looked ten years younger.

"The architect of Esther's journey back to life was Annabella Serna of Buenas Días Geriatrico, whom she met four years ago. Esther and this psychologist not only became bosom friends but each other's educators. What Annabella acquired from Esther in the first session must have been the basic secrets of charming men. At first sight of this girl with glasses, ten years younger than me, I took a liking to her. In the past six months I've lost both my grandparents, and I plan to marry her as soon as my period of bitter mourning comes to an end ..."

With a mind at peace, Fernando Ruibial refilled our wine glasses. As he wrote down the address of the Buenos Días Geriatrico, he made me promise to keep him informed about the Ali-Esther reunion. He didn't intend to diminish the suspense of the final scene by sharing the news of Ali's presence in town with Annabella. The heaviness I felt getting into the car probably wasn't caused by the three glasses of wine I'd had. I was practically nodding off as I conveyed, without much dramatization, the story to Ariel. I revived somewhat when we got to the hotel, and there was almost a spring to my step as I walked to my room. I was eager to talk to Professor Ali but was disheartened to hear, when I checked my messages, that he'd gone out for dinner with Dr. Armenak. I called room service for food and went out onto the balcony. I realized that I missed hearing the evening *ezan*. I went down to the deserted bar in the lobby, where I drank beer and read every page of the *Buenos Aires Herald*, which somebody had left on my table. When a noisy group of tourists sat down next to me I escaped to my room and looked for a tango station on the radio that would help me sleep.

Professor Ali was tipsy when he woke me at midnight. He told me that during their Anatolian dinner at an Armenian restaurant he felt like getting up and dancing the *horon*. "Tomorrow we can take a tour of the town and then pack our bags," he concluded, which didn't exactly put me at ease. As I recounted what Fernando Ruibial had told me he groaned, "Kemal, I hope you're not joking with me," and as I concluded my report he collapsed into my arms.

*

The professor's ankle hadn't completely healed. He was walking with some difficulty, and if there was somebody's arm to grab he seized the opportunity. I knew that he was going to choose his best outfit that morning. His efforts to pretend that he was relieved were in vain. As we went down to breakfast he assured me, "Don't worry. I'm ready for anything."

He perked up on hearing that Buenos Días Geriatrico was next door to the Evita Museum. The brochure at the empty reception desk in the foyer said, "Nos estaba buscando?" "Is it us you were looking for?" Ariel went to find somebody in charge while I concentrated on the dim lobby that smelled like a medicine cabinet. Quite a few old people were drowsing to the accompaniment of classical music; the Aphrodite statues at each corner seemed amused by them. When our guide came back with the good news that Esther's room number was 211, I feared that Ali would drop dead on the spot. I told Ariel to wait in the lobby and helped my patient-as-a-stone neighbor walk to the elevator. The door to her room was ajar. We stood hesitantly in the doorway, through which only silence was seeping. The woman sitting in the plain room's single armchair was knitting furiously and humming what sounded like an Aegean song to herself. She looked no older than sixty-seven and adopted a noble posture. I thought I should give a friendly nudge to Professor Ali, who stood frozen, his lips trembling.

"Ess-therr," he moaned softly, and my heart fell to pieces.

A brief flash of her violet eyes made me believe everything I had heard about this legendary İzmir woman.

"Esther, it's meee," said the professor, and lapsed into silence.

Squinting in our direction, she said, "Aa-liii?" Had they traveled like a flash of lightning before my eyes back to their university days? She jumped from her chair, repeating "Aa-liii," and I dragged the Professor into the room. They embraced hesitantly, timidly, and I found Esther's not noticing me very poetic. I returned to the doorway and watched the scene that I deserved to enjoy all alone. Having survived the first shock, they tightened their embrace, then, like teenagers, began whispering and giggling to each other.

When Esther started to cry Professor Ali sat her down on the bed. He put her head on his shoulder and caressed her hair and started to cry too. They were closing the account, I thought, of those missing forty-five years that were snipped from their lives like the middle of a reel of film. In their interlocked and trembling hands I saw their determination to bet everything they had on the time left to them. My heart eased, I shut the door and strolled up and down the corridor. I studied the cheap reproductions that cluttered the walls and bulletin boards. I phoned Fernando Ruibial and relayed the news. Instead of a joyous exclamation, he said, "I've made dinner reservations for five at Cabañas Las Lilas."

Forty minutes later I was summoned back to the room. I was a bit apprehensive about whether there would be a whiff of embarrassment or self-consciousness. Esther stood and looked at me as if we had known each other a long time. As she took my face in both her hands I felt I was being squeezed between Greta Garbo and Doris Day.

"Back home I used to feel envious whenever the Muslims said something like *Allah razı olsun*. 'May God be pleased with you.'" She spoke in Turkish that hadn't rusted. "During my marriage I always knew that those three words would never flow from my mouth because I was constantly cursing. But after hearing what you did for us I think that you're a saint come down to earth. *Allah razı olsun*. May God be pleased with you, my kind-hearted boy."

She took her hands away just before the tears trickling from my eyes reached them. I felt a pleasant warmth rising in my breast. Was this the ultimate state of satisfaction, reserved for helping a friend in need? I committed the feeling to memory.

Professor Ali delivered a few words of gratitude and kissed me ineptly on the cheek. I was stunned when he whispered in my ear, "I know it was you who sent me that note, but I don't mind anymore." At last I understood the reason for the cynical expression on his face when he listened to my scouting reports. But it was too late for me to reply that I had suspected him of the same thing. The same demonic character had sent me to Mahmudiye, Tirebolu, Ayvalık, and Buenos Aires: I was thoroughly disgusted with Suat Altan, who was toying with me as if I were his pet guinea pig.

We left the rest home with Ariel. He could sense that I was agitated, but that I would be furious with him if he uttered a word about it to anyone. It didn't help contemplating the rows of arid books in his shop. I strolled down Avenida Corrientes and my mind cleared somewhat. Was I being unfair to Suat, who flashed in and out of my life for the purpose of pushing my buttons like a robot? It was the clue he sent that had brought his ex-neighbor Ali and Esther together. As I walked the Buenos Aires streets, I realized the psycho was probably following me. I supposed his next gambit would be to hook me up with Haluk' granddaughter Sim. I wondered if he knew that this girl, whom I knew only from a painting, was blind? I strongly suspected that his role as "remote-control Cupid" was a cover-up for an even more deeply hidden agenda. I smiled to myself like Suat's naïve puppet, but I was hatching a plan to spring a trap of my own. Marching vigorously into a music shop, I prepared for the second act of the drama by buying thirty tango CDs recommended by the salesman.

The dinner party composed of Ali and Esther, Fernando and Annabella, and the companionless Kemal never grew dull. Conversations in Turkish, Spanish, and English ricocheted around the room. The freckle-faced Annabella reminded me of my primary-school teacher Miss Nimet, whom I loved and feared (her response to my lack of interest in Rumi's poetry was totally artificial). Professor Ali, whose ankle had suddenly healed, wouldn't leave the city before getting married. I had decided to leave the next day. The prospective groom had once told me that Gogol, as he lay dying, cried, "A ladder, quickly, a ladder." I was warming up for the game ...

VI

The flight back to Buenos Aires wasn't full. Before falling asleep in a row of empty seats, I tried to decode the meaning of the checkers pieces my mysterious benefactor had spilled on the table in front of me. Suat Altan had no twin brother: it was he himself who emerged onstage in the role of Fuat. (The Poe character Sami, who admitted he had never seen them together, might well be on Suat's permanent staff.) I had been sent on Haluk's trail because of a clue from Count Nadolsky, who was the ex-tenant of the flat that had been bequeathed, first, to Suat by his uncle Izak Toledo, and second, to me by Suat. (What if an old letter or photograph were even now awaiting me in the study, which I'd considered a laboratory for some time now?) Whoever had attacked me in the building doorway at midnight and helped Professor Ali give me aid belonged to Suat. He knew that the incident would result in the professor and I becoming close. (I didn't wonder that Sami, who rarely went out even in daylight, happened to be away at midnight. I could imagine him on the fringe of the gang of attackers.) Izak Toledo and Luna were good friends of Ali and Esther. Perhaps when Luna emigrated to Israel and saw Izak, who was already living there, she let it slip that Esther had never actually died. (An interesting detail was how Esther's first Buenos Aires address had been passed on to Suat; but we all know the things diaries are capable of in romantic novels.)

*

I began feeling restless as my taxi from the airport drove into Balat. It had never occurred to me before how ready I was for another week of zigzagging behind Esther through the labyrinth of Buenos Aires. As I hauled my exhausted suitcase past Professor Ali's apartment I felt a twinge of concern about who the next tenant might be, after Ali married his Esther and moved—probably—to upper-class Maçka. Another problematic and marginalized individual? Thanks to the amount of cheap soap and detergent lavished on it by Aunt Cevher, my living room smelled truly like a laboratory. I threw myself on the bed. My eyes were too tired to scan the ceiling for a secret camera before I nodded off to sleep fully dressed.

I rose to the evening *ezan* and had my much-missed

"meditative shower." I was out of excuses not to go into the study. Since the day I'd moved in, I'd never looked inside the closed cabinets below the library shelves. I must have subconsciously been dreading what I might find. I greeted the ringing of the doorbell enthusiastically; it was Sami. He agreed to accompany me to the Black Sea *pide* restaurant. Edip the cook asked whether "my commander" had gone to his home town, which seemed a poetic idea to me. "Close enough," I answered, thinking my soul would quiver with bandoneon melodies. Sami didn't take much pleasure in the fact that the professor and Esther had found each other, but when I told him I was about to lay hands on the thugs who attacked me his ears seemed to prick up. Thinking that I'd been too quick to doubt his integrity, I was suddenly unsure whether I'd moved my checkers correctly.

Back home I sluggishly unpacked my suitcase. My mood improved when I realized that I had money left from the $5,000 Ali had given me. I dressed and went to Disco Eden according to my usual custom. I don't know how many glasses of vodka I drank before my attention came to rest on the Slavic girls dancing with each other on the little stage. The dark-haired one with a turned-up nose was dancing enthusiastically in front of me. I was curious to know what her sweat would smell like, so I had her called over to my table. As the head waiter brought the large girl, I knew he whispered in her ear that I was a V.I.P. When it came time to introduce myself I said, "My name is Salvador Buenos Aires."

*

The next day my mood was that of a falcon growing accustomed to its cage. The noon *ezan* was just starting as I began rummaging through those closed cabinets in the library. By the time I extracted my haul of notebooks and journals from different periods, metal vases engraved with gothic designs, curious atlases, a pair of calligraphy scissors, two icons, pen cases painted with erotic motifs, silver Ottoman and Persian cigarette cases, an antique revolver, naïve wooden animal figurines, a sailboat in a bottle, geometrically cut ruby-red glass objects, a stuffed baby shark, a jar of dried seahorses, and four documentary videos and DVDs, the last strains of the evening *ezan* were dying away.

I carried two stylish notebooks of Venetian workmanship, a leather-bound diary, and a DVD marked SERENDIPITY to my desk, feeling as pleased as if I had pillaged a small museum. The first twenty pages of the A4 notebook were filled with dozens of pen-and-ink drawings of Edgar Allan Poe. The next section began with the portrait of a sad-looking girl above a caption that read, "Virginia Clemm (ANNABEL LEE)," and ended with a parade of theatrical characters whose surnames were all Poe or Allan. I think it was Kenneth Silverman's biography, *Edgar A. Poe: Mournful and Never-ending Remembrance*, that I pulled from the POE corner of the library to verify the names. I wasn't surprised, on comparing the photographs in the book with the drawings, to note that the latter were as lively as photocopies.

OFFERING TO THE MASTER was how the last section began, and I wasn't wrong, as it proved, to be startled. It must have taken weeks out of the life of a paranoid student to complete this letter, which was obviously written very slowly in gothic script. When I discovered the rationale behind the strange color of the ink that stood out dramatically on the white paper, I could scarcely credit my senses. Flabbergasted by the bizarre passage, I read it again, as though that would ease my heart:

19 January 1999

To the Prophet of Mystery, Master Edgar A. Poe,
Your disciple, who always hearkens to you when you descend to him in his dreams, desires—if you so permit—to offer his personal sentiments on your one-hundred-and-ninetieth birthday. Words fail me, Master, when it comes to explaining the bitter reason why I have added my own blood to the ink in my fountain pen.

In order to put to good use the talent of their wonder-child Elizabeth (Eliza) Arnold, her family migrates from England to America and establishes a theater company. At ten Eliza (1787–1811) is already a star in the making. The theater company's comedian, Charles D. Hopkins, to whom they marry her five years later, dies mysteriously a year into the marriage. Eliza and the dancer David Poe, whom the company hires to replace her first husband, fall in love at first sight. Handsome and mysterious, Poe is a talented law-school graduate. His father, a general who presides over the customs house, is disappointed by his obstinate son's passion for art. Eliza and David marry in 1806. Their first son, William Henry Poe, is born in 1807. The husband and wife are locked in constant strife and the theater business is not doing well. The grandfather takes over the job of looking after William Henry. In the year Edgar is born (1809), his alcoholic father is running away from home every chance he gets; he can't stand living in his wife's shadow. The year their daughter Rosalie is born (1810), David's body is found in a pathetic hotel room in Chicago. At her first opportunity the poor and sick Eliza moves to Richmond with her two babies. Before she can succeed in obtaining the lead role in Romeo and Juliet, she dies of tuberculosis. Only with difficulty can the three-year-old Edgar, now an or-phan, be pulled away from Eliza's dead body. He has never seen his mother looking so beautiful and peaceful. Whereas humankind in general does not remember anything that happens before the age of four, Edgar begins to demonstrate a natural affinity with death as a three-year-old. Certain opportunistic and shallow scholars have in their biographies represented Poe as the victim of a tragic fate since the day he was born. In fact he was a genius blessed not only with a rich inner world but loaded with the advantages of having two artists as parents; and therefore he was, from birth, a member of THE ELECT!

Edgar and Rosalie are adopted by two wealthy families from Richmond, the tobacco center. The unrefined merchant John Allan cannot appreciate the actor's son Edgar but his wife Frances, who has the soul of an artist, adores him until her death. The year Edgar begins primary school the Allans move to Great Britain for five years. The adopted child, spared their last name, attends Stoke Newington, a church school in the outskirts of London. John Barnaby, the priest and headmaster, possesses an unusual philosophy of education: the basic principle is to rely on textbooks as little as possible. If, for instance, it is the four mathematical operations that are to be taught, the birth and death dates on the tombstones in the neighboring graveyard may be used. If a funeral is in the offing, students may take turns at grave-digging in lieu of gym class. Edgar quickly grows accustomed to the atmosphere of this school located on the street where Daniel Defoe was born. He is warmed by the anecdotes of ill omen traded back and forth so spiritedly by his churchgoing teachers. When he wants to hear more elaborate stories, he sneaks into the pub patronized by old soldiers and sailors.

The year he becomes a sixth-former, the family returns to Richmond. His classmates don't much like this "newcomer" with an English attitude who seems to be looking down on them. But the burgeoning genius of Edgar, who achieves marked success with little effort in every class he takes, is recognized in the end even by the tobacco man, John Allan. His favorite subjects are literature and foreign languages, and there is no classical work that he hasn't devoured. He declares himself the guardian of his frail classmate Richard.

Although he does not cease to write love letters and poems to his sister Rosalie's friends, he falls in love with Richard's mother J. When J. takes to her bed with a fatal illness, Edgar compares her more and more to his own mother. He visits her every day; he is at her bedside as she dies in excruciating pain. There isn't a night when he fails to visit her grave. For a whole year he can only find solace, after every session of weeping, by wandering through the cemetery with his eyes tightly shut. His family is not disturbed by his peculiarities because they are all sympathetic to the mysterious vibrations of genius. In the year of his graduation from high school he has a dream that is like a divine revelation: as sounds pouring from the beak of a coal-black bird flutter and turn into a column of numbers running from top to bottom, clouds wafted by a sea breeze turn into letters of the Greek and Roman alphabets and parade before him from left to right. The numbers and letters hover and soar until he memorizes them. When he wakes in the morning he easily deciphers the meaning of the two sets of symbols, which he has converted into type fonts. The sentences he records in his personal journal are: "One day the whole world will admire your genius" and "You won't be on earth to see that day." He keeps this dream a secret even from Frances; I am the only other person who knows about it.

1826! He registers at the University of Virginia, founded by the third president of the United States of America. He will immediately become the " wonder boy" of the literature department. His devotion to the classics and his talent for foreign languages at first intimidate his *professors. He is in the spotlight also in drama and sports. He seizes every opportunity to use his rhetorical skills to protect the bookworms from the bullies—Virginia is a school favored by the children of the rich. Wishing to punish Edgar, John Allan withholds the moderate sum necessary for his school expenses. Edgar has to borrow money and, when it emerges that he gambles at cards to pay off his debts, is expelled. (This outcome does not affect him unduly. His private journal contains an entry known only to me: "My sole profit in the university adventure has been the absorption of cryptology.") John Allan of course does not overlook this opportunity to evict Edgar from his home. Even Frances cannot soften his heart this time; Edgar has to enlist in the army for a five-year hitch. Just before he joins his company, his first book of poems is published under a pseudonym. (A copy of this 1827 volume, the source of his first and last literary frustration, recently sold for $200,000; the immortal copy in my possession is graced with the Master's signature.) In two years he is bored with the military although he has risen to the rank of sergeant. He writes apologetic letters to John Allan asking permission to return home. No answer until Frances, whom he calls "Mother", dies of tuberculosis. Bowing to his wife's wishes, in 1830 John Allan uses his influence to get Edgar admitted to the famous West Point military academy, but again success eludes him. Although he excels at military strategy, he is expelled in 1831 for continued breaches of discipline (the first was failure to attend religion classes). In the same year his alcoholic older brother William Henry Poe—poet,* *exhausted journalist, and ex-sailor who lived with his aunt Maria Clemm—dies of tuberculosis at twenty-four. Edgar is clapped in jail because he cannot pay his brother's debts, for which he is guarantor. His period of education concludes without the punctuation of a diploma. However, he manages to achieve something much more important: he has acquired a store of material for his writing life.*

After several odd jobs culminating in confusion, he decides to go on with writing. In 1832 he takes refuge in Baltimore with his poor aunt, Maria Clemm. He falls in love at first sight with his cousin, the 'sorrow virtuoso' Virginia Clemm (then ten years old). Maria grants permission for a wedding three years hence. He prefers reading and idleness to the work of writing, except for letters—with judicious intervals between them—to John Allan asking for money. This time Allan, who has already remarried, is sympathetic. Edgar cannot enter into sexual relations with Virginia, whom he marries in 1835, for the first year. In twelve years of marriage their fondness for each other never wavers. Playing childish games with his thirteen-year-old bride makes him perfectly happy. He teaches her math and literature and helps with her piano and singing lessons. He is editor and columnist for several newspapers and magazines in different East Coast cities. His mystery stories are little favored, and the musical and experimentalist touches in his poetry go unremarked. He is constantly changing jobs but is consistently poor. (I am the only one, until now, to have read this in his journal: "A hundred years from now hundreds of writers will follow me and hundreds of thousands of people will read me.") In 1845 his poem, 'The Raven,' brings him recognition. In 1847, when his beloved wife dies of tuberculosis at twenty-five, he doesn't even have a blanket of his own to cover her with. Under pressure from his publisher, he changes the title of the farewell poem he's written for Virginia Clemm Poe. 'Annabel Lee' shocks its readers, from slave to president. Edgar A. Poe is now a famous—but still poverty-stricken—writer.

He cannot pull himself together after his wife's death. He increases his alcohol intake and looks for chances to challenge the people around him. Unable to fall in love again, he attempts to commit suicide. He completes the poems of his mature period; he is forced to go on the lecture circuit to make money. (On the last page of his notebook he writes, "Eagerly to feel the approach of a gray tunnel.") He was forty when they found him groaning on a Baltimore back street one foggy autumn morning. There are several explanations for his death. Even I wouldn't know why the clothes he had on when they brought him to the hospital were not his ...

Master, I discovered your work when I was in middle school, and by the time I was a lycée student had memorized it all. I enthusiastically followed your footsteps to the University of Virginia 170 years behind you. I may well have been to every place you stepped foot in between Richmond and Boston. In Charlottesville there was an antique shop called "Vintagia" on the edge of the university campus. In this place, which had a lot of things from the nineteenth century, my attention was drawn to a black hard-cover notebook. Its yellowing pages contained certain codes that had been formed by combining Latin and Greek letters and double-digit numbers. The writer had the dexterous hands of a calligrapher. The notebook had the charm of a holograph manuscript. I seized it eagerly and rushed home. As I cracked the codes with a kind of divine exultation I could not of course have foreseen that this would change my life. What made the hair on my head stand up was the suspicion that the notebook, encompassing reactions to certain literary and socioeconomic agendas which in turn provoked aphorisms and prophecies regarding the future, might actually be yours. Yet the last entry, in the year of your departure from earth, coincided perfectly with the anecdote about "the lost suitcase in Richmond." I was elated to realize that your biographies had missed the substance of your inner world, which was protected by these codes. I did not feel like announcing the presence of this notebook to the world at large. It was my happy destiny to be the one and only creature on this perishable earth who had managed to decode you. As it imprinted itself on my brain line by line, I was at the same time crushed by the awareness of your genius. I felt as if I were entrusted with "the book of immortality," and that if I failed to do what had to be done, I would incur your wrath, O Master!

I threw myself into the labyrinth of intellectual coordinates such as heaven/hell, past/future, and day/night and made them my own. By the time I emerged from this cul-de-sac I had become a Poe character myself. To do justice to my role it was necessary to become financially powerful and never to remove the cloak of mystery.

You broadened the horizons of thousands of writ-

ers, beginning with masters like Walt Whitman, William Faulkner, Herman Melville, Flannery O'Connor, Charles Baudelaire, Stephane Mallarmé, Paul Valéry, Marcel Proust, W. H. Auden, Fyodor Dostoyevsky, H.G. Wells, Jules Verne, Robert L. Stevenson, George B. Shaw, Thomas Mann, Vladimir Nabokov, Arthur C. Doyle, Jorge Louis Borges, and Julio Cortázar. You saved the book world from being overrun by sentimental novels and academic critics. You widened the horizons of hundreds of millions of people. Furthermore, no love poem has surpassed "Annabel Lee" for the last 150 years.

I am moreover well aware of your use of mystery as a tool in "the dispensation of justice." In 2009, on the 200th anniversary of your birth, I am determined to settle accounts on your behalf, O Master!

Your servant,
S.A.

Why was this letter addressed to Poe? Was it perhaps written when Suat was a student to prove his admiration for his master's ghost, or more recently to confuse me?

As I finished this letter, I remembered the abridged Poe stories we had read on our English courses. I would have to study his Master's longer stories and essays to determine how far Suat's psycho-manifestation had exaggerated the facts.

The passionate move of my right hand toward the notebook in grayish-red leather startled me. Like a tentative periscope I surveyed the room. I stood and picked out a

Branford Marsalis CD, and as "The Ruby and the Pearl" began to fill the room, cautiously lifted the cover on the notebook. The lines, "If I went I wouldn't know it / Not even my shadow can come along" used as a preface seemed superficial. I followed the parade of Poe characters on the light pink pages. Every drawing looked like it was waiting, to be certified as a graphic-novel hero. Detective Auguste Dupin was endowed with two different expressions so that he resembled both Poe and Suat. I came up with the inane idea that if Suat's life were made into a film, he would be played by Johnny Depp. After drawings of tigers, gorillas, and wild birds there was an innocent section in which, I think, all the alphabetical letters in the history of civilization were listed from top to bottom. They danced like the designs on a naturally dyed kilim. As I brought them together before my eyes, they seemed to escape from the page with the speed of light.

The third section consisted of place names written in different colors with a ballpoint pen. Apart from Aden, Artvin, Auckland, and Bhutan I had never heard of them, but I wasn't concerned. There was a red circle around Serendipity (Serendip). I resorted to the Internet: the word "Serendipity" had Persian roots and meant "while questing for one beauty to run into another." "Serendip," on the other hand, was the legendary name of Sri Lanka. With relief and deep satisfaction at having discovered Suat's base, I stood and took a short victory tour of the house. But the meaninglessness of my discovery soon sank in, and I came back to my desk and plunged into the final section of the notebook, which was called "Haiku-Sized Stories."

Miniature poems in Japanese were called haiku, weren't they? I scanned the sixth one in the collection of seventy-seven:

Dr. B., who stumbled upon his hunchbacked older brother and his wife kissing, discovered the next morning when he woke up that all his hair had turned white. After the divorce, he left the country. He moved happily to Ushuaia, the birthplace of the mulatto Argentinian nurse whom he met in Vancouver and married. This quiet town was the closest spot on the continent to the South Pole. On the day his young wife broke the happy news that she was pregnant he received another piece of news regarding an accident: a van on a Patagonia expedition had fallen into a ravine and two people were seriously injured. The tourist couple ended up in Dr. B's operating room fighting for their lives. They were his ex-wife and his brother, who had funded his medical education. Owing to hospital conditions and the shortage of time, he would be able to save only one of them …

I must confess that the characters whom I encountered in the passages I hastily read grew on me. The fact that in almost all of them a justice prevailed that was beyond God's own reminded me of something that Suat—as Fuat—had once said to me. Suat had been discharged from the army just forty-eight hours before the driver who had killed his father was found dead in his taxi. I was grappling with the rising tension in the stories. I would have to finish them on the journey I felt I would soon be taking.

Next I took up a worn diary covered in blue plastic. It was clear that this nosegay-of-days composed in the Cyrillic alphabet had been Vlad Nadolsky's. Once Suat had had this document—a month-by-month chronicle of the period from 1917 to 1987—translated into Turkish, he possessed all the information he needed to send me on my mini Anatolian tour. Wedged in the back cover of the thick diary were two photographs taken perhaps sixty years before depicting Haluk and his patron arm in arm. I saw in Count Nadolsky's attractive face a calmness deriving from the final acceptance of the state of exile. These photographs, and the musty diary, were temptation enough to visit Haluk once again. It was too late to worry about the fact that they'd been planted in the library while I was in Buenos Aires.

"SERENDIPITY," the front cover of the CD proclaimed; and on the back was written, "This is not Sri Lanka." I smiled ruefully when I realized that Suat had foreseen how easily I would be sucked in. Eagerly I inserted the disk into the player; the soundless images ran for twenty minutes. First Suat tried to impress me with footage of his compound shot from ground level and then from the air. Within this private world, separated from the outer world by high stone walls, there were: a postmodern chateau, a forest of trees I did not recognize, an artificial lake with a dock, and three rows of outbuildings. The swaggering postures adopted by a cluster of security guards at the main entrance were frightening. Suat was swimming in a pool of sharks and stingrays and tugging a horrific gorilla along the bank of the lake on a leash. The entry hall of his opulent mansion was bristling with busts and portraits of Poe. Then the dining room scene: at the table, among Suat's Japanese and Negro advisers, sat an attractive young mulatto girl. Their eyes were shadowed with fear. At first I thought the object on Suat's left was a porcelain statue. It turned out to be, however, a Siberian tiger that licked Suat's hand whenever he extended it. The huge creature was sitting motionless, eyes half closed, as if it wanted to avoid disturbing the others at the table. Following this series of self-promotional images, the final statement on the screen—"Imagination, thoughtlessness, yearning for solitude, belittling the present while nourishing an intense passion for the future: my life has been about nothing else"—must have belonged to Edgar A. Poe.

I got a bottle of beer from the fridge. I felt like watching the DVD again, but I couldn't, though I tried more than once: the recording had erased itself. It reminded me of *Mission Impossible*. An acute pain sprang up on the left side of my head. I stood and opened the window and focused on the view of the Golden Horn. I waited until the distant siren of an ambulance disappeared into silence. As I withdrew from the window I felt the satisfaction of a decision reached: in accordance with the wishes of Suat, the Master of Mystery, I would visit Haluk and meet his blind granddaughter.

VII

Ali and Esther Uzel came home to Istanbul for good and I was spared from traveling to C. in the hellish August heat. I took great pleasure in watching them move into the Maçka house. It seemed they would never tire of one another. When I said, "I can't visualize you as husband and wife," Esther giggled and replied, "I hope God made you say that." The professor informed me that he intended to keep his Balat flat empty; I was delighted. At the beginning of September the Uzels went off to Heybeliada to spend two weeks in a friend's villa, and I prepared for my Ayvalık trip.

I needn't have bothered looking up the so-called lawyer on the Internet merely to note the global rhyme between the names "Suat" and "Stuart." I called Haluk Erçelik at the number on the crumpled card he'd given me and delivered my prepared speech without faltering. I knew he would be dubious on hearing that I'd found Count Nadolsky's diaries, and I knew he would be suspicious on hearing that I'd brought CDs—sorrowful but not depressing—from Buenos Aires for Sim. He said, "This time I'm not going to let you go before we have a good sit-down at the *raki* table." I recalled an old saying that went something like, "He's following me, and he doesn't like it that I'm doubling back on my own trail."

The wheezing bus to Ayvalık wasn't full. I was glad to find that Ayvalık had lost its excess tourist weight, but I felt the heart of my gladness evaporate immediately. When we got to the terminal the late-afternoon *ezan* was in the air, which warmed my heart, but when the hotel receptionist greeted me for the second time in English I was annoyed. I restrained myself from asking, in my sternest voice, why their establishment didn't smell of olive oil.

Together with the adventurous Pasadeos couple from Mytilene whom I met in the lobby, I crossed over the next day to neighboring Cunda Island. These retired teachers' purpose in coming here was to buy a new wardrobe. I told them that I was a classical-music DJ at an Istanbul radio station. They told me that the best *mezes* in the whole of the Aegean region were to be found at the Bay Nihat fish restaurant. I paid our check, grateful not to be asked why I wasn't yet married. On the way back the smell of olive oil overwhelmed the center of town. It sobered me up slightly. In my room I began reading *Old Love* by Isaac Bashevis Singer. Its cover depicted a pair of Jewish lovers in their eighties, hand in hand. I attributed the plain language of the Nobel laureate to his being a rabbi's son. The arithmetical organization of his sentence structure reminded me of Bach, which made me in turn think of Ariel. And as the bandoneon melodies rising heavily from the southern hemisphere besieged my soul, I fell asleep.

*

Haluk told me to drop by in the late afternoon, so after breakfast I paid a visit to the neighboring town, Bergama, which Konstantin Pasadeos once declared "Rome's rival" as a center of culture. Inhaling the antique perfume radiated by the objects in the Archeology Museum, I wished I were in bed for a good long sleep. On the way to C., I finished the Singer book. The dark-haired driver, who kept even his name to himself, looked like he was about to cry when I offered him a generous tip. As the gate to the olive grove opened, Arrow barked twice and the distant sound of a *ney* fell silent. Climbing the footpath, I wondered if it was Nalan who had selected its jewel-like pebbles. As I followed the trail of shining geometrical stones, I encountered all the compositions I had admired from childhood to ennui, from Bach to Adamo.

Haluk was waiting for me on the veranda behind the stone house, sitting at a table piled high with food, like a chess player with his first three moves prepared. In addition to the usual *raki* table *mezes*, there were delicacies of the region like spicy olive paste, seaweed, and nettle pastry. I took mental note for Professor Ali. I would have been skeptical about Haluk's kissing me on the cheek had his breath not reeked of anise. He could not conceal his joy as he took the Nadolsky diaries from me and said, "This means you've found the twisted maniac who played that bad joke on you."

"Yes," I said, "I found him, but I can't settle accounts with him because he's hiding somewhere beyond my reach."

"Does this pervert have a lot of money?"

"He's plenty rich and plenty smart too," I replied, trying to indicate with a look that his choice of words was perhaps a little extreme.

"You don't seem to want to talk a lot about it," he said. "Well, bring your glass here and let's drink to other things …"

The porch at the top of the tree-covered hill had the ambience of a retired sultan's royal caique. The view of the misty Aegean from this shady eyrie transported me. The soft wind fell back into the sea after sighing up the hill to kiss my face, and fresh fragrances filled the air as the sun sank, producing a peaceful feeling that the buzzing of the locusts only increased: the joy of it all made me feel that my chair might become slowly airborne, until Haluk said, "There's so much oxygen on this hillside that a man can't quench his thirst." When our conversation turned to the confessional, he spoke first, as I expected he would, of his deceased wife.

"Women go through a more basic change in the ageing process than men," he said, opening the second bottle. "I wore myself out trying to deal with Nalan, who was a very fragile woman … But ever since we challenged the world hand-in-hand when we were twenty-one we overcame every crisis together … The moment my wife died I turned into a zombie, Kemal. I woke up every day only to feel the pain worsen. If my hand went out to a *raki* glass, I remembered the first day our eyes met. Following my doctor's advice I cut my drinking to every other day, and I spend at least two hours at Nalan's grave on my sober days. When Sim heard that I'd fallen asleep in the plot I reserved for myself next to Nalan's, she said, 'Are you rehearsing?'

"No, Kemal, even in the soap operas you won't see such things as have befallen my granddaughter, who is my reason for enduring all this!

"… Sim fell in love with a kid younger than herself, a student in the School of Architecture at the same university. The Rasputinesque Rebii Güler was 'by birth a potential world-class architect and painter.' But what Nalan said about this insipid hanger-on of Sim's was, 'There's no spark of love in that boy's eyes.'

"Two years ago Rebii was drunk and driving his Jeep when he crashed into a minibus on the Bosphorus road. Sim was in the front seat. Her seat belt came undone and she flew through the windshield. At the hospital, where we could hardly bear to look at her lacerated face, we learned that she had lost her sight. The accident report declared that the boy had not been under the influence of alcohol and that Sim's seat belt had not been well fastened. It did no good, of course, when my granddaughter regained consciousness, to learn that it was a fraudulent report. Rebii's father was a wealthy dentist with powerful connections. This unscrupulous man immediately packed his son off to Paris and discharged his obligations to us with a reluctantly apologetic phone call.

"Day and night for six months we took turns being tormented in hospitals reeking of death in Istanbul and London ... We suffered a severe meltdown both emotionally and financially. The stress of this period muted our jubilation over the success of the reconstructive surgery. Sim's face was recovering even as she mourned Rebii's disappearance. It was her ophthalmologist who broke the news that with a cornea transplant my granddaughter would be able to see again. I knocked literally on every possible door until I found a suitable pair of corneas ... The surgery too was a success. The next day, when she opened her eyes, Sim announced timidly that she could see, but only in gray tones. We returned home when she reached the point of 'seeing the world like a Nazmi Ziya painting behind tulle.' We sacrificed a lamb in thanksgiving. But that was it; our happiness could go no further. Within a month the poor girl's eyes had closed again. According to the officious professor who performed the surgery, her body had rejected the corneas. He told us we could apply to an American clinic specializing in this type of case—if we happened to have a few hundred thousand dollars to spare. I could have spat in his face.

"Sim was in fact getting stronger, but when she lost her grandmother she fell apart again. The psychiatrist indicated that she could recover from her depression in two years or so with medicine and moral support. It's been more than a year now since my wife died. And if you ask me she's no better.

"If we'd simply told her that the new resident of Vlad Baba's house had brought her a CD from Buenos Aires she wouldn't have bothered to come out of her room. But when she heard about your accident—which tore you away from the military but not from life … You'll be meeting Sim when you have your coffee."

We passed into the empty living room of the stone house, which was as luminous as a ghost in the descending darkness. It was good that he kept his eye on me as he brought Sim into the room and took our orders for coffee. Her smoke-colored glasses could not conceal her attractive face. Her hair was tied in a pony-tail, making her broad forehead more prominent. (Hayri Abi used to say that women with large foreheads were both intelligent and obstinate.) She could be considered tall. She wore a pale pink T-shirt and gray trousers. As she approached me I was startled by Haluk's signal to rise and shake her hand. She said, in a lucid and sad voice, as she seated herself next to her grandfather, "I heard that you survived a terrible accident. I hope you're all right now."

Empowered by the fact that she was four years younger, I said, "We should both be grateful that we're still alive. But you seem luckier than I, since you'll be able to start seeing and painting after your operation. Me, on the other hand, they wouldn't even give a helicopter for safekeeping." This made her grandfather nod his head in earnest. My tongue was loosened. I thought the story of Professor Ali and

Esther would entertain them both, so I held nothing back except for the clue laid down by Suat. When Sim scolded her grandfather for dozing off, I felt as relieved as a nanny who's just passed a test posed by a difficult child she's about to start minding.

I received an invitation to breakfast the next morning, which I couldn't refuse, although Haluk's request that I punctuate it with a musical presentation of the CDs I'd brought along seemed a bit much. Zakir's son drove me back to the hotel in Sim's purple Jeep. Samsun was the name of this fellow, who was earnestly trying to be macho by complaining about how easy his military service on the Bulgarian border had been. It was probably the umpteenth time he'd explained how he got his name: his father had named him after his prison cellmate's hometown. He added that his sister's name, Renk—"color"—was "a gift from Miss Sim." It was clear that he would be gratified by a question like, "How long have you been working for Haluk Bey?"

"When my father got out of prison he came to Ayvalık for seasonal work. The year I was about to start grade school, he called me and my mother to C. because he was going to work for Haluk Bey. That was fifteen years ago. Hereabouts they always called me Kurdish Samsun, Captain. Our boss always paid for my education, so when he almost went broke I quit school. He's our provider and we've become a natural part of the olive grove now. We're all upset about what happened to Mrs. Nalan and Miss Sim, Captain. Each one of us came and bowed to our patron and said that we were ready to give an eye for our miss any time he wanted. The boss thanked us and said if this was possible he would have given both of his own eyes. I swear by the holy book that it wasn't a joke when I asked him to let me go and cut the eyes out of that shameless boy and his worthless dishonorable father, Captain. Mr. Haluk said that people without honor will get their reward in the other world if not this one. Right now the main thing is for Sim to get well enough to be operated on again. Once there was a deserter from the army, a private I knew, his name was Dervish, and he said that the angels and devils are inside us and not outside and that hell and heaven are on earth and all this stuff has got me mixed up real bad …"

"Samsun, please stop calling me 'Captain'," I said, trying to calm this potential self-sacrificer. "If your deserter had been an F-16 pilot he would have known that heaven is not on earth. And Mr. Haluk is not worried about Sim; by next year at the latest he will send her to a specialist clinic in America for an operation."

"My mother heard our boss talking to his granddaughter and saying that he might have to sell both olive groves to raise the money for the operation. Miss Sim yelled, 'I won't let those groves be sold for a risky operation.' Since I heard this I buy a lottery ticket three times a month and play lotto once a week."

I said hello to the night shift in the lobby and went up to my room to gaze at the lights on the point. The satisfying duet between darkness and silence brought me to my senses. A trickle of olive-oil aroma entered the midnight mosaic, somehow reminding me of the Rameau concert I'd missed on the radio. I think Suat had had two expectations when he bequeathed me an apartment and a salary: the first was that I would help Ali and Esther get together; as for the second, I didn't know how I was supposed to help a blind girl. As I undressed for bed I should have been considering my limitations. Instead, what was on my mind was the line, "Alone under a shooting star, a girl undressing." I was sifting my memory for its author when I dozed off ...

I wondered how I must have looked to Samsun, who, when he came to pick me up the next morning and take me to the stone house, could say nothing more than "Good morning, Captain." The host and hostess attended breakfast in fashionable attire. I set up for my presentation, and it was amusing to see them take the chairs closest to the stereo. "I chose one piece each from twenty tango singers. If you feel you've been hearing the same thing after number five, please alert me," I said before starting. Maybe this was why they managed to look interested all the way through.

After the music, when Haluk proposed that I read to Sim, I could have shouted, "Yes! Gladly!" I was startled when he linked our arms together for the climb to the second floor. Three walls of the spacious salon were covered with paintings. "Do you like painting?" asked Sim with a kind of moan. Nothing could more precisely have expressed the pain of being unable to see.

I probably disappointed my inner voice by composing a reply like, "Actually, I tend to feel as if I'm both reading poems and viewing paintings when I'm listening to baroque music, Sim."

The gray cat curled up at the end of the brass bed snarled at me. Momentarily animated, Sim said, "And this is my roommate, Ash." I noticed the lively colors of the hand-woven rug on the floor. Then I saw the seven thick books on the antique desk that was a gift from Count Nadolsky. I was stunned. Marcel Proust's magnum opus was to be read, according to Nalan Erçelik, when one reached the age of thirty-five. "I've aged ten years in the last two." said Sim, "I'm ready for *Remembrance of Things Past*."

We took our places in the two bamboo chairs across from the desk and I began to read *Swann's Way*:

> For a long time I used to go to bed early. Sometimes,
> when I had put out my candle, my eyes would
> close so quickly that I had not even time to
> say to myself, "I'm falling asleep." And
> half an hour later the thought that it
> was time to go to sleep would
> awaken me; I would wake as
> if to put away the book which
> I imagined was still in my
> hands, and to blow out
> the light; I had
> gone on
> thinking,
>
> ...

*

Those lines were the overture to a three-thousand-page symphony of prose. While the sentences tasted of poetry, the paragraphs tasted of tirades. I paid no attention to the sardonic smile brought, no doubt, to Sim's face by my naïve enthusiasm. My listener fell asleep during our reading session, and as I pulled a purple bedspread over her, on which was written, "The Limits of My Colors are the Limits of my World," I felt as if I'd known her for months. The jealous Ash snarled as I wiped the perspiration from her brow with tissue paper, but I felt as relieved as a private who's survived his first watch. Sim rarely went out and when she did she needed assistance. Dutifully I walked arm-in-arm with her through the olive groves after our afternoon tea. She gathered that I was an anti-humorist. To set her at ease, I told her a little about my life.

That evening, as I returned for what would be my last night at the hotel, I was feeling restless. Next morning I was to move into the stone house. We were passing the "Welcome to Ayvalık" sign when Samsun said, "Captain, you can see now that Miss Sim is a lot higher caliber than those Istanbul girls angling to get married, even if she can't see. My mother sends her regards to you. She says if the lead pilot marries Sim, she and Renk will be at their service twenty-four hours a day. And me, I say that if you were to marry our angel, the lowly Samsun would be yours to command until he dies …"

From the window of my room on the ground floor of the stone house, the surrounding landscape looked like a gray-green ski run. I might have exercised my imagination by chasing a gray tulle curtain stretched like a line on the horizon between me and the sea. I grew familiar with the voices of the morning chorus perched in the wild fruit trees next to my room. As for the evening concert of migrating birds, it usually ended when the furious and arrogant wind blew down from Mount Ida. Sorrow, Solitude, Serenity, Scribe, Saddle, Sobriety, Scrap, Sigh, Spleen, Sortie: of the names Haluk's wife Nalan had bestowed on the tree-dervishes of the olive grove, these were the ones that stuck in my mind. Ever since my accident I'd been unable to fall asleep unless I lay face down, hugging my pillow. But now as soon as I turned off the lights and stretched out on the bed, glad not to know how many nights I would be there, my eyes closed before I had time to worry about getting to sleep. Even Arrow was aware that my presence had eased the tension in the grove. Whenever I went outside he ran up to allow me to pat his head respectfully. When we were eye to eye, I understood that, unlike Samsun, whatever he might do for me would be free of conditions. I started wondering whether it was nature that had set me up to settle down in this quiet olive orchard.

We thought that if I read 120 pages a day, we wouldn't tire the novel's delicate characters nor would we be startled by the twists and turns of Proust's time tunnel. *To chase the time that was left* we would head for the beach or visit other local attractions. Renk in her maxi-skirts would come along to C.'s unspoiled beaches. On the road to Mount Ida or Edremit, Sim would scold Samsun, saying, "Don't drive this Jeep like you're quarreling with it." I didn't mind it when the busybody siblings left us alone together to increase the efficacy of their mission.

Sim tried not to be a burden on me, but her concern was unnecessary. I got used to her taking my arm on our strolls, and was duly annoyed by the stares of the young layabouts whose eyes, full of bad intentions, followed her. To me it was absurd that she didn't believe I took pleasure in reading restaurant menus to her or cutting up the meat on her plate. She never acted impulsively and never uttered a frivolous word. That she possessed a rich inner world was clear from her questions and conversation. Anyway, I wasn't expecting to become her confidant. On our fourth day we started *Within a Budding Grove*. Since Haluk had gone to Cunda to meet his hunting pals, we were on our own. At dinner that evening I was surprised when Sim slipped into the familiar "you" after two glasses of wine.

"I'm sure that my grandfather has explained down to the smallest detail what I've been through. Well, I hope *you* haven't been hurt by love too," she said as Arrow announced his presence by pressing his nose against my right arm. The giant Kangal dog stood like a totem beside me, reminding me of Suat's tiger. Suddenly I felt like a mortal confined within a comic book. It took me a few seconds to decide not to think about what I might do were I not intimidated by my inner voice. Sim had found a way to enable me to offer her moral support.

"As a young boy I was in love with a ghost whose small tombstone was in Z. cemetery." I said "Her name was Aslı. After that there was Dolores O'Riordan and France Gall, for the sake of their husky voices … at the Air Force Academy I lost interest in my girlfriend, whose inner world seemed to have shrunk the two years I'd known her. The truth is—I've never told anyone else this—my secret love up until the time I crashed it was my F-16 …"

I never liked couples who, after making so-called vows of love and marriage, went for each other's jugular. After the story of Esther and Ali I began thinking that marriages— like art—should be kneaded out of talent and achievement. As I was wondering whether the author of my clumsily improvised response was really me, I guessed that Sim had already figured out that I didn't bear a love scar.

At the end of my first week we began *The Guermantes Way*. By then I'd met all the expectations that went along with the "savior" status which befriending Sim had conferred upon me. But there were also awkward moments, such as when I asked Haluk, "Sir, haven't you had a lot to drink?" Or when I offended Zakir and his family by failing even to ask them to fetch some water when they had averred their eternal service. The first one to notice me had been Arrow, the establishment's secret philosopher. Now, when Haluk remarked, "I don't think this dog takes anybody but you so seriously," Arrow for the first time seemed to regard me with suspicion.

One day while we were listening to Albinoni's oboe concerto Sim said, "Before you came, the only thing there was to do was to paint abstract pictures with virtual brushes on the virtual canvasses that I stretched on my imagination." I failed to grasp this as an early warning. Next morning Sim yelled at her grandfather and didn't come down for breakfast. Behaving like a psychologist, I went to her room. She was in bed with the cat in her arms. No, she didn't want me to open the window. I wasn't offended by this; I sat down in my usual chair and began to read. The treacherous cat snarled at me and left the room. After an hour, thinking she was asleep, I pulled the bedspread over her, but jumped back when she threw it off. In fact I'd always felt hesitant about looking directly into her face, as though it were a sorrowful painting, because I was afraid she might feel my gaze on her and get the wrong idea. By evening she had not emerged from her room. Haluk went out to see an old friend of his from his lycée years in Ören. I drank three beers while dining alone, then made a last sally to her room. She was listening to a radio program called "From Inside Evening." I was touched. "Do you have a problem?" did not seem like a question that would elicit the right kind of reply. Still, I should not have asked, just to make conversation, who the abstract artist was whose reproductions were hanging on the walls of my room.

"He's the greatest living painter in the world. If you could manage to understand Howard Hodgkin's work you would realize that its music and its poetry are beyond categorization."

I didn't think I deserved such a sharp-tongued reply. I went back downstairs to share my troubles with Arrow, and decided abruptly to get out of this depressing place.

It was the last morning. Just as I read "The thing I needed was to have Madame de Stemaria ..." Sim's cell phone rang for the first time in nine days. I was so happy to hear that two of her university friends were arriving next morning to spend a week with her. Sim tried politely to keep the room arrangements she was making with Bereket a secret from me, but I assured her, "I'm going back today." She acted surprised, but as I expected, she didn't insist on my staying. I packed my bags, angry with myself for having caricatured my personal problems just to amuse her. I was certain that I'd paid my debt to Suat. (Or were his expectations confined to my passing along Count Nadolsky's diary to Haluk?)

Fearful of upsetting Sim, the olive-grove folk saw me off rather formally. As we set out for Ayvalık, Arrow chased the Jeep until he was out of breath, as I knew he would. Samsun found me a seat on the bus to Istanbul. He probably felt embarrassed about my manner of leaving, but I had no intention of consoling the would-be self-sacrificing loyalist. As we bid farewell he said, "Captain, you are the marshal of our hearts; may God's grace be with you," and kissed my hand; and I looked forward to being alone again.

On the bus I settled down with my iPod and closed my eyes. I tried to marshal the names that Nalan had allocated to her favorite trees: Afife, Bacchus, Ceberut, Demeter, Ebabil, Flora, Gazel, Hera, Imza, Jupiter, Kanca ...

VIII

I liked the way Esther and Ali Uzel were disappointed if I didn't show up for dinner and spend the night with them at least once a week. My respect for Esther only grew because she never tried to match me with some rich family's daughter.

Rifat Demren, the cousin of Esther's neighbor, heard somehow about my passion for music and said he wanted to meet me. He was the director of Radio Estanbul. This radio station, which addressed itself to the city's art lovers, happened to be my favorite. It was on the air twenty hours a day with jazz, classical, and world music, as well as short pieces on art, archaeology, and travel. Except for occasionally plugging a big contributor, it was commercial-free; and the assertive female voice left no doubt that if you wanted news and weather you were in the wrong place. Every night the station signed off by recommending a CD or a book to listeners still awake and then sank into silence with a nostalgic song. This lullaby changed monthly, and some nights I stayed up until three just to hear it.

It was for Esther's sake that I agreed to meet Rifat. Even if he made a job offer, I wouldn't have dreamt of accepting. The dank smell issuing from the second floor warned me that I was traveling into the past. There were Ottoman-era name plates on the third-floor doors, which opened probably once a year. The fourth-floor offices were occupied by pseudo-foreign companies. I recognized those with Jewish agents by their framed inscriptions, and those with Armenians by the accented curses oozing out through the doors. On the fifth floor all but two doors sported Radio Estanbul signs in blue and black. I approached the door with a brass plate that said "Aesthete Platform," and was disturbed when I realized its significance. Had the huge gray and pink stained-glass skylight above me not caught my attention I would have hurried out of that building. But while I ruminated on why I might be fixating on that particular color harmony, a melodious voice called my name. A woman with an artificial leg apologized on behalf of her boss for the five-minute delay and escorted me to his office.

The walls were covered with giant pictures of Cappadocia. Rifat Demren walked in and sat down behind his desk. He looked to be in his sixties, a little tubby but lovable. His gray beard didn't surprise me. He wore blue jeans. Perhaps because he wanted to downplay his expertise, he focused his gaze on the antique pen case on his desk. Skillfully he put me through my paces. I regretted criticizing the station for producing so many programs for the newly-initiated and not enough for the cognoscenti. When we both took a breather, it dawned on me that what the noticeably large pictures contributed to the room was serenity. I assumed that Rifat Demren was mentally preparing a job offer, which I was mentally preparing to refuse, but I was wrong.

"My aunt used to tell me, 'You can't become a diplomat but maybe you should be an MP.' I had a better idea: I was going to wage war, all on my own, on the malaise in this country by establishing the most highly specialized radio station in the world, at the risk of making no money at all. We think we've been pretty successful, judging by the kind of reaction we've been getting.

"The most significant asset of this station is the attitude of its DJs. These able and honest people with unassuming artistic hearts have taken good care of Radio Estanbul. For a long time now I've covered our financial losses by using most of my rental income, and I've kept the station from being gobbled up by the local global media giants. My life's mission is to keep it alive as it aspires to perfection ..."

As I prepared to take my leave he uttered the sentence that compelled me to accept his job offer: "This country needs a *classical music DJ* as badly as it needs an F-16 pilot."

I joined Radio Estanbul, waiving the symbolic fee they proffered. My program was called "Bar Bar Baroque" and it was well established by the second broadcast. I tried to keep my patter plain and simple, avoiding technical details. I knew that statements like "I thought it was Allah speaking when I heard the *ney* for the first time," or "I learned from the papers that the man who turned me into a classical music addict was a drug dealer" wouldn't attract the wrong kind of attention. At the end of my first month I took on another program, "Since Stravinsky," where I introduced twentieth-century composers to our audience. And, at Rifat Bey's request, I wrote personal essays under a pseudonym for a music magazine called *Klass*.

Most of the DJs got together every couple of weeks for dinner. They counted their meals in the dim restaurant as the fees they refused to accept. I came to like this team of academics, writers, poets, retired musicians, civil servants, and *rentiers*, who refrained from bringing sports and politics into the conversation. The youngest of them was ten years older than me. The reservations they at first had about me, probably because of my spell in the military, were hilarious. I warmed to Rifat Demren, who was like a walking encyclopedia. He was an idealist full of secrets. He'd made a substitute home out of some rooms next to the studio, and he spent more time there than he did in his Gümüşsüyü flat with the sea view. I had the notion, during my nights on Istiklal, that he read Bruce Chatwin as he sat listening to the radio transmissions from the other side of the wall.

He liked to think that he extracted pleasure from life frame by frame. He would tire himself out running from football to ballet, from the horse races to the opera; he knew every kebab master and sushi chef in town. Rumor had it that this refined man, whose passion for radio was like mine for my deceased F-16, was asexual. (I was sure, on the other hand, that being alone simply increased his pleasure in life.) He would invite me to his office after my shift, where his conversations about radio never failed to interest me. We went out to dinner every other week. After the second glass of wine would come the boring reminiscences of school years, but he would raise his head like a cobra whenever the talk turned to radio. I respected the fact that he never gave me the nostalgic lover's sob story.

I took him to the Golden Fish in Cibali. The specialty of this restaurant, whose ambience, after Professor Ali advised them to change the lighting, stirred the desire to drink, was sea bass in paper, prepared again according to the professor's recipe. The place was two-thirds empty on that pleasant autumn evening. On the other side of the Golden Horn, Pera looked as proud as a steamer about to set sail on its maiden voyage to center stage in a Fellini film. As my boss talked, I finished choosing the pieces for my Von Biber program.

Suddenly an explosion of atonal and fake laughter caused everyone in the room to crane toward a table in the corner. I studied the two middle-aged dandies thoroughly; their derision seemed to be directed toward our table.

"Those two drunks are newspaper columnists," said Rifat Demren. "They belong to that class of journalists who regard lack of principle as a virtue and who write what they get paid to write. I turned down the bearded one's programming suggestions, and pointed out that the wigged one was a plagiarist. Now they think they're ridiculing me. If they see we're ignoring them completely, they'll shut up …"

I wasn't convinced. When it became clear that I was right, I sent Akif the waiter over to have a word with them. This time, words like *pilot*, *pilaf*, and *piyaz* began rising from the corner, from which I understood that Akif had been spreading rumors about me. With alacrity I stepped over to their table. They looked alarmed.

"Are you looking for trouble?" I asked. The beard tried to rise, but I pushed him down like a sack of dirt. My hand was on his shoulder and I could feel him trembling. With my right foot I stepped on the other one's left foot; he was holding back for fear that I would snatch his wig off.

"Actually the cheap wine you're drinking says more about the kind of journalists you are than your lousy prose styles," I said. I took the bottle from their table and poured it in their plates and then over their heads. "I'll give you five minutes to get out of here before I come back with a bottle of Sarafin and wash your faces in it. And if you're thinking of stopping by my table on your way out, I'll mop up the floor with you as sure as there's a hell for media disgraces like yourselves!"

I studied the dessert menu as they got up and left. I shouldn't have said, as I started in on my chocolate halva, "Am I too set in my ways ever to become an aesthete, Abi?" The poor man felt compelled to say, "No, you're beyond being an aesthete; you're an intellectual with courage." I consoled myself by remembering that it's always the good guy who comes out on the bottom in the New Wave movies.

*

I assumed that this period of Balatian hospitality and gentility would end in due time, but I wasn't really concerned about when that would happen.

I no longer went in much for part-time idleness, with three days of my week now taken up by radio and journalistic responsibilities. I referred to my wanderings around the Golden Horn as "Strolling through Arafistan," *araf* meaning something like the line between heaven and hell. These were occasions for me to plan my radio shows and essay topics. At *Klass* I had at least managed to find a crowd my own age; I was twenty years younger than the other DJs I'd met at the radio station, and thirty years younger than my concert companions. The editor of *Klass* was Halide Ishakoğlu, a fan of C. W. Gluck. This middle-aged woman wore a beret summer and winter, and would only answer to "Halhal." She surprised me by discovering "the compassion of a lighthouse" in my eyes. Thanks to a slim volume (*Ba*, by Birhan Keskin) she brought as a gift when she came to my place once for dinner, I stopped belittling the younger poets.

I read somewhere that there are over 4,000 pieces of music specially composed for pianists who've lost a hand through war, disease, or accident. Paul Wittgenstein, the pianist brother of the man Professor Ali called the last century's most significant philosopher, Ludwig Wittgenstein, suffered the amputation of his right arm after being wounded in the First World War, in which he'd volunteered to fight. Among the composers whom the wealthy Paul commissioned to write pieces for him—he was himself a student of Theodore Leschetizky—were Strauss, Prokofiev, Ravel, and Benjamin Britten. As I played the compositions these masters had written for the mediocre pianist, I thought of Sim and got goose bumps. I was annoyed with myself for thanking Allah that I hadn't lost my hearing when my F-16 and I crashed to the ground.

The next evening I was getting ready to go to Disco Eden when who should call but Haluk. I couldn't pretend I didn't understand the meaning of "You've made yourself missed" was "Come and read books to my bitter granddaughter."

"I'd like to be there with you," I said, "but I'm working now," and went on to tell him about my two jobs, even though the money I made from them both wouldn't pay for a bus ticket to work. The following evening I was playing chess with Sami when who should call but Samsun.

"Captain, my respects," he said. "I'm not disturbing you, I hope?"

"Good evening, Samsun. I'm playing chess with my neighbor. If you cut it short, maybe he'll fall into the trap I set."

"Captain, I'm coming to Istanbul tomorrow. With your permission, it would be my honor to pay my respects to you tomorrow evening."

"If you're not going to drag me back to Ayvalık by playing

on my emotions, okay, Samsun. I'll expect you."

"Oh, I would never be so bold as all that, Captain," he said. It didn't occur to me to suspect the unusual cheerfulness with which he uttered those last words.

I had my nose buried in a book when two hesitant rings of the doorbell reminded me that I was expecting Samsun. His orange-green shirt and black velvet trousers were dazzling. Despite the thick coat of gel encasing his hair, he looked like an overweight jockey. He didn't come in. Standing at the threshold, he looked down at the floor and said, "I have something to tell you if you won't be mad at me."

"You rogue! I can promise you I'll try, but that's all."

"Thank you, Captain. You came down to us like a saint from heaven. We only realized how much we liked you after you went away. Poor Miss Sim fell into a big depression. That novel you two started reading … it wasn't even half finished, Captain. She knew I was coming to Istanbul to see my army friend Muho, who is now a Kasımpaşa taxi driver, and asked if she could come along. She insisted, so I brought her. She's downstairs in Muho's taxi. If she could just be your guest until you get to the end of that novel …? If you say the word, I'll bring her up. If not, we'll take her back and take care of her ourselves. May you be happy in your life, Captain."

With the panic of a new mother who's left her baby on the street I ran down the stairs cursing Samsun, who followed me with a grin on his face. The chunky young man leaning against a car, who looked like he was eating a cigarette, must have been Muho. He bowed his head gravely in greeting, as if he were a man on a difficult mission. I opened the wrong door as Sim emerged from the other one and stood waiting. "You look very chic," I said, even before "Welcome," and kissed her on both cheeks. Extending my arm to escort her to the entrance, I already felt the stress of having a blind female houseguest. Samsun followed us with Sim's suitcase. At the threshold he whispered, "If it's the will of fate, I'll pick her up when the time comes. May the Almighty turn everything you touch to gold, Captain," and tried to kiss my hand.

Sim asked for a glass of water so she could take a pill. I left her on the living-room couch and rushed to the kitchen. She followed me in.

"Kemal, I owe you an apology and an explanation. Since the day I lost my sight, the only time I ever had any peace was with you. And when I saw that with every passing day I was feeling more attached to you, I got scared. I was afraid that when your period of charity came to an end and you left, even the early days would look good by comparison. I rejoiced when my old friends called in the middle of my dilemma. I thought that if I shared my loneliness with them I could rescue myself from your spell. But I could hardly put up with those two pretentious wretches for a week. I felt that they weren't really sorry for what had happened to me. With every giggle of theirs I remembered how expert they used to be in making up gossip about me at school. The only good to come out of that small-scale nightmare they brought on was that I remembered the sweetness hidden in your voice. On our way home from Ayvalık after we saw them off, I tried not to believe Samsun when he told me he'd seen my grandfather in tears over that quarrel of ours.

"That night for the first time I analyzed my situation. Despite his excessive fondness for me, I was constantly quarreling with my grandfather—mostly because of what he did to my grandmother and father, and maybe too because he's a man. I was ashamed of what I had done to this person who showered me with affection and was ready to sacrifice everything he had for my operation. If nothing else I should at least have been able to live with him in peace. And expecting the people who look after me to make me the center of their lives was wrong too. I have to be content with what they can do, and I should certainly not be afraid of flirting in the dark ...

"I'd planned to come to Istanbul to buy clothes for the fall season and to stay at Banu's house. She's the painter who did that portrait of me on the wall in the living room; we supposedly pick out my clothes together. The day before we were to leave, she called and said she was going to Tokat for four days. But Samsun insisted on not postponing the trip, so I went along with him. Your uninvited guest will try her best not to be a burden to you until Banu Tanalp gets back to town. And if you feel like it you can go on reading Proust to me ..."

Two months before, when I was telling Professor Ali about what had befallen me in C., he said, "What you've told me reminds me of Yakup Kadri's story, 'A Blind Eye and a Blind Heart.'

"Zeliha, a village girl blind from birth, falls in love with the imam Hafız Şerif. This man, who has no virtues other than a beautiful voice, is unaware of the situation. When he is appointed imam of a mosque across the sea, poor Zeliha follows him on foot 'for the sake of breathing the same air as he does.' She takes up begging at the door of his mosque. In a letter home to his village, Hafız Şerif writes that he has run into Zeliha and has done his best to help her, but since everything has its limits, the girl's family should come and rescue her. Not even the story's narrator knows how this bizarre passion ends ... Kemal, son, you can't be unaware that Sim has developed similar feelings for you."

Listening to Sim now, I was enjoying the thought that the professor had been wrong. My guest, whose four-day stay was looming larger and larger, was still trying to make peace with life. I didn't bother to reassure her that I wasn't upset with her. I suppose I'd already started my countdown to the day when I would hand her over in one piece to her friend Banu. At her request we took two tours of the flat, fifteen minutes apart. As she organized her closet she said, "Don't worry, you won't have to help me dress. I have a technique of recognizing my own clothes." When she came into the living room on her own, she had *The Guermantes Way* in her hand. Opening it to page 103, she put it in my hand. We sat on the couch side by side. Once more I bowed to the splendor of this word symphony, eager to perform eloquently:

What I required was to possess Madame de Stermaria, for during the last few days, with an incessant activity, my desires had been preparing this pleasure, in my imagination, and this pleasure alone, for any other kind (pleasure, that is, taken with another woman) would not have been ready, pleasure being but the realization of a previous wish, and of one which is not always the same, but changes according to the endless combinations of one's fancies, the accidents of one's memory, the state of one's temperament, the variability of one's desires, the most recently granted of which lie dormant until the disappointment of their satisfaction has been to some extent forgotten; I should not have been prepared, I had already turned from the main road of general desires and had ventured along the bridle-path of a particular desire; I should have had, in order to wish for a different assignation, to retrace my steps too far before rejoining the main road and taking another path.

*

The Sevil Barber Shop was the tiniest in the city and Taci was the slowest barber. I knew that I'd plunged into serious civilianhood when I began finding it odd that he refused to work without wearing a white shirt and tie. Taci only used his cell phone to quarrel with his wife, and deeply lamented his failure to find a nice Golden Horn girl for me to marry. I liked his daughter, who thought a sergeant out-ranked a colonel. I relied on Rabia, a veteran student, to help out with

Sim when I left the house. The first day I came home as soon as I finished work at the magazine. I was eager to take Sim on a tour of her forefathers' neighborhood and wanted to test my skills at creating vivid descriptions of Balat by following the changes in her facial expression. (On her first shift Rabia asked my houseguest whether she distinguished colors by sniffing them.)

Sim smiled to hear that we were starting our excursion on Half Balat Street. We took our first break in front of a signless storefront at a crossroads that doubled as a recruitment office. Then on past the early retirees who sat idly on small stools or wandered among the miniature shops; the dispirited youngsters doubtfully eyeing the small Ottoman bazaar; the robust women hurrying along narrow streets exempt from the cries of happy children; the stuttering but melodious street peddlers; the old crones who cursed when they stopped for a breather at every third step up the hill; the area cutting in from the coast and rising to a level of greater and greater obsolescence, where I found passages of Buenos Aires sorrow and Venetian mystery: at which point I get tired of the sound of my own voice. Sim was growing tired too, so we rested on the edge of a dry Ottoman fountain at the top of the hill. Irked by the constant pressure of her arm on mine, I calculated that eighty hours remained before I would be rid of her.

I gave Sim her medication when she woke. I read Proust to her. As a pleasant fall evening came on, we walked down to the shoreline of the Golden Horn. But when the time came to describe the luxuriant ivy and clumps of fig trees tying together scenes of havoc along the 1,400-year-old walls, I lost my enthusiasm: I remembered that Sim had been able to see until two years ago. I suppressed my comparison of the buildings in Galata, on the other side, to mercenary soldiers kept waiting hundreds of years for home leave. But I confessed that I'd been dreaming of going to Genoa to check the degree of its kinship with Istanbul.

The evening *ezan* had to start up for me to realize how much I'd been talking. As we stood up to go, Sim remarked, "I guess the reason for the Golden Horn's color is that it can't decide whether it's a river or a stream." For dinner we went to Albanian Bahri's place, where even the soup came in clay bowls. Sim didn't seem impressed by the discovery of the childhood friendship between her grandfather and the restaurant owner. On our way out Bahri whispered in my ear, "Who knows which of Haluk's sins this *houri* is atoning for?" We went over to Londracula, which I knew I would find deserted whenever I dropped in. I warned Sim that I was taking her to the strangest bar in Beyoğlu.

She thirstily downed a glass of cognac before beginning.

"I was so lucky to be reared by my grandmother. She was as refined and delicate as a porcelain figurine. She was my mother, sister, and best friend. My *joie de vivre* increased with every 'Good morning' we exchanged; and every 'Good night' came after a day made richer by her every gesture. The first thing she taught me was to love color—which was why

I never believed she'd be able to cope with my blindness.

"My father came to see us once a year, and my grandfather tried not to be at home then. As soon as my father and grandmother had greeted one another, the quarreling would begin. I knew that he held me responsible for my mother's death. And I knew that he hated the fact that I looked so much like her. I was frightened of his erratic behavior and the wrong toys he always brought me. Despite his protruding eyes and gray hair he was handsome. I suppose I envied him because he looked like my grandmother. He had earned Master's degrees in literature and computer programming, but not even his mother knew what his job was. 'Maybe Yusuf has a very important position in the computer division of a secret organization,' she used to say hopefully.

"I decided he must be a high-ranking English spy when I heard him yelling on the phone in English, but changed my mind when he finished in coded Turkish. I wasn't terribly sorry that we never saw him again after that summer between my second and third year of high school. He told me when we saw each other for the last time, 'My daughter, I don't know whether it was lucky for you that your grandmother first practiced her parenting skills on me, but it's definitely a good thing that you've got your artistic mother's looks rather than mine.' I was annoyed that he referred to me as 'my daughter' but also relieved, as it seemed to me another sign that he was leaving for good. We decided we would tell people he had died in a car accident. But I'm pretty sure he's still alive and that, moreover, he comes once a year to gaze at me from a distance, like a perverted peeping tom.

"The first time I shouted with joy was when I got the news that I'd been accepted by the Art Department of Mimar Sinan University. I knew I'd never become an important painter, so I set my sights on the academic world. I took more pleasure in observing than in painting anyway. After classes I'd visit an exhibition or two. It used to bother me if I couldn't find a story or poem hidden in the paintings. I amused myself by working on my pet theory: the colors humans wear always clash; the colors nature wears always harmonize. I always found a way to meet painters whose work I liked and I never went to bed without reading from the biography of a master.

"I was in my third year when I noticed the freshman Rebii, who always sat sketching in the library. He had a relaxed attitude and an enigmatic face. He was bohemian yet chic. I was impressed by the sketches of his that I sneaked a peek at, so I decided to introduce myself to him. He seemed to be an agreeable, well-mannered kind of guy. Since his father, the high-society dentist Nebi Güler, objected to his becoming a painter, he'd decided to be an architect instead. I gradually got used to taking the lead in our relationship—I guess I thought I was molding the passive Rebii into the ideal husband-to-be.

"My grandfather must have told you about the accident. What really killed me was Rebii's running away. I was afraid I would end up struggling alone in the dark when my grandfather succumbed to alcohol and my grandmother to death. You yourself know how I drove away a real friend who came to help. My psychiatrist—a collector of poor engravings—told me, 'Those pills I gave you can only cure your headaches. You'll have to find your real medicine in time and in yourself.' Time did what it was supposed to do, but I was hopeless about myself until I heard that tribute to Ingmar Bergman on the radio. He was my favorite film director. Although I had trouble connecting with his dignified characters, they still looked magnificent to me. A sentence by Bergman's son-in-law, the writer Manning Henkel, made me stop and think. 'Bergman increasingly took refuge in music as his eyesight failed him,' he said. I think this was the divine portent I was waiting for. I stopped seeing myself as the most pitiable girl on earth and a talent lost forever to the art world, and relaxed a bit. I reached a conclusion, as you know: peace with yourself, peace with those around you. Now the next test is my check-up in two months. I hope I won't collapse if they say that another operation won't help. But if they do say there's hope, I don't even want to know if the money we have left is enough: all I know is I can't ask my grandfather to give away his olive gardens ..."

Like a teacher rewarding a student for an enthusiastic reading of her composition, I caressed Sim's cheek. I didn't much like the phony tone of my voice saying, "Something in me is happily telling me that you'll see again. And don't forget that I'll be there whenever you need me."

Next morning we started *Cities of the Plain*. We discussed our misfortunes in a quiet Golden Horn café. Nobody else was in the cinema where we went to see Nuri Bilge Ceylan's *The Seasons*. We were invited to the Uzels for dinner. I knew Sim would impress them. "She looks like Audrey Hepburn rehearsing the role of a blind girl," Esther said, which sounded right when I remembered the looks she got from the men on the street. I thought my houseguest would be pleased by this delayed compliment but I was mistaken.

For breakfast the next morning we dipped our fresh warm *pide* into Ayvalık olive oil, then with *Cities of the Plain* under my left arm we set out toward the nicely named Unkapanı. I narrated to her the misty Ottoman streets between Zeyrek and Horhor inch by inch and color by color. I read Proust to her in dim cafés under the pitying gaze of tactless retirees. I became self-conscious when I realized that I was producing a different voice and rhythm for each character. (Was this the ploy of a restless father expecting the daughter to whom he is reading fairy tales to quickly fall asleep?) We had lunch at Tirebolu Pide in Fatih. I raked the couple at the next table with my eyes when they stared at me for tearing Sim's *pide* into smaller pieces. Sim liked wandering around the antique dealers' shops on Horhor Street. She fell asleep as soon as we got into the taxi to go home. This time I didn't have the heart to pull my shoulder out from under her head.

I was relieved to hear why she'd turned down my invitation to go to a concert: she needed to get ready to go to her friend Banu's the next morning. (I was now about seventy hours behind in my plans for Disco Eden.) Together we packed her suitcase, and I didn't find helping her dry her hair so tedious. Reluctantly we finished the longest volume of *Remembrance of Things Past*.

I had to admit that I was getting used to Sim. She was an agreeable person who knew when to listen and when to ask questions. For the first time since my infirmity I had revealed my own inner world to someone. Walking down Sofyalı Street with Sim on my right arm and her suitcase in my left hand, I said, "Let me remind you that we still have three volumes to go."

"I have *The Captive* with me," she said. "I never thought we'd get past the fifth one."

"I'll pick up the last two," I said. "You've got three days ahead of you to make up for lost time with your Banu."

I liked the studio just inside the entrance of the gloomy *han* that housed pious foundations, trade unions, and the offices of never-to-be-retired lawyers. Was the mess in the studio compensated for by the Puccini opera surging from the stereo next to the antique stove? I almost started describing the colors and sorrowful tales of the huge paintings on the walls to Sim. Banu Tanalp was an attractive woman in her fifties with an elegant look that made one want to pull oneself together. When she told me that she was one of my listeners, I found her ironic smile less fearsome. Sim had already told me that she was an artist who didn't strive desperately to be recognized. On her graduation from the Fine Arts Academy she had married a sculptor thirty years older than herself. It was an exceptionally happy marriage, envied by all her friends, lasting until her husband died four

years ago. I was impressed by this artist with the mournful
eyes, whose son had risen to the second-violin chair in a
California city orchestra. Later I would understand why she
had looked down at the floor when I told her I would come
back in three days to collect Sim.

*

The inevitability of two-year-old magazines at the dentist's
and two-day-old newspapers at the barber's. As I sat
patiently waiting my turn at the Sevil Barber Shop, Taci
seemed to be slowing down just to annoy me. A news story
and photograph in a tabloid paper with unsolved crossword
puzzles caught my eye: the well-known society dentist
Nebi Güler's historical mansion on Büyükada had burned
to ashes along with everything inside it. The cause of the
fire, in which no one had died, was under investigation. The
fact that the museum-quality contents of the house were
uninsured was emphasized.

I went outside immediately and called Samsun on his
cell phone.

"Where can I track you down, you teller of tall tales?"

"I'm in Istanbul, Captain, and with good luck I'll be back
in C. tomorrow."

"Did you and Muho burn down the mansion?"

"I don't get what you're sayin', Captain."

"I just read about it in an old newspaper. Sim's old
boyfriend's mansion completely burnt to the ground. Thank
God nobody died."

"The papers I could buy if I had enough money only cover fires in the boondocks, Captain. And in my book we ain't supposed to light an empty house on fire and run away. I wish I'd been there when those Nebi and Rebii scumbags were at home so I could have shot their eyes out. But Haluk Bey wouldn't let me go, Captain."

If I believed in Samsun's innocence, I had no difficulty figuring out who the arsonist was.

"Captain, if you please, I got somethin' to tell you."

"No more than three sentences, Samsun, and let them be your last words. My mind is confused all of a sudden ..."

"Now we talkin' man-to-man, Captain. I made up that story for Sim about Haluk Bey crying because of her, to soften her heart. (*This worked.*) To set her up for a stay in Balat, I asked Mrs. Banu for help, and so she pretended to go to Tokat. (*This worked too, didn't it?*) My apologies and my thanks, Captain."

"If you were here I'd strangle you, Samsun! Are you practicing an internship in meddling, you interfering rat?"

"If necessary, poor Samsun will sacrifice himself for you, Captain."

I knew that the Master of Twilight, Suat, wouldn't be satisfied with arson alone if he had decided to punish the Gülers. I googled the name on the Net. The news that Nebi Güler was last seen in Cyprus with a model on his arm, and that the Nazmi Ziya paintings Aydeniz Güler had bought were fakes, was offered almost gleefully. It occurred to me how I might get some information on Rebii. I found his father's phone numbers and went to Taksim. I found a wine-whiff-free phone booth and dialed the non-rhythmic number of the Güler Dental Clinic. The secretary broke off her canned response mid-stream, asking abruptly, "How can I help you?"

I asked for Rebii Güler's number, knowing that she would scarcely want to help.

"Who's calling?"

"An old university friend of his, Sadık Kaçmaz. I wanted to express my condolences."

"He lives in New York now and unfortunately we don't have his phone number."

"Okay then. How is he getting along, may I ask?"

"Have you just heard about that horrible accident he had last summer?"

"It would be a comfort to me if you could fill me in on his latest condition."

"Rebii Bey was walking in Manhattan that night when a motorcycle hit him from behind and knocked him down. Just as he was about to get up, a van ran over him. Both of his legs were severed at the knee, sadly ..."

I hung up, my head pounding. My inner voice probably thought it would soothe me to say, "Be patient until you meet your benefactor, that postmodern Robin Hood." I went home and took two sleeping pills and went to bed. That evening I was playing chess with Sami for pizza. (Sim never liked him and once said, "This guy with the firecracker voice, is it fake art he makes?") I was concerned when he

MANY AND MANY A YEAR AGO

met my bad moves with even worse ones.

"Sami, I know my mind is confused, but what about yours?"

"There's a rumor going around the bazaar."

"The Grand Bazaar or the Mirror Bazaar?"

"The bazaar says that when Professor Ali gets Sim's eyes opened with an operation, you're going to marry her."

"So then, Master Sami, did you step up and say, 'Hey bazaar, I live in the same building as those two poor people and I would know if there was anything between them. Lieutenant Kuray has taken a disabled person into his home for the sake of humanity.' Did you?"

"The young bazaar folk want you to have a big colorful Golden Horn wedding. I have some dollars saved up, and if necessary ..."

"I restrained myself when you said that Pink Floyd was more important than Tchaikovsky, but this is too much nonsense even for you, Sami. You'd better get out of this house, or lab, or whatever it is, and don't come back for ten years even if I implore you!"

Hayri Abi used to say, "Don't use music like an aspirin by taking it only when you're mad." I looked in my drawer for money to go to Disco Eden, but there wasn't enough, so I went down to the shore instead. I sat on the first bench I found and tried to make the best of the cool night air. For a while I listened to the cars hissing by in even intervals on the wet street behind me. Then the surface of the water trembled slightly, and I perked up as though I were about to see a ghostly sailing ship slip by like a Byzantine souvenir.

*

As we headed toward Asmalımescit I had a goal in mind that I kept secret even from my inner voice: to have a quiet, good-natured girlfriend who loved music and possessed a rich inner life. When poor Sim, for whom I would always have a prayer or two to spare, went back to C., I would begin a new period by undertaking a quest of the heart free of time constraints and ulterior motives.

I was pleased to find Sim less cheerful than when I had left her. I cursed Samsun as I struggled to convince Banu that my feelings for Sim were those of a compassionate older brother. On the way back to Balat I had the feeling that Sim was preparing what she wanted to say to me. As we were putting her things in the closet I said, "I think of Samsun as a major character who pretends to be a minor one. Do you think I'm wrong?"

"If I answered in a word it wouldn't be fair to him. As a child he had problems adapting to C. He ran away from school when the other kids made fun of his name and accent. My grandfather, with a whip in his hand, taught him how to read and write and so saved him from prison. Samsun is devoted to all of us, but he worships my grandfather. When he was drinking in the bars until the early mornings it was Samsun who waited at the door, carried him home, put him to bed, and gave him his medicine. Another one of Samsun's jobs is dealing with the migrant workers who pick the olives at harvest time. I think you already noticed how sorry he was not to be given the additional responsibility of family bodyguard.

"He's able to multiply four-digit numbers in his head. So as not to be an extra burden to us, he turned in an empty paper for his university entrance exams. He reads radical newspapers and magazines and strange philosophical books. He has a peculiar sense of humor. He goes to the mosque on Friday and fasts during Rammadan. And whenever he falls into his father's folksy Turkish, he's definitely up to something.

"He never used the polite *hanım* in speaking to me until I started university. One day he came to my room and asked, very shyly, 'Sister dear, do you think people have the right to fall in love just once?' I think he's still in love with the actress Meg Ryan. I'm worried that he might upset the applecart by doing something outrageous just as he's trying to make things right ..." (If Sami was Suat Altan's Balat agent, then Samsun must be his man in Ayvalık. I no longer found this theory comical.)

We finished *The Sweet Cheat Gone* and *The Past Recaptured* in a week. As we neared the end of the masterpiece, it felt as if both the writer and his characters were getting a bit bored. (Was it perhaps the author's choice to consume the poetry like the last few grains of sand in an hourglass?) We went out every day as soon as we'd satisfied our reading quota. I could never be bored in the studio of the artist Sali Turan, who lived and breathed paint, or at the art gallery of Evin Iyem, an elegant woman with rapidly blinking eyes. At the concert I took Sim to I told her, "I won't let go of your hand until the second I feel that you're not bored." I made her laugh by reading headlines I found in the tabloids left behind on the old ferries. At the Ahırkapı lighthouse forty ships sailed by before we noticed the rain falling on us. Together we took my latest article to the magazine office. When she was with me in the studio, my radio programs seemed more successful. She impressed Rifat Demren, as I knew she would. When she dozed off while watching a DVD of Ingmar Bergman's "Winter Light" I carried her to bed in my arms. On her last day we rushed off to the Akmerkez mall to buy her a hat. I gave the useless and comically dressed short-legged salesgirl, who was simultaneously sneering at and pitying my houseguest, a look that said, "It's because you know she's worth five of you even in her present condition that you're bursting with envy."

Samsun came with the Jeep to collect Sim and her three suitcases and almost collapsed with laughter when I said, "What's 9,876 times 5,432?"

"I used to feel bad at being treated like a monkey, when everybody I met tried to test my meaningless talent, so I started giving them perfectly wrong answers. But when they continued to be impressed, I started enjoying myself. They usually give me numbers from nine to two in descending order ..." he said.

I was happy to think that he'd ended his period of flattery. If he was trying to send me a message, I didn't care.

Sim said she would stay with me when she came for her check-up in six weeks time. Once I learned that she'd reached C. safely, I went out to Disco Eden, but it was closed. I didn't feel like going home so I climbed the stairs of Radio Estanbul in the dark, knowing I would find Rifat Demren reading in what he thought of as his temple.

"Rifat Bey," I said. "After seeing Sim off, a weird thing happened to me. I'm irritated by the silence in my house, which I used to like just because it was silent."

"I once saw a documentary about the octopus. It seems that the male turns completely scarlet when he touches the female, perhaps out of embarrassment. The female, on the other hand, stops eating after laying her eggs and waits five months for her offspring to emerge. When she sees them slip into the water, she dies in peace."

He uttered a heart-rending whistle and returned to scribbling notes in the margins of his rare book.

"Brother, I'm not sure I understand what you mean, but if you're suggesting I'm in love with Sim, you're mistaken," I said.

I woke up in a meaningless flurry of anxiety and felt like I needed an excuse to leave the house. I opened the living-room window to the pleasant crispness of the air and the gray sky. I put the Giuseppe and Giovanni Sammartini CDs in the beige bag that was a gift from Sim. I'd never walked to the station from home before. Along the way I realized that for the first time I'd left without shaving and eating breakfast. By the time I reached the Unkapanı Bridge

I was missing the warmth of Sim's hand on my right arm. I speculated on when the feeling would leave. I decided not to bother with my "quest of the heart"; if it was in the stars, the woman of my life would find me. I stopped at a deserted buffet at the Tünel plaza and called Sim while waiting for my toast and sausages. I felt more at ease on hearing her, but the joy in her voice unsettled me. I said that I owed her a "Thank you" and that she owed me an apology: "I enjoyed very much having you as my houseguest, but you're damaging my relationship with my solitude."

While recording in the studio I had to convince myself that Sim wasn't there too, sitting across from me. I listened to Adriana Varela over dinner, which consisted of a pastrami sandwich with pickled cabbage and a Malbec wine, followed by *tulumba* for dessert. I called Sami and said, "As long as you don't mention Sim's name, you can come over and I'll teach you chess."

*

Next morning?

The thousands of musical notes flying toward each other from the four corners of my bed and the warm spring-like breeze wafting against my body were making me uneasy. I feared opening my eyes would cause me to miss a fantastic show. I turned on my side carefully, as if I were protecting a precious gift entrusted to me. And then the sublime nature of my inner voice dawned on me. I'd been anticipating instructions from it in vain. It had turned away from me and departed. I realized, as my eyes slowly opened, I was a new man.

I knew that her smiling image would greet my open eyes and I would feel her presence within me. Whether Suat Altan wanted it or not, I had fallen in love with Sim Erçelik. Having made this private announcement to myself, I leapt out of bed and threw myself face-down on the bed where she'd slept for a whole week. As I inhaled her fragrance I wondered whether the reason we got on so well was that she was blind. I felt like I was flying in the ocean and swimming in the clouds, growing lighter and lighter by the minute.

I jumped up again and rushed to the study. I took down the big dictionary and bemusedly looked up the word "love." (If my life were a novel, the preceding sentence would be erased.) I was reassured to see that I met the parameters of the definition. Still, I thought the word should have had a more earth-shattering definition in view of the uniqueness of each case. On a sudden impulse I read Poe's "Annabel Lee" in Suat's manuscript once again. It struck me that the phrase "Many and many a year ago" was sufficient unto itself as a manifesto of true love.

Having resolved my crisis of joy, I called Professor Ali. He chuckled and said, "Let's meet at the Marmara Café." He didn't take his eyes off the glass in front of him until I said, "My only fear is that, true, Sim won't refuse me now, but one day if she can see she might leave me."

"I don't think you rushed into this thing too quickly. Everybody around you was saying what a nice couple you'd make and how when you walked arm in arm you became almost one body. I knew you'd call me after she went back. I'll make one and only one comment on this matter: just listen to your heart, my son.

"Now here's something else I have to tell you. Esther and I don't intend to leave anything behind us when we leave this world. The house we live in is yours. Besides that, I've got a good buyer for my old flat in Balat. I made a deal with Ken Melling, an American translator and lecturer at Kadir Has University, to sell him the place for $185,000. Your new neighbor-to-be is a likeable person in his sixties. I'll put the money in your bank account. It might come in handy for Sim's eye operation.

"Esther's bridge partner Perihan has a physician son who is coming from Boston to Istanbul for five days for a wedding. Kamil is on the staff of a well-known eye clinic there, and if you wish, he'll take a look at Sim's eyes.

My eyes filled with tears. "Professor, I don't know what to say. This is too much."

"You deserve no less, son," he said.

Perhaps because of the heightened emotion, I gave him a quick summary of how Suat Altan had become my benefactor. Seeing that he wasn't particularly impressed, I kept the part about Suat playing Cupid to us to myself. I walked him to the Taksim metro. There were tears in our eyes as we embraced goodbye.

I dove into Sıraselviler Avenue on the heels of a nervous ambulance. Then I remembered that Rifat Demren's favorite restaurant wasn't open for lunch. I leaned against the Changa Restaurant's closed iron door and phoned Sim.

"I wonder myself what words are going to come out of my mouth," I started by saying. "You were my houseguest for just ten days but what you left behind is ten years' worth of yearning. I planned to infuse the joy of life into you because your eyes were shut, but you taught me to see a myriad of hues with my own eyes. When I go walking now I feel the absence of your warmth like a missing piece of my own body. Whatever I see in the city I feel like describing it to you in all its colors, and when I feel your absence something in me falls to pieces. You ruined my relationship with Bach and Vivaldi. Your eyes are the most alluring in the world, even if they're not open. If I don't say 'I love you,' it's because it sounds too ordinary. And if you say 'Yes' to my coming to you, I'll never leave you again, Sim!"

"Yes, come immediately," she replied. Staggered by the force of the fireworks that exploded inside me upon these words, I collapsed. When I opened my eyes again I was a strange bird. I got up and walked, and I was a line of musical notes. Swinging and swaying I made my way back home …

The sturdy man I ran into on the stairs was Ken Melling. I invited him in for green tea and gave him a tour of the house. Standing before an out-of-the-way shelf in the library he said, "I don't know rare books all that well, but there are two leatherbound volumes with coats-of-arms there that could be valuable."

As he left he said, "They're about to start major repairs

on my apartment. I'll move in after the new year, and the first thing I want to do is to teach you backgammon. I'd better go now, you look as pale as a new lover about to meet his beloved for the first time."

IX

Arrow met me at the garden gate. I sensed some reproach in the way he jumped up on me. I was wrestling with him for the sake of old times when Zakir appeared at the door of the annex. His bowed legs, discolored sweat pants and baggy sweater made him look like a character out of "The Pink Panther."

"Haluk Bey and Samsun have gone to İzmir on business," he said. My guess was that his son had plotted this trip in order to leave Sim and I alone.

"And I suppose Bereket and Renk have also gone to the village?"

"They have, I swear on the Koran!"

I imagined the olive trees that leaned back as I passed before them were like the gods of Mount Olympus who turned into forms of vegetation during sacred rites. Before

I rang the bell of the stone house I shot a glance through the living-room window: Sim was listening to a small radio on her lap and—I hoped—waiting for me. She sat upright in her armchair as if posing for Banu. She was wearing a beautiful orange and gray dress. She looked as haughty as a model and as vulnerable as an abandoned kitten. I rang the bell determinedly, but had no idea what my opening lines would be. The door opened and I barged in wordlessly and wrapped my arms around her as tightly as I could. My mouth opened to speak, but instead I kissed her.

"I'll never forget that you're a gift to me, Sim," I said. She leaned her head on my chest, put her arms around me, and started to cry.

I stayed at the stone house for three days, and on the fourth we went to Ayvalık to buy engagement rings. Haluk accompanied us. His expression seemed to say, "I knew from the first glance that this guy would be my son-in-law." (Do we need to analyze this?) After lunch we all went to the village cemetery. Arrow tried to join the party, so Zakir gladly stayed behind with him: as far as he was concerned, the old suit he wore might as well have been a set of fetters.

It was no surprise to see that the only monument belonged to Nalan. Her epitaph, carved in white marble in the shape of a book, read:

> You alone are near when you are far
> Loneliness comes from the road you go down.

Haluk Bey knelt before the well-kept grave. As he cleared

away the moss nobody else could see, he seemed to be bringing his wife up to date on recent events. We waited for him to stop crying before we put the rings on our fingers. He embraced us and said, "The reason you were both spared from these fatal accidents was to strengthen your togetherness."

Samsun took us to the Ayvalık station to catch a bus to Istanbul, stopping off at a gas station restroom on the way. The litter of radical journals and bedraggled fanzines on the front seat made me wonder what might be in the glove compartment. *Thus Spake Zarathustra* by Nietzsche, *Three Anatolian Legends* by Yashar Kemal, CDs by Leonard Cohen and the left-wing folk singer Edip Akbayram, Sudoku puzzle magazines: were these his carnival masks? Before I climbed onto the bus I told him, "I owe you a debt of gratitude because, while you were trying to save your lady from loneliness, you did me an even greater favor. But if I ever see you again in whatever mask you choose, I'll make sure you regret it."

I almost added, "After, of course, I deal with your boss."

*

Dr. Kamil Polat was a man in his forties with curly hair and slanting eyes; and he was tiny. Perhaps this was why, I thought, he tried to look like a rhetorician. He examined Sim at a clinic on the Asian side of Istanbul, where a medical-school friend of his worked. I appreciated the fact that he never referred to the erroneous treatment my fiancée had already undergone.

"It's a very challenging corneal disk detachment. It wouldn't be an easy operation. And time is against her; she has to be operated on soon. I would recommend Dr. Carl Cooper. He is a partner in the Wishion Eye Clinic where I work and a legend in his field. They call him C. C. for short. His initials, you see, sound like "See, see" in English—a happy and deserved coincidence. If you've got $250,000 I'll start begging immediately."

I couldn't think of anything to say but, "We'll be grateful to you."

"I'll call you in forty-eight hours. Otherwise my mother's words—'If you don't arrange an operation for Sim I'll never speak to you again!'—will come true."

Dr. Kamil Polat called when he said he would. Dr. Cooper had received the X-rays and other files and would operate on the morning of 19 January. We were to be in Boston three days before the surgery for a final examination. More good news was that he'd obtained a ten percent reduction on our bill. As the words *Allah razı olsun* rolled off my tongue, it didn't occur to me that I had only $185,000 in my account.

*

I was taking Sim to visit the radio announcer Saadet Gülmez, her one-time neighbor in İzmir and an old high-school friend. I was excited at the prospect of at last seeing the labyrinthine interior of the Istanbul Radio House where he worked. But on seeing Sim's young friend playing her voice like a virtuoso, I sneaked out of the gloomy building at the first opportunity; it would have embarrassed me to be introduced to her as a professional colleague.

I walked toward the book dealer whom I used to see when I was staying at the Pera Palace. I had to find at least $45,000 for Sim's surgery. Strangely, I didn't think it necessary to make any plans beyond ascertaining the market value of the two books Ken Melling had pointed out to me in the library that day. On the inside front cover of the books was written N. ZERVUDAKI. I was glad that I had no time to think about how Suat had acquired these books that Count Noldolsky had inherited from his beloved's husband. As I opened the door of the tiny shop at Galatasaray, a middle-aged man with glasses was holding forth: "No, it was Yashar Kemal who told the greatest love story of Turkish literature in *The Legend of Mount Ararat*." The smiling book dealer and a young woman sitting on the only chair in the store were listening to him, but I couldn't tell whether it was out of respect or just because he was a regular customer. He looked like a bureaucrat or a failed writer played by Peter Sellers. When his hand reached toward the two books I pulled out of my briefcase, I assumed that he was the dealer's secret partner.

"If these two masterpieces of the Ottoman era are to be sold for any reason other than marriage or illness, I'll be heartbroken," he said.

"I'm suffering from both," I said.

"Then I can direct you to someone who can speedily solve your problem. There's a small bookseller just five minutes from here on foot. ANKA specializes in rare and historical books, maps, and photography. Open by appointment only. The owner is İsmail Bayramoğlu. He's a serious collector of Ottoman books in foreign languages. He lives in Paris and Istanbul and is an honest perfectionist. Shall I call him?"

Despite the florid phrases of gratitude choking my throat, all I could get out was, "I would be glad of that, sir." He went out to use his cell phone and I shifted awkwardly on my feet, too self-conscious to examine the books on the shelves. My new fairy godmother said, as he gave me the address, "Ismail won't charge a commission if he can set a good value on the books."

I walked down Balo Street among the tiny buildings camouflaged in beige and gray paint and climbed the stairs to the third floor of one adorned in faded red. ANKA looked like a book museum. Had I seen this plain smiling man, Mr. Bayramoğlu, on the street, I never would have taken him for a world-class collector. As he took his cigar out of his mouth his age dropped from the forties to the twenties.

"These books are important and in good condition," he observed. "And especially if these coats-of-arms prove to be what I think they are ..."

He held a magnifying glass to the insignia. He sniffed the bindings. He put on his gloves and ran his fingers over them. He consulted other books, brochures, the Internet. After speaking in French to two different people on the phone he concluded, "These books came from the library of Emperor Napoleon the Third." If I waited for the Paris auction I might get 130,000 euros, but there were Turkish customers who would pay 90,000 to 110,000 euros right away.

I was trying to work out what that would be in dollars when İsmail, seeing my helpless expression, said, "I'm talking at least $125,000. When do you need the money?"

"Tomorrow, if not today," I said with quavering lips.

He tucked a receipt for the books in my pocket as I left. Although I knew Balo Street was full of bars, the James Joyce Irish Pub had escaped my attention before. I plunged into the dimly lit interior, where I downed a double cognac and reviewed the train of events. If Suat Altan and/or his counterparts were really planning to push me into a blind cul-de-sac after first opening one door after another, I wasn't going to let them have the last laugh. Whatever they might think, even if Sim left the operating room as blind as she came in, it would not matter that much to me.

Next day, when İsmail Bayramoğlu called to inform me that he had deposited $125,000 into my account, my parting words were, "Sir, can you tell me who the man was who sent me to you?"

"That was the retired banker Selçuk Altar. He dislikes the limelight, but in my opinion he's one of the country's most important book collectors."

I rushed to Yapı Kredi Bank to get my credit card limit increased to $185,000. I bought two open New York-Istanbul plane tickets and Sim and I went to the U.S. consulate to start the tedious rigmarole of obtaining visas.

*

During our last week in town we were treated like "brave conscripts." The day before our flight, after taking Sim to the painter Sevinç Altan's studio apartment in Galata, I dropped by Radio Estanbul to say goodbye to Rifat Demren and leave him six weeks' worth of taped material to broadcast.

I needed to drop a spare set of house keys off with Sami. He brought me linden tea and said, "They say there's a ninety-nine-year-old woman at Ayvansaray who tells fortunes. The bazaar got together and had Sim's fortune read. She said at least one of her eyes will be saved."

I couldn't bear this.

"Sami, are you a lousy liar or are you just imitating one? If you could only hear the sound of your own blabbering voice, your spirits would be the first to sink."

*

Boston! The receptionist who checked us in to our hotel offered us a room on the twenty-fourth floor with a view of the river. I was slightly offended when I realized that the Wishion Clinic had recommended this luxury hotel because it was specially equipped for the handicapped. Sim went to bed and quickly fell asleep. I sat in front of the large window to view the cityscape at night. The Charles River, embraced by a body of light on either side, looked tame. I couldn't help comparing it to the archaic Golden Horn that was lake, river, and sea all at once. I was glad the sight of the red lights glowing from our neighbouring hotel didn't produce butterflies in my stomach as it brought to mind Disco Eden. I liked the soulless house next to it for the feeble light leaking out of one or two windows. A plane groaned overhead.

Dr. Kamil Polat managed to make us laugh by playing the Fenerbahçe soccer club's fight songs in his car on the way to the clinic. I loved the campus town feel of Cambridge on the other side of the river. I tried to describe to Sim the harmony of color and height between the brick buildings and the green vegetation surrounding them in the skyscraper-free district. It was reassuring to see the Wishion Clinic, composed of blue glass and gray aluminum, on the deserted Arrow Street. There for three long days, while Sim exhausted herself going into one examination after another, I meditatively roamed the building's corridors. I prayed for the visually impaired who approached me with little steps, and said hello to those who extended an arm.

On the evening of 18 January we were ushered into the presence of Dr. Carl Cooper. He was a gentleman in his sixties who seemed firm but fair. He inspired trust when he refused to give hope. "There is great damage to her left eye," he said. "We'll be very careful to avoid leaving any scars." I went to the cashier to put down a fat sum as an advance. Not to seem disrespectful to Kamil Polat, I signed the release form without reading it. They told us Sim would stay that night in a private room. That evening Dr. Polat and I went to an Italian restaurant on Newbury Street with overly attentive waiters. He drank only one glass of white wine since he would attend Sim's operation the next morning. As he dropped me off at the hotel he said, "Well, the good thing about eye surgeries is that they don't end in death," which did nothing to decrease my anxiety. Like an adolescent, I was on the brink of saying, "Kamil, I love Sim the way she is now. What if gaining her sight back is the cause of my losing her?"

Back in my room I chose three cocktails at random from the minibar. I pressed against the window to look for the farthest point of light in this town that combined the skyscrapers of New York with the red brick of London. No more merciless a joke than losing Sim as she regained her vision came to mind. I imagined a narrative in which she abandoned me for the love of a genius painter. I wondered what Ahmet of *The Legend of Mount Ararat* would do in this case.

They let me see Sim for five minutes before the operation. As they escorted me out I said, "If worse comes to worst, we can always start where we left off," recognizing the cliché even as I uttered it. Dr. Polat asked me to return in three hours.

Disturbed by the icy cold of the empty streets, I sought comfort first in the Lame Duck bookstore and then in Grolier, which carried only poetry. I bought *Averno* by Louise Glück for the sake of her beautiful name. As I wandered the Harvard campus it occurred to me that a school isn't the most significant factor in one's education. I took shelter at the Pamplona Café and drank organic teas whose names I was hearing for the first time. I experienced the juvenile ambivalence of a child waiting for his mother at the maternity hospital, excited about the prospect of a sibling but uneasy about sharing his mother's love.

At 12.50 I stood up and walked to Arrow Street. Dr. Cooper had already indicated that he could save Sim's right eye, but I was worried about the next stage. Not knowing how well I could play the part of acting euphoric about a successful outcome, had I found a strategy worthy of Ahmet of *The Legend of Mount Ararat*?

Kamil Polat gave me a thumbs-up and advised me not to embrace her too powerfully—as in the Turkish movies—when he allowed me to see Sim for ten minutes. I poked my head through the half-open door and said, "If my face is uglier than you expected, my body won't bother to come in." That she had put her pillow upright behind her and was sitting up was a positive sign.

"Come three steps closer and wait for my decision like a good soldier," she replied, in a voice that seemed to have gained volume. Squinting, she stretched her arms toward me and said, "You're neither as handsome as Samsun described nor as ugly as my grandfather implied." I hugged her like she was cotton candy and didn't let her go until the nurse warned me. The pure and genuine light in her eye scattered all the dark clouds inside me. That revitalizing green was enough for me. I said, "You look like you've put on new make-up, Sim. It becomes you very well."

In order to maintain the precision of her sight, the clinic wanted to keep Sim two more days for observation. I called our dearest friends, beginning with her grandfather, to bring them up to date. I left Sami until last. When I came to him, I said, "Sami, you're nothing but an indecent soothsayer. When I get back I may decide to settle our accounts for my fiancée's unopened left eye by closing one of yours."

We stayed in Boston for five more days, attending the clinic every morning. I knew Sim wouldn't utter any clichés about her joyful recovery, and I was glad of that. As we wandered the city she didn't let go of my right hand, and if she forgot herself and clung to my arm, we smiled at each other ruefully. We took the metro from our hotel to one of the most luxurious malls in town, where Sim leafed through almost every magazine in the bookstore. I rejoiced to watch her looking at the paintings and sculptures in the Boston Museum of Fine Art and the Isabella S. Gardner Museum. She was reluctant to leave the splendid New England Aquarium, saying, "Sharks are wonders of design."

"Sim needs two more examinations a week apart. You can go to New York as long as you're back here on Wednesday afternoons," Dr. Cooper told us. Kamil Polat was going to Buffalo for a conference, so his high-school daughter Türkay hosted us on our last night in Boston. The young woman looked as if she hadn't fully enjoyed her childhood. This observation took me back to L., whereupon I realized I hadn't even thought about my mother. We were off to the Charles Playhouse to see a mime performance.

As we turned into Warrenton Street, which lived its days and nights all in the same gray tones, Türkay said, "Edgar Allan Poe was born in a house on this street." And as we took our seats in the theatre I remembered that Sim's eye operation had taken place on Poe's birthday. I refrained, however, from constructing a complex theory around this. Suat's marionettes had fulfilled their duties and we had all reached a happy cinematic ending together. I assumed that he had no more expectations of me. My deeper anxiety was for Sim, who thought that it was I who was her savior—an assumption far more worrying than her growing attachment.

*

In New York we acted like a carefree honeymoon couple. I patiently escorted Sim to famous stores and museums whose names I forgot instantly. In the evenings, if we had time to spare from Broadway musicals, we went to concerts at Lincoln Center. When she saw Picasso's "The Blind Man's Meal" at the Metropolitan Museum, my fiancée sighed like a repentant sinner who's run into his unrepentant partner in crime. There were constant queues of people snaking out of shops where they sold coffee like lime juice. I missed Balat.

Sim's favorite university professor Selime Hanım was now working at the Baltimore Museum of Art. We were due to go and see her on Sunday.

We caught the train at Penn Station, which resembled an ant's nest. Selime and her husband met us in Baltimore.

Selime was a wide-eyed, charming brunette. Her plump banker husband's excessively subservient attitude toward his wife discomfited me, although I had yet to be disturbed by his exaggerated hospitality. He took us on a tour of the city in his Cadillac. To me Baltimore resembled the set of a psychological thriller, and the Baltimoreans were actors unhappy with their pay. We were sipping our coffees at the Inner Harbor, when Doug said, "Well, I don't blame you if you don't like Baltimore—it's under the curse of Edgar Allan Poe." (The conceit of living in the city where Poe was buried and being indifferent to it.)

We had lunch at the museum where Selime worked. Actually the Baltimore Museum of Art, with its famous Matisse collection, bored me. (I couldn't, of course, tell them that if I saw one Matisse I felt like I'd seen them all.) My fiancée wanted to stay longer, so Selime assigned her husband to entertain me in town. I could hardly believe how easily the words spilled out of my mouth when I asked Doug to take me to Poe's grave.

There was a theory that Poe had been attacked by religious fanatics when he was found on a Baltimore back street struggling for his life in 1849. Even if this theory were false, it was possible that his soul wouldn't have appreciated this memorial with the caricature-like relief of Poe carved on it. I underlined two sentences that I read twice in *Frommer's Maryland and Delaware*, which I'd picked up before boarding the train:

After his death as his relatives were preparing his grave a train derailed and hit his headstone, alone of those in the cemetery. And every 19 January, one of his admirers visits his grave and leaves half a bottle of cognac and three red roses.

(Ah, the pleasant glow stirred by coming across Suat Altan's trail in a guidebook!) The small, not to say *boutique*, cemetery of Westminster Church, situated at a busy intersection, reminded me of the graveyards of our neighborhood mosques. Doug, sensing that I wasn't overwhelmed, proposed to take me to the Poe museum. The lack of desire in his voice increased mine.

The squat two-story building had belonged to Poe's aunt, and it was during his stay here from 1835 to 1837 that he fell in love with Virginia Clemm. The unskillfully polished bricks made the miniscule museum look like a toy building. N. Amity street had long since become an African-American neighborhood. The youngsters standing around looked like mannequins brought in to lure visitors to the museum with their bright-eyed looks. The rooms inside were as claustrophobic as solitary-confinement cells.

I was stuck in front of a notice on the bulletin board. A headline in large print proclaimed, "Greatest Literary Prize After the Nobel," and under it was an announcement that a "first novel" competition—with a first prize of $200,000—had been organized in honor of the bicentennial of Poe's birthday in 2009. The deadline for entries (not to exceed

60,000 words) was 19 January 2008. In my opinion the name of the sponsor was as exciting as the grand prize.

I wrote down the address of the NEVAR Foundation in my guidebook. The word "NEVAR" was more than simply the reverse of the title of Poe's poem "The Raven," which had brought him fame. In Turkish it meant "What's up?" The phrase rang distant bells even for Doug, whose father had been the director of a global medical company in Istanbul for five years. I had no time to waste; my mysterious benefactor was summoning me.

As soon as we got back to New York I got on the hotel's Internet. NEVAR was a foundation newly established to support research on Edgar Allan Poe. I wasn't surprised to find the founders' names unmentioned. Next morning I called the foundation to speak to the person in charge. I nearly said, "Ne var?" instead of "Good morning."

"Who's calling?" asked an authoritative female voice.

"I'm a friend of Suat Altan from Istanbul," I said.

A new voice came on the phone, claiming to be Dr. Rodney Quinn, who probably thought he could get rid of me by saying, "There's nobody of that name working here."

"I'm pretty sure that Suat Altan does work there, Dr. Quinn," I said. "But he would be the founder."

"I'm not authorized to give out the names of our founders, nor to take messages for them," he said. His response obviously contained coded congratulations on discovering Suat's trail.

"I'll send him a fax today in Turkish," I said. "If you have nothing to do with Mr. Altan then you can tear it up."

As soon as Sim retired for a nap, I found a piece of hotel stationery and eagerly set to work. The rest of it was taken over by my right hand.

Dear Suat,

I'm writing to thank you, though I don't know how exactly to express my gratitude and how to express my ingratitude. In any case you're a man who likes ambivalence.

You are a dangerously intelligent and powerful man, yet a benign master of ceremonies. If you weren't, I would have abandoned the game as soon as I realized that Suat and Fuat are one and the same; and that you were actually using the house you gave me as a kind of laboratory.

Because of the unsigned letter you sent, a saintly man was reunited with his long-lost but never-forgotten beloved.

Because of the clues provided by the so-called lawyer you sent, a young girl was brought back to life and I was given a reason to live again.

Perhaps you're proud of how your puppets performed, but I pray to you as our Eros and miracle-working physician.

I hesitate to tell you how I tracked you down. I'm under the impression that you know everything anyway.

We'll be back in Istanbul in a week and I will marry my fiancée at the first opportunity. I'll name my first child after you, whether it's a boy or a girl.

You will call me one day ...

Sincerely,
Kemal Kuray

My hastily scribbled letter was flowing through the fax lines of the hotel and I was experiencing the satisfaction of paying my spiritual debts, but I couldn't stop myself from reading through what I'd written.

*

Contented with Sim's last check-up, Dr. Carl Cooper let us go for six months.

We were leaving for Istanbul in three days. Banu Tanalp's fellow academic and artist friend Peter Hristoff had taken my fiancée to visit the School of Visual Arts where he teaches.

There was a pleasant bite in the air outside, but I was hooked on the classical music station a black taxi driver told me about the night before. Last night, at a pizzeria named Angelos, I had tried to explain to Sim the Suat Altan concept. I'd have felt better about it if she hadn't had a smile playing on her lips the whole time.

I got up to look at the distant ocean that hung outside my window like a travel poster. The message button on the phone was blinking nervously, so I went down to the lobby. There were two blue envelopes inside the large orange one the courier handed me. I recognized the handwriting immediately, and was climbing Jacob's ladder. A check fell out of the embossed envelope; I couldn't look at the figure. In the other one was a letter and color photocopies of two photographs. I was devastated to see Suat and Fuat as children standing hand in hand.

The letter read:

Commander,
I've gone no further than to make a sincere gesture on behalf of someone who is for me a brilliant paragon but also a friend suffering misfortune. If you received an unsigned note, or were visited by a phony lawyer, it was not I who sent them.

I have good reason not to be seen in the open. One day I'll come to see my namesake.

Your friend,
Suat

Tired of pacing up and down, I pressed my face and arms to the window. I singled out "five new tricksters", and I didn't care whether they worked independently or as a team. I didn't worry about who had sent the unsigned note or the deceptive lawyer. Suddenly two balloons, one red and the other blue, appeared in the sky. They flew over the tops of the skyscrapers and disappeared from view. My right hand began to itch sweetly, and I went down again to the lobby. There I exchanged a dollar tip to the doorman for the address of the nearest stationery store. At Staples I bought a thick spiral notebook, a dozen pencils, and an eraser.

The first-novel contest sponsored by NEVAR, in honor of Poe, was not something that I could avoid entering. It was only eleven months until 19 January 2009, but I knew what I would write. Perhaps Ken Melling had been sent by fate— or someone else—to the flat below mine just to translate my novel. I opened the notebook and wrote the title in capital letters: MANY AND MANY A YEAR AGO.

Muttering a *Bismillah,* I turned to the first page. From here on in I would be unable to meddle in the work of my right hand:

> What is to come will not cause us to mourn for what is gone, says my inner voice. Should I trust it? Does eluding death mean losing the will to live? Is it a reward or punishment? My inner voice warned me once too about my passion for music. It was when I was five and lost in a solo on that unearthly flute, the ney. Turning to my aunt, I said, "It's Allah Baba talking, isn't it?"